Praise for *Adama*

'Explosive ... We look forward to the second and third volumes of the trilogy.'

TLS

'*Adama* is not only a warm, funny and fascinating book, it is also a very brave one. It deserves to be read.'

The Times

'Al-Hamad has written a charming and involving coming-of-age tale. Always humane and often humourous, *Adama* has much to say about the foibles of the adolescent mind.'

Boyd Tonkin, *The Independent*

'A seemingly whimsical novel banned for its political curiosity.'

Mariella Frostrup, *Open Book*

'I loved this book, which exposes the secrets of the inner and the outer life of the people of Saudi Arabia and made them vividly real to me; writing this book was a great act of courage.'

Maggie Gee

'Hisham's priapic adventures in Riyadh capture something of the nervousness and electric excitement of late adolescence, with all of their rowdy expletives and *arak*-fuelled wrestling matches.'

Cairo Times

Also by Turki al-Hamad

Adama

Turki al-Hamad

SHUMAISI

SAQI

British Library Cataloguing-in-Publication Data
A catalogue record for this book is available from the British Library

ISBN 0 86356 911 0
EAN 9 780863 569111

This edition first published 2005

SAQI
26 Westbourne Grove
London W2 5RH
www.saqibooks.com

1

His room seemed ready now. He'd got everything he needed: a small metal bed, a rack for his clothes, a wooden table and chair, a bookshelf, a gas cooker, a radio and second-hand tape recorder, and a large blue lamp that gave the room a particular glow and a hidden beauty that the soul felt before the eye saw it. He'd bought it all at an auction and it hadn't cost him much. He still had most of the money he had brought with him from Dammam. It would be enough to see him through until he received his first instalment from college. He had turned the window sill into a small store, where he put tinned foods and fruit: tins of milk concentrate, yellow cheese, melon jam, tea, sugar, an orange or apple or banana, and the remains of a loaf, always wrapped in newspaper and usually thrown away after going stale before anyone had touched it, especially once Ahmad's raids on his modest store had stopped. Moudhi had given him a small silver teapot, a saucepan for boiling water and several glasses, which he put on a wooden fruit box draped with a piece of blue cloth, not far from the door, beside the gas cooker. This was despite Moudhi's protests; she didn't think that there was any call for him to make tea for himself. She was always there, and he had only to give the order. But he persuaded her when he pointed out that she went to bed early and he needed tea late at night, which she grudgingly accepted. However, she continued to make tea for him without his asking and he didn't object, since it pleased her. The fact was that he didn't like the weak tea made in Riyadh, which was usually very sweet, with a colour more like leaf tea than proper tea.

His room was lovely, despite its simple furnishings – better than Ahmad's and Abd al-Rahman's which, though they were filled with splendid furniture, still lacked beauty. Moudhi cleaned and tidied his room every day herself. She sprinkled rosewater on his bed, and sometimes lemon balm, which made it wonderfully fragrant. She took no notice of Abd al-Rahman's grumblings and protests as she left his room to be cleaned by Said. 'You are a disgrace,' she said to him, 'and your room is a tip! Hisham's room doesn't need any effort to clean or tidy. As for your room … God Almighty, it needs a whole army of workers!' Then she would laugh and go away, leaving Abd al-Rahman to snort and pick his nose, which he always did when he was angry but unable to find a retort. Hisham went out of his way to relieve Moudhi of her chores. He made his bed as soon as he got up and usually didn't sleep in it except in the afternoon, for at night he slept on the roof with the others. There were just those stubborn patches of dust that defied all his attempts at cleaning.

The room became a refuge for his cousins, who came as their own needs dictated. Ahmad would raid it at midnight, devouring any food he could find and enjoying Hisham's hot tea without bothering to bring replenishment. If Abd al-Rahman wanted to smoke, the room was his favourite place. Several times he had declared his intention to bring girls round, but Hisham was adamant on this point. Abd al-Rahman gave in, sorry that he had not realised the value of the room until Hisham moved in. As for

Hamad, he would bring his supply of *arak*, no more than a bottle, or part of a bottle. Sometimes it would be in a plastic bag, forcing Hisham to pour it into a bottle so that it did not split and spill its revolting-smelling contents all over the room. Hamad would hide the *arak* and, when he felt like getting tipsy before going out, would make for the secret store in the room and have a glass or two. No one at home would be awake apart from Hisham, who was normally reading or studying. Hamad had tried to persuade Hisham to join him in a drink, but he flatly refused. Hamad always smiled and shook his head. 'Idiot!' he would say. 'Just like your uncle's children, you don't know a good thing when you see one.' Then he would gulp down the *arak* and chatter on, unheard by Hisham, who was immersed in the book in his hands. To begin with, Hisham was afraid that Moudhi might find the *arak* and he spoke frankly to Hamad about his fear. Hamad replied with a shout of laughter that almost made his eyes disappear up into his head. 'Don't you worry,' he said, 'Moudhi doesn't know the difference between water and *arak*. And she has no idea what wine is, either! I used to leave it in *my* room. When she was good enough to clean it sometimes, she took no notice of what she found. You're above suspicion in her eyes, so don't worry about her or Said, he's a stupid fellow.' Then Hamad laughed loudly again and returned to his glass. When Hisham asked why he didn't keep the *arak* in his own room, he said he was just being cautious, and that anyway he liked the company. Hisham couldn't object. Hamad's family owned the house, and he was their guest; he didn't want to antagonise his cousins at any cost.

Hamad was almost right. When Moudhi found the bottle she did ask Hisham about the foul liquid inside. But he told her it was something to do with his studies, and she didn't suspect anything and sighed. 'If only my father had let me finish my education, I would be like you today. But praise be to God, I can at least read. I have my elementary certificate.' Her eyes glistened behind her veil as she spoke. 'My poor sister Munira,' she went on sadly, 'never went to school at all. May God forgive our father. Everything about him was fine, except that he was afraid of girls' education. But never mind. What God has chosen is best.' Then she took the used glasses and went off to clean them. After that, Moudhi looked after the bottle with great care, like a woman fussing over her child. Hisham would smile, feeling his stomach contract painfully when he saw what she was doing. As for Muhammad, Hisham never saw him except occasionally at lunchtime, or when they had breakfast together. As the oldest son, Muhammad was always preoccupied with his work, his wife and his two children in the other part of the house.

2

Two days before the start of term, on Thursday to be precise, he
had a surprise encounter that signalled the return of his stomach
cramps. He was relaxing with Abd al-Rahman in his room after
lunch, pretending to be buried in a magazine in an effort to escape
Abd al-Rahman's never-ending complaints about his father, his
work and the dawn prayers, not to mention his brother Ahmad
and his unbelievable stinginess. Hisham could tell when Abd al-
Rahman was really annoyed – when the words started coming out
of his nose. Right now he was snorting and pulling at his nose while
he remembered Ahmad's behaviour at the lunch table. Their father
had finished and left as usual, when Ahmad cut up the remaining
meat, chewed on it, then put it back on the plate. The oldest brother
Muhammad had already left, immediately after his father. He only
ate a little, knowing that his wife Anoud would be waiting for him
with a special lunch for his own little family. Hamad was only half
there – at lunch he was only ever half there, and often left the table
without saying anything. He only ate properly after he'd had a
siesta to make up for the sleep he had missed the night before.

So for all intents and purposes only Abd al-Rahman and Hisham were witness to this particular lunchtime incident. Hisham was stunned by Ahmad's behaviour. Abd al-Rahman, however, did not take it lying down, but took a piece of the mangled meat and chewed it himself. Ahmad watched and fiddled with his nose. Then he grabbed the two remaining pieces of meat. At this Abd al-Rahman got up from the table snorting, 'God curse you, Ahmad. Anything goes with you. You don't respect God's bounty or anyone else's.' Ahmad just laughed, then carried on eating, the drops of fat dripping from his fingers as he moulded more meat into a large lump of rice.

Abd al-Rahman was ranting and raving about this incident when Moudhi suddenly came into Hisham's room. 'There are two people at the door asking for you,' she said. Hisham felt as if he had swallowed a lump of lead, and his thoughts lurched towards prison. Now his turn had come. They had to be from the authorities. He got slowly up from the bed, heart racing. In no time at all, his hair had become drenched with sweat. Yet despite this, he felt horribly cold. He was shivering – in August. In a state of extreme agitation he dragged himself down the stairs, unaware of Moudhi behind him.

The front door was ajar. He pushed it open, hands trembling and dripping with sweat. He almost fainted as he looked at the two people waiting there, fully expecting them to grab him by the collar as soon as they caught sight of him. But his eyes widened further when he recognised his two friends Abd al-Muhsin al-Taghiri, whom he knew as Muhaysin, and Muhammad al-Ghubayra. He felt as if every friend he had made last summer in Nejd stood there grinning on the doorstep. Without thinking he rushed towards them, embracing them roughly. 'How happy I am to see you!' he exclaimed, laughing and hugging them all over again. The other two were taken aback by Hisham's unusual display of emotion. They had seen nothing like it when they had all been together in Qusaim.

Hisham invited them in and they went up to his room, where he introduced them to Abd al-Rahman. He was about to offer them refreshments, but Moudhi was too quick; in only a few moments Said brought tea and a small plate of salty biscuits of the kind usually only offered to unfamiliar guests, especially women. As soon as everyone had settled down on the floor, Muhaysin handed Hisham the small paper bag he was carrying.

'I didn't want to come empty-handed,' he said, smiling. 'I've brought you something that my mother gave me for my life in exile.' He laughed. 'She thinks that living in Riyadh is the worst exile of all.'

Hisham smiled back, taking the bag and opening it immediately to reveal four pastries. He took two of them out of the bag, put them on the tea tray, then carefully wrapped the other two and put them in his little store by the window. He promised himself to move them later, fearing one of Ahmad's midnight raids. Then he went back to his seat. 'What a delicious surprise! ... Oh. And the two of you,' he said, jokingly. He smiled as he poured the tea and offered it to his guests, while Muhaysin said fervently, 'These aren't just any old pastries ... They're homemade by my mother. Everything in them is the real thing, cardamom, sugar, treacle, flour, fat – you name it.' Hisham took the round pastry, cut off a piece for himself and bit into it. He washed it down with a quick sip of tea. Then he offered the rest of the pastry to Abd al-Rahman. The leftovers from the cake crumbled from his mouth.

'You haven't told me how you knew where I was living,' he said, as soon as could speak again.

'That's easy,' replied Muhammad. 'You told us in Qusaim that you would be living with your uncle in Shumaisi. We asked around for him here, and a couple of people showed us to his house. That's all there is to it.'

'Anyway,' said Muhaysin, laughing. 'A Bedouin moves on and just asks, isn't that so?'

They all laughed. 'How long have you two been in Riyadh?' asked Hisham.

'Over a week,' replied Muhammad, crunching on a dry biscuit.

'A week!' reproached Hisham. 'A whole week, and you only inquire about me today, when term is about to start!'

'We were busy,' said Muhaysin. 'First of all, we were looking for a suitable house to stay in, then we were furnishing it, and before that we had to present our papers to the university. We were almost turned down, as we were late for the submission deadline, but God arranged a go-between for us in the shape of some acquaintances of Muhammad's father, who smoothed our path. We only began to sort things out yesterday, and today we've been out looking for you.'

A silence descended, broken only by the sound of slurping tea and crunching biscuits. Abd al-Rahman popped the last bit of pastry into his mouth; then Hisham broke the silence, saying, 'You haven't told me yet where you are staying.'

'In a house not far from here,' replied Muhammad.

'A clean, spacious house,' said Muhaysin, 'with four rooms, a large hall and a big roof, even though it is a bit expensive. Four thousand *riyals* a year. The landlords of cheap houses refuse to rent to unmarried men. But never mind, there are four of us to share the rent.'

'Four people?' asked Hisham quietly.

'Yes,' replied Muhaysin. 'As well as us, there are Dais al-Dais and Muhanna al-Tairi ... I think you know them.'

Muhaysin and Muhammad exchanged furtive glances as they said Muhanna al-Tairi's name, and Hisham, who had never got on with Muhanna, was annoyed to hear it mentioned, but he tried not to show it and busied himself pouring more tea while Muhammad said, 'Why don't you come with us so that we can show you the house? It isn't far from the Umm Salim roundabout.'

Hisham cheered up at the mention of the roundabout, remembering Raqiyya and her moist, wild triangle. This had been his introduction to Riyadh's forbidden pleasures. He and Abd al-Rahman had picked Raqiyya up at the Umm Salim roundabout before driving off for that unforgettable afternoon in the desert. He looked at his cousin, smiling. Abd al-Rahman grinned back before gulping down the rest of the tea. 'Why not? Let's go,' he said, getting up, with the others following. Hisham took off his house *tob* and put on his outdoor *tob*, with his headdress and skullcap. He slipped his feet into his expensive Nejdi slippers then hurried outside, where everyone was already waiting. Abd al-Rahman invited the two young men to lunch the following day. They accepted, and asked him to come with them to their new house, but he excused himself on the grounds that he was busy while looking at Hisham out of the corner of his eye and smirking. The three old friends hurried off in the direction of New Shumaisi Street, exchanging fond memories of Qusaim and its picnics.

3

Their house was in a narrow alley that branched off one of the streets leading from the Umm Salim roundabout. It was mudbrick, with a narrow iron gate bordered with rust that led directly to a short, narrow corridor. The most spacious room in the house stood on the left of the entrance. On the right was a small bathroom. The corridor ended in a door leading to a hall that took up most of the house. On the left of the hall were two smaller rooms. The hall ended in a door leading to a kitchen linked to another tiny room. On the other side, a stairway led to the roof. The kitchen held a small gas stove and an enormous earthenware jar covered by a wooden slab on which sat a large, shining aluminium water jug, a medium-sized pan and large cooking pot, a saucepan for boiling water, a teapot and some tea glasses and spoons thrown carelessly into a washing-up bowl. In the little room to the side lay bags of rice and sugar, a small bag of coarse salt, a box of tea, some tins of tomato paste, a bag of onions, a tin of vegetable oil and a few cockroaches looking for food, which disappeared as soon as they entered various crevices in the walls. As for the roof terrace, it was quite spacious. It overlooked the alley and the rest of the neighbours' roofs, where one could usually see a woman or girl hanging out washing or making beds, her face covered by a fine veil that revealed more than it hid.

Muhaysin showed Hisham around, then took him back to the room where Muhammad was sitting, having made tea. This was the nicest and most spacious room, with a white fan hanging from the ceiling and a large window overlooking the alley. A red carpet completely covered the floor; it had a metal bed like Hisham's and a desk with a dark wooden chair. None of the other rooms had fans or windows. In fact, the room beside the kitchen was unbearably hot, damp, dirty and dark. As they sipped their bittersweet tea, Muhaysin explained that he had kept this room for himself in exchange for paying a larger share of the rent than Muhammad or Dais, while Muhanna had chosen the small room in exchange for paying less.

Under the dreamy breeze from the fan, revolving lazily and noisily, Hisham suddenly said, 'It's a strange thing, that water jar … Why didn't you buy a fridge? Wouldn't that be better than a jar?' Muhammad and Muhaysin hurriedly exchanged glances before the latter replied, 'You're right. That was our original plan, but Muhanna persuaded us there was no need, so long as we bought what we needed on a day-to-day basis.'

'The person responsible for the household that day,' interrupted Muhammad, 'buys a quarter-of-a-kilo of lamb for a *riyal* and a half, or half a kilo of camel meat for the same price, and some tomatoes, then prepares the *kabsa* stew. Actually, we usually make it without tomatoes, just with tomato paste. So there's really no need for a fridge; there's nothing to put in it.'

'What about breakfast and supper?' asked Hisham.

'Everyone looks after himself; that's what we agreed, except on special occasions,' replied Muhaysin.

'But wouldn't it be easier to buy what you need once a week

and keep it in a fridge, as well as cold water?' asked Hisham, offhandedly.

Muhaysin said, pointedly, 'We talked it over when we rented the house, but Muhanna said that it would cause us difficulties we could do without.'

'Like what?' probed Hisham.

'If we split up, for instance, who would get the fridge? What would we do if none of us wanted it? Problems like that ...' said Muhaysin, before hastily adding, 'Besides, water from the jar is as cold as water from any fridge.' He sprang up and left the room, then came back carrying a bowl full of water. He thrust it towards Hisham, saying, 'Here you are; taste it and judge for yourself.' Without enthusiasm, Hisham took the bowl, took a quick sip of water, and handed it back.

'You're right,' he said. 'It's very cold. I had no idea earthenware jars were so good at keeping water cool.'

Muhaysin smiled and sat down again. He poured himself a glass of black, stewed tea and gulped it down with relish. Hisham was humouring his friend; the water wasn't cold at all. As for Muhammad, he had been silent the whole time, with the trace of a smile on his lips. Hisham couldn't stop himself wondering about the hold Muhanna seemed to have over them. 'What's up between Muhanna and yourselves?' he asked eventually. 'Do you do everything he says?' Again Muhaysin and Muhammad exchanged glances.

'The fact is he's a lot older than us,' said Muhammad, as if to apologise. 'He got his school-leaving certificate from night classes, because he worked during the day. He resigned from his job to enrol in medical school, so our families have a lot of faith in him. They were very pleased when they found out that we would be living together in one house. That's why we've left control of the household affairs to him.'

Hisham nodded to show that he understood, even though deep

down he had misgivings. He sipped his cold black tea quietly, without enjoying it much. They all fell silent, as the gentle moaning of the fan induced a feeling of lethargy. After asking his friends if they minded, he slumped back against the wall and stretched out his legs, and his two friends followed suit. He soon dozed off, but was woken by the sound of the front door being opened. He straightened as Dais, with his thin body and tall frame, came into the room with a book under his arm. Hisham stood up. They shook hands and embraced, exchanging kisses and the traditional greetings, then sat down as Dais tried to shake the last drops of tea from the pot.

'I've just come from the Ibn Qasim auction beside the big mosque,' he said, with obvious enthusiasm. 'What a place!' Draining the dregs from his glass he added, 'You can find things there you'd never imagine. Even banned books – books that have been burned – you can find them there dirt cheap!' He fiddled with the teapot again. 'Can you believe it? I found this book there and bought it for just one *riyal*. If the bookseller had asked for two I'd have given it to him.' He chucked the book down in the middle of the floor for them to see. Muhammad picked it up and read out the title in a loud voice. '*The Philosophy of the Revolution*, by Gamal Abdel-Nasser.' Then Hisham took it and began to flip through its pages. He had already made up his mind to go to the auction again. He had been there before when he was buying stuff for his room and found a lot of books he hadn't expected to see such as the Baathist Aflaq's *On the Path to Revival*; Munif Razzaz's *Features of the New Arab Life*; an extremely ragged copy of the first part of Marx's *Das Kapital*; two stories by Maxim Gorky and Fyodor Dostoevsky; as well as a complete set of the *Pillars of Freedom* series by Qadri Qalaji.

'Muhanna will be so pleased to get a book like this,' said Dais happily, looking at Muhammad and Muhaysin, who glanced at Hisham. This Muhanna, who appeared as a shadowy presence behind everything they said and did ... Hisham was beginning to get annoyed at hearing his name repeated at every turn. He got up and excused himself. 'I have some things I must do before term begins,' he said, and making for the door he said goodbye. Their farewells trailed after him. But before the alley could swallow him up, Muhaysin leaned out of the window and shouted after him.

Hisham turned back. 'Is everything all right?'

'Yes,' said Muhaysin. 'But some friends will be spending the evening with us tonight. Why don't you come? It'll be a reunion for the Qusaim holiday!'

'Okay. I'll come – God willing,' said Hisham. He began to walk back towards the Umm Salim roundabout. Before reaching the end of the alley, however, he turned back towards the students' house and saw Muhaysin still leaning his elbows on the windowsill, and a girl standing outside the door of the house opposite. She had covered her face with a thin veil, and was putting the rubbish out in a way that seemed slightly too casual. He gave it no further thought, however, and carried on walking. The *muezzin* was about to call people to the sunset prayers.

4

When he returned to the house that evening, he found everyone gathered in the hall around the teapot. As well as the regular members of the household, there were three newcomers. He already knew Salim al-Sinnur and Salih al-Tarthut, whom he had met before in Qusaim, and he was introduced to the third man but instantly forgot his name. Muhanna al-Tairi sat in the middle and everyone hovered around him. He was talking about the latest Rogers peace initiative, and the reasons that had induced Nasser to accept it. Muhanna was not enthusiastic about Hisham's presence. He had looked at him with suspicion when he came in and only got up sluggishly to greet him. The smile on his face was obviously forced as he said, 'Greetings to the newcomer! Greetings to the shepherd of Marx!' Hisham gave an equally forced smile. They exchanged cold kisses, then Hisham said, 'How nice to see you, brother Muhanna!'

'May you have good health, brother Hisham … Or should I say "comrade"?' Muhanna sniggered. He reminded Hisham of a cornered rat, the way his gaze shifted round everyone. Then he went back to where he had been sitting, while Hisham chose a place in the circle between Muhaysin and Muhammad. Before Muhanna started talking again he studied Hisham, frowning.

'By the way, brother Hisham,' he asked, 'are you still a communist?' While speaking his eyes once more shifted around the gathering, then he turned back to Hisham who answered coolly, trying to hide his anger.

'Who told you I was a communist? I'm a socialist. Isn't Gamal Abdel-Nasser one too?'

'Yes,' answered Muhanna. 'But he's not an atheist like you. I mean, like the communists.'

'Who told you I'm an atheist? Or is that an accusation?' retorted Hisham angrily. Muhanna was silent for a moment, then started talking about the Rogers initiative again, and how wise Nasser had been to accept it just at this precise moment, now that the war of attrition had achieved its objectives. Hisham listened silently, his thoughts returning to the time of the organisation.* He was furious, not hearing a word of what was being said around him, until Muhaysin dragged him out of his gloom. 'Are you really a communist?' he asked in a whisper.

'You asked me before, and I gave you an answer.'

'It was a vague answer. I want a precise answer, yes or no.'

'There is no definite "yes" or "no" here. Yes, Marxism attracts me. But no, I am not a communist.'

'What's the difference? The one implies the other.'

'Not exactly. It's a long story. We'll discuss it later.' At this point, Muhammad, who had been listening to their whispering, interrupted.

'Do you really not love Nasser?' he asked, also in a whisper. Before Hisham could reply, Muhammad added, 'I can't imagine

---

* While at school, Hisham joined an ill-fated illegal political organisation. See *Adama*.

20

that there is anyone who doesn't love Nasser ... except for traitors and agents. And sorry, I don't think you're one of them.'

'It's not a question of love or hate, but a matter of principle. I don't hate Nasser personally. On the contrary, I love and admire him totally. But he doesn't satisfy me intellectually, that's all there is to it.'

Hisham was whispering without paying attention to the blazing looks Muhanna was directing at him. He soon felt their heat, however, when, in a voice clearly betraying intense anger, Muhanna challenged, 'What's all this whispering, *friends*? If you don't want to talk to us, why don't you go elsewhere?'

Muhammad and Muhaysin were silenced by Muhanna's outburst. They lowered their heads and stared at the ground. But Hisham was unable to bear the insult. He couldn't curb his headstrong nature. With wide eyes and reddening cheeks he said in a voice quivering with rage, 'Brother Muhanna. You are simply talking to yourself. You're giving a lecture, and I, for one, am not obliged to listen.' He got up, making as if to leave, but Muhaysin grabbed him by the hem of his *tob*.

'Hisham, stay,' he begged. 'It's too early to leave.' Then he looked at Muhanna. 'He's our guest, Muhanna,' he said weakly. 'At the very least, he's *my* guest.'

'Yes, yes, he's a guest, Muhanna,' repeated Muhammad and Dais. Muhanna sighed stagily, glaring at Hisham, who smiled evilly and sat back down. Now Muhanna could not remember where he had left off, and started to flounder and stop before reaching the ends of his sentences. He got up suddenly and made for his room, adding in a tone he made as sarcastic as possible, 'Reading is better than all this time-wasting. I'm going to reread the 30 March Declaration, the best political document of the age.' He gave Hisham a filthy sideways glance.

As soon as Muhanna had shut his bedroom door, Salih al-Tarthuth shouted, 'Cards! Cards! Who will play?' Then the company became heated and began to shout. Muhammad got up to get the playing cards from his room, while Dais went into the kitchen to make tea.

5

Term began. On Saturday, Hisham went to College, which was packed with students, unlike the day he had first visited it. He was tense and fearful as he embarked on this new phase of his life. Doubtless everything would be totally different to what he had been used to at school. Here 'doctors', not teachers, gave the instruction. The mere mention of the word 'doctor' was enough to conjure fear and awe, so how would it be when they were seeing them and dealing with them every day? Here there were 'lectures', not 'classes', and only oneself to rely on instead of everything being completely mapped out as it had been at secondary school.

When he entered the big hall there was a large crowd at the announcements board, which listed the names of the students, their level of study, their lecture rooms and the names of the doctors who were lecturing. He joined the crowd and, once he'd found his name on the board, wrote down all the vital information.

The first lecture was on economics, a subject he had studied a lot in order to crack the riddles of *Das Kapital* – a book he still couldn't touch without a slight feeling of awe and a strange tremor passing through his whole being.

In came Doctor Mahmud Behnis Jaljali, Professor of Economics. Unlike the other doctors he did not wear the traditional head cord, and he would even take off his headdress, throwing it down on the table in front of him until he had finished his lecture, when he would sling it over his shoulder and leave. Doctor Mahmud was a typical Meccan, from a traditional quarter of the town. He was witty and well-versed in his subject, but he was also demanding. He asked them to buy an enormous book – *The Principles of Economics* by Paul Samuelson – then told them that this book would be no more than a work of reference; the meat of the subject would lie in what he had to say during lectures. Some of the students disliked Doctor Mahmud for his strictness and pedantry, so in order to explain away the humour and courage he displayed in tackling political subjects normally reckoned off-limits, they accused him of drinking before he came to lectures, and some of them swore blind they'd smelled whisky on his breath while he was speaking.

The second lecture was on 'General Administration' by Laith Abd al-Wadud. He made a bad impression from the start. Gloomy and morose, he looked as though he carried the burdens of the world on his shoulders; when he did occasionally smile, he looked as though his jaw cracked in the process. Their dislike of him was increased by the fact that he didn't require one set book but a whole collection, most of which were not to be found in the bookshops of Riyadh or the college library. When they told him this, he gave one of his rare smiles and said, 'Not my problem. I give you the references, it's up to you to get hold of the books.' Despite the fact that he tried to be more human later, they maintained a deep dislike for him.

The third lecture, 'Political Principles', was given by Doctor Muharib al-Khayzurani. He stood out immediately because he was very tall and extremely heavily built, with a tiny, delicate voice. The words twittered from his mouth with a speed and harmony that was utterly captivating. On top of all this, to relieve the atmosphere from time to time he would smile and crack jokes in a broad Gulf accent. What made them like him even more was that he didn't give them any references, but said that if they came to his lectures and listened attentively that would be enough. His lectures, despite their richness, were more like stories and folktales – which made politics the most popular subject among the students.

The last lecture that day was on the subject of general international law, and was given by Doctor Ahmad al-Mukannaz. He came into the room with a glass of tea in his hand, which he put down on the table in front of him. He then began to sip it noisily, speaking slowly and chewing over his words in a way that made sleep tickle their eyelids. He asked them to get a copy of Ali Sadiq Abu Hayf's book, *General International Law*, then told them it was unavailable in the commercial bookshops and that they would need to ask someone to bring it from abroad. Doctor Ahmad was uncouth in his appearance and in his behaviour. His habit of always bringing tea into the lecture room was roundly condemned. They had had to get used to a long list of 'don'ts' in the lecture room, including eating and drinking. When some students concluded that behaving like this must be a natural thing to do in the university, and brought glasses of tea with them into one of Doctor Ahmad's lectures, he reprimanded them severely and turned them out of the room while he himself went back to noisily slurping his tea. He and Doctor Laith were the butt of the students' jokes, sarcasm and vehement dislike.

The day's lectures were over. Some of the tension and fear that had dogged Hisham all morning disappeared. It was still early, only a little after twelve o'clock, and he didn't want to go back to his room yet. The college caretakers were rolling out decorated carpets in readiness for the noon prayers, and some students were already sitting on them while others were heading for the canteen at the back of the building, from where you could see the walls of the Agricultural College. Hisham made for the canteen and ordered an egg sandwich and cola from Amm Wardan, who was in charge, choosing an out-of-the-way seat at one of the wooden tables spread around. He looked around as he ate and drank, filling his lungs with air that was heavy with the smell of cow dung – a smell that is quite acceptable, even pleasant, once you are used to it. Amm Wardan was extremely thin and tall, and quite dark. His eyes were always red, tinged with a hint of yellow, and he had very fine features with prominent veins on his forehead and hands. He always wore a white, flowing *tob* and a striped skullcap, which could not hide the bald head that shone through the holes in its design. Despite his attempts to look stern, it became clear that he was extremely kind, and that this stern expression was just a first line of defence against the students' horseplay.

Hisham munched quietly and took it all in. His old sense of wonder returned. Why all this architectural extravagance, as if the university were a towering palace? Again he looked around: just a handful of students and Amm Wardan, leaning on the edge of the serving window enjoying a cigarette after getting the students' orders. Hisham went up to him and ordered a glass of tea. As he made it Hisham asked – trying to seem casual – 'It's strange, this place. More like a palace than a college.' Amm Wardan laughed as he stirred the sugar in the glass, revealing a gappy mixture of black, yellow and white teeth. In one corner of his mouth glittered a gold tooth. Handing the tea to Hisham, he spoke in a rapid Sudanese dialect: 'It *was* a palace, man ... It was a palace belonging to one of the elite.' He took the quarter *riyal* for the drink, then added with a meaningful smile, 'But he moved to a new residence, and leased his palace to the university. That's the story.' He moved away as he spoke, ready to greet a customer. Hisham returned to his seat and drank his treacly tea. He didn't finish but got up, resolving to stop by his friends' house for a short time before going home.

6

The lectures continued over the following days, and Hisham's fear of university finally disappeared as he got to know the rest of the lecturers. They were a collection of peculiar and contradictory types. There was Doctor Najar al-Shatartun, an inexcusably ill-tempered man who behaved as if he were perpetually at war with the rest of the human race. He demanded that they read a lot of references in addition to what he said in lectures, in spite of the fact that his academic shallowness was obvious from the start. Although they did everything they were told, they could never get good marks from this professor until one of the students discovered his secret: he used a book not mentioned in his list of references, and had borrowed all the copies to be found in the college and university libraries. The students managed to get hold of copies of this book, which they passed among themselves with smiles on their faces; Doctor Najar turned into a walking question and exclamation mark all in one, which increased his extraordinarily bad temper.

There was Doctor Talba Abd al-Mutajalli, Professor of Business

27

Management, who fiddled with his nose the whole time. A fine spray flew from his mouth as he spoke, which encouraged everyone to avoid the front row of the lecture hall. Doctor Hasan Luzanji, Professor of Economic Resources, was so relaxed with the students that he even cracked some risqué jokes during his lectures and had no embarrassment about mentioning matters that are not usually brought up in public. There was Doctor Muhammad al-Hizbar, Professor of Accounting, who caused them considerable anguish despite his strength of personality and depth of knowledge, for he squinted so badly that if he asked one of the students a question, that student wouldn't reply, thinking that the professor meant the person next to him. The professor would then explode with anger and castigate him in a broad Upper Egyptian accent, then hastily apologise with exaggerated politeness, pointing with his finger at the pupil he actually meant. Doctor Muhammad was one of the professors dearest to their hearts. He was extremely learned, with a strong personality and fluent style, and on top of all that he was pleasant company. He was the exact opposite of Doctor Najar al-Shatartun.

Then there was Doctor Said al-Ghadban, Professor of Islamic Culture. He spent most of the time talking about himself before starting his lecture, so that the bell would ring almost before the lecture had got underway. The main concern of Doctor Sutuhi al-Mifakk, Professor of General Finance, was to get to know the students from rich families so that he could cadge a lift home with them at the end of the teaching day. There was also Doctor Mutawalli Shahtuti, Professor of Financial Mathematics, who was constantly talking about his failure to take the opportunity of settling in America when he had been a student on a scholarship there. But he was one of the best-loved professors by the students … because he was so often absent.

The fear and tension finally disappeared. Hisham soon saw that it was simply a matter of a change of names; at heart it was just the same as school. The teacher had turned into a doctor, the school into a college, the class into a lecture and the classroom into a lecture theatre. As the lectures went on, he became frustrated as he worked out that the knowledge he was seeking wasn't to be found here. He wanted to study capitalism, socialism, Marxism and the political and economic systems he had fallen in love with since reading *Studies in Systems and Regimes* by Louis Awad and *Major Economic Systems* by Rashid al-Barawi. Here, though, they taught subjects that he not only did not like but actually felt an aversion to, because they bore no relation to what was going on in his mind: Accounting, Business Management, General Administration, Insurance, Mathematics, Statistics, Law. Even the economics they taught in college had no connection with political economy, the basics of which he already knew but into which wanted to delve deeper. They learned the law of scarcity, advantage and diminishing returns and the complexities of supply and demand, without any mention of capitalism, socialism or their historical laws. As time went on, he felt that they were teaching him capitalism and its laws on the basis that this *was* economics. He realised that Marx had been right when he talked about warped consciousness, and about the ruling class imposing this consciousness as the true consciousness. Despite the fact that he found something in politics to quench his thirst, it wasn't enough.

When he went back to his out-of-the-way room, taking the college coach that spared him walking or being herded into the local bus, he shut himself in and made tea, then began to read what really interested him, as well as forcing himself to study the college subjects he didn't like. When he got bored with revising or reading, he would go to his friends' house, and spend hours with Muhaysin, chatting and drinking tea in his room. Sometimes Muhammad and Dais would join them. As for Muhanna, he was either be out or in his room, sometimes reading but more usually twiddling the knob on his radio. The needle would invariably come to rest on the 'Voice of the Arabs', after a long detour that took in London, the 'Voice of America' and the Moscow Arabic service.

7

One afternoon, bored with reading and with Abd al-Rahman's
never-ending complaints, Hisham went to his friends' house.
He knocked on the door several times, but no one answered. It
seemed his friends were out. He turned away, intending reluctantly
to go back the way he had come, and happened to turn towards
Muhaysin's closed window. Through the blind, he spotted a fan
turning. He was surprised that Muhaysin should be so extravagant
as to leave the fan turning when he was out. As he stepped from
the threshold, he thought he heard a whisper. He listened more
carefully, but heard nothing. Again he was about to leave, when
this time he heard the sound of a stifled laugh. He was sure he
wasn't just imagining it. With nothing else to do, and overcome by
a burning curiosity to know what was happening in Muhaysin's
room, he retraced his steps to the top of the alley and waited at
the first corner, watching the house with great anticipation. Then
the call to evening prayers sang out. A few minutes later the door
opened and Muhaysin's head popped out and looked anxiously
left and right. As soon as he was certain there was no one walking

down the street, he disappeared. A girl wrapped in black slipped from the house and headed quickly for one of the houses opposite. She ducked inside and shut the door quietly behind her. Hisham smiled and sensed the ghost of Raqiyya teasing him again. Tension and lust consumed him. He waited for ages, he didn't know how long, until he saw the window open and Muhaysin's head emerge briefly. Then he walked back to the house and casually knocked on the door. Muhaysin's head soon emerged again, this time smiling to greet him. He opened the door wearing a white vest and a pair of white trousers that reached just short of his knees. Droplets of sweat had gathered on his brow.

The two of them went into the room that to Hisham's mind still bore all the hallmarks of a female guest. Muhaysin donned a white *tob* that was hanging from a wall-hook. There was little out of the ordinary about his room, just a tea tray with two glasses and a small silver teapot on the desk, and a small towel lying on the floor. Hisham looked at the towel, then up at his friend, with a knowing smile. Muhaysin flushed. He snatched up the towel and chucked it into the bathroom, then came back, saying in a sheepish voice, 'Forgive me. A bachelor's mess, as you can see.' Hisham said nothing but smiled – an inscrutable smile that seemed to Muhaysin to conceal a multitude of meanings.

The two sat on the floor, Hisham still smiling, while Muhaysin continued to look very embarrassed. He soon got up, saying quickly, 'I'll make some tea … excuse me.' He shot off to the kitchen with the tea tray. Hisham followed him with his eyes. A few minutes later his friend returned carrying two glasses and the small silver teapot.

'I saw her,' said Hisham, after his first sip of tea, staring hard at Muhaysin and smiling. Muhaysin squirmed uncomfortably, in the process spilling tea on his clothes. 'I saw her slipping out of the house like a snake.' Hisham gave a short laugh, while Muhaysin smiled faintly, looking from Hisham to the floor and back. 'It was the first time, wasn't it?' he continued coolly. Muhaysin did not reply, but concentrated on pouring more tea. 'The first time is always hard,' added Hisham. 'What's the story? Tell me how it happened?' Hisham remembered what Abd al-Rahman had told him about his first time on the Kharis Road. He was eager to hear what had happened between Muhaysin and the girl, and whether his feelings about her were like his own feelings about Raqiyya.

Muhaysin was reluctant to talk but Hisham insisted, and in the end his friend said falteringly, 'The fact is ... the fact is ... this wasn't the first time. The first time hasn't happened yet ...'

'I don't understand. You are talking in riddles,' said Hisham, turning to face Muhaysin, whose brow dripped with sweat which he wiped away from time to time with his hand. 'I've had several relationships in the past,' said Muhaysin. 'And this was a relationship of the same sort. Nothing more ...'

'You mean you didn't go the whole way?'

'Yes. We do everything except ... you know. There have been other girls, and the one you saw was the same ...'

'Yes, yes,' said Hisham, again thinking of Raqiyya and the Kharis Road and his conflicting feelings and emotions at the time. He wanted to say something, but Muhaysin spoke first: 'And you?'

'And you?' he said again, swallowing half a glass of tea in a single gulp. 'Haven't you tried it? I mean ... Well, you know what I mean.' Hisham remembered Raqiyya, then thought of Noura in Dammam. But he immediately thrust Noura from his mind, ashamed of himself for comparing her with Raqiyya. It was Raqiyya he had in mind when he said, 'There have been some opportunities, but nothing happened. Even what you have been doing yourself, hasn't happened. The fact is, I haven't dared ...'

'It will happen, it will happen,' said Muhaysin, giggling. All traces of embarrassment and confusion had vanished from his face. Hisham laughed with him and they sipped their tea, each sunk in his own reverie.

8

After this revelation, Hisham visited his friends' house only when
he was certain from the open window that Muhaysin was inside
and alone. If the window was shut but the fan was on, these were
sure signs that one of his 'guests' was there. Muhaysin's window
was not closed much – in fact it was only closed twice after that
first episode – but Hisham stuck to the new ritual. His relationship
with Muhaysin grew stronger, so much so that he was reluctant to
see the others when Muhaysin wasn't there except occasionally, and
then only Muhammad and Dais. As for Muhanna, it was obvious
that the two of them did not get on. It wasn't hatred, but it was
something pretty near it – a kind of aversion or incompatibility.

The discovery of Muhaysin's exploits stirred a strange desire in
Hisham that he had never suffered from before; an overpowering
lust controlled him completely, so that he was aroused by the least
movement or mere suggestion of a woman. Everywhere he looked
he saw the arousing parts of a woman's body. For days he could
not banish women from his imagination. At last he decided to do
something about it. He approached Abd al-Rahman and asked

him to arrange a meeting with Raqiyya, or some other woman he knew. His cousin simply laughed. 'Just what are you suggesting?' he taunted. Hisham shrank with embarrassment, but his lust was tearing him to pieces inside. 'Can you or can't you?' he demanded. Abd al-Rahman snorted with laughter. 'My God!' he said. 'At this time of day! Are you giving me orders, Hisham, my friend?' But the following day Abd al-Rahman brought him the good news: Friday, after the afternoon prayers, with Raqiyya. Desire flooded Hisham's veins. His body was a furnace on the point of exploding. Friday, the best day of the week!

Friday came. From the moment he awoke he was gripped with excitement. But the nearer his appointment got, the more he felt his nerves would betray him. In a flash he remembered the bottle of *arak* hidden under his wooden box. He found it more than a third full. His face lit up. He could have hugged his cousin Hamad. Hisham had heard that alcohol put an end to embarrassment and nerves, and this was exactly what he needed today. He said the Friday prayers with his uncle and his cousins and went back to his room. He was driven to distraction by all his conflicting emotions. He felt amorous, but also afraid and confused, and at the same time he was plagued by a sense of worthlessness. These feelings became more oppressive as the minutes passed and the appointment drew nearer, but he struggled to suppress them. This time he was determined to see the experience through to the end.

When they returned from the mosque after afternoon prayers, Abd al-Rahman told Hisham that he would wait for him in the car in ten minutes' time. Hisham went up to his room with his heart pounding. He put the bottle of *arak* and a bottle of cola in a paper bag – Hamad had once told him, by way of encouraging him to drink, that the flavour of *arak* was greatly improved by cola. Then he went down the outside stairs, to where Abd al-Rahman waited for him in the car.

To Hisham's surprise Abd al-Rahman headed for the General

Government Hospital. 'Is everything okay?' he asked. 'I see that this time we're going to the hospital!'

'The hospital is safer today than anywhere else,' said Abd al-Rahman. 'She can get in with us without anyone having the slightest suspicion. They'll think we're her male relatives, come to get her after some treatment. Also, going to the hospital is a convincing excuse for her to leave her own house.' Abd al-Rahman laughed loudly. 'A really amazing situation: everything forbidden and outlawed, but everything also permitted in an unimaginable way.' Hisham glanced at him and smiled, saying nothing, while Abd al-Rahman spotted the bag Hisham was clutching.

'What's that in your hand?'

'Nothing,' Hisham smiled. 'Just some cola if we're thirsty. Though it may have other uses ...' The two of them laughed as their car approached the hospital.

They approached from the east, so Abd al-Rahman drove round until he was parallel with its western perimeter. From there, he drove on a little until he reached one of the outpatient clinics. The pavement outside thronged with black *abayas*. He stopped the car some metres away from the crowd, then got out a cigarette, which he smoked while waiting quietly. Hisham was terrified, but he was slightly reassured when he saw women getting into a number of other waiting cars. After a few minutes, Abd al-Rahman opened the back door and a moving lump slipped inside, swathed in black from head to foot. As soon as she had settled in the car, Abd al-Rahman set off east towards the Kharis Road.

The Kharis Road was crowded that day, as it was every Friday. It was as if the whole city had come out to gather there. Abd al-Rahman smacked the steering wheel angrily. 'I should have thought! ... It's Friday. Everyone comes to the Kharis Road or the Salbukh Road today. How stupid of me!' No one spoke. He jostled through the other cars, swearing and cursing at them nervously. The jam forced them to drive further than before, through Khashm al-An, until they were less than ninety kilometres from Kharis itself. Here, Abd al-Rahman turned the car off into the soft sand and drove for some distance, following the tracks of a desert road for fear of 'spies'. When the trail gave out he parked the car in some very soft sand.

Like last time, Abd al-Rahman got a carpet out of the car and spread it on the sand, then he fetched tea and water. Raqiyya meanwhile threw her *abaya* and veil as far as she could and spread herself out on the golden sand beside the carpet. Hisham stared at her with awe and lust. This time she was wearing a black dress that revealed the tops of her breasts, while the remainder was clearly discernible beneath her dress. He grasped his paper bag and made towards the carpet where Abd al-Rahman squatted, smoking a cigarette. Raqiyya wriggled about on the soft sand, arousing, seductive and enticing all at the same time. Hisham sat down beside Abd al-Rahman and produced the bottle of *arak*, which he put between them saying, 'What do you think of this little surprise?' Abd al-Rahman looked at him, nonplussed. 'Water? Where's the surprise in that?' But Raqiyya understood the nature of the surprise. She sat up, made for the carpet and grabbed the plastic bottle. She took out the stopper, held the bottle to her nose, inhaled deeply and smiled; her eyes closed in a daze and she squealed, '*Arak*! This will certainly help things along!'

She reached for a glass, filled it roughly half-full of *arak*, and then added some water, joking, 'I don't suppose you have any ice.' Downing the glass in one, she poured herself a second. 'Very thoughtful,' she laughed. 'How sweet of you!' She drank a quarter of the second glass, and then lowered her eyes. Her full mouth opened into a foolish smile, 'Should I drink all alone? I don't think so. The pleasure of drinking is in company.' She laughed coquettishly, pushing the bottle between them. Hisham and Abd al-Rahman exchanged glances, then Hisham produced the bottle of cola and looked around for something to open it with. Raqiyya snatched it with a merry laugh and used her teeth. She passed it to Hisham, saying in an impish voice, 'Here you are, my darling.' Again that coquettish laugh. 'How nice you are,' she repeated. 'How kind, how thoughtful. Cola and *arak*, indeed. You have reminded me of my youth ...'

Hisham poured a quarter of a glass of *arak*, added cola and took a quick swig, which he savoured in his mouth. Then he swallowed the whole lot. His throat burned with a fire that moved straight to his stomach. Saliva poured into his mouth and he felt like vomiting, but he got a grip on himself. More saliva poured into his mouth and then he felt a certain comfort in his stomach. At the same moment a curiously pleasurable ache pervaded his head. He drank another quarter, and more saliva flowed into his mouth, but the burning sensation was weaker this time. He pushed the glass to Abd al-Rahman, who refused it: 'Cigarettes are as much as I can take.' Hisham swallowed the rest of the glass, this time without any burning sensation at all, and then turned to look at Raqiyya. She had become extremely beautiful. In fact, everything had become extremely beautiful. His guilt and awkwardness vanished, as had his embarrassment. His mother's face appeared to him clearly, but he carried on gazing at Raqiyya, not caring. He felt the urge to slap his mother, but the thought pained him, so he banished her image from his mind and immersed himself in Raqiyya. Nothing concerned him any longer except Raqiyya; life was Raqiyya. He leaned over her, and she quickly took his lips. For a few moments, they were unconscious of everything around them. Everything inside him became aroused, and everything in Raqiyya as well. He poured himself another glass and drank half, while Raqiyya drank the other half. She took a cigarette and smoked it greedily. Then she took a deep breath, held it in and moved closer to Hisham. She held her lips against his and blew her smoke inside him. It made him cough for ages, but nothing mattered. Pleasure and a feeling of total release came over him. He felt like the first person at the beginning of creation, when nothing was taboo or forbidden. Raqiyya was completely at ease. She looked like a dark Aphrodite with Oriental features. Abd al-Rahman slipped away, and everything closed in on everything else … just like a flood …

On the way back, Raqiyya wrapped herself in her black *abaya* and Abd al-Rahman lost himself in a cigarette. The voice of Fawzi Mahsun flooded out from the radio: 'Oh birds, why do you cry?' Hisham himself was lost in the memory of that moment when pleasure had taken him from himself. The delicious headache still gripped him, and he was dozing off with his pleasurable thoughts. It was amazing, this life. How could one thing be a source of ugliness and beauty at the same time, a source both of pain and pleasure? He remembered how Raqiyya and her wet, tangled triangle had disgusted him last time, yet today she was beauty personified, pure pleasure. He wished he could stretch out his hand and touch her soft skin again but the road was crowded with lines of cars returning from their Friday excursions, so he abandoned the idea. Still, he had been mortally embarrassed when Abd al-Rahman said Raqiyya cried out so loudly during orgasm that he had been scared and would have run away if the crying hadn't suddenly stopped – this was by way of a joke.

They dropped Raqiyya off near her house. She was a little drunk. Hisham grudgingly gave her ten *riyal*s, which she slipped nonchalantly between her breasts, then walked off, swaying slightly.

When he entered his room that evening, the pleasurable headache had gone. In its place was a different kind of headache; one that made him giddy and nauseous. He ran to the bathroom and spewed out the contents of his stomach, then drank a lot of water, which soothed him a little even though the nausea lingered. He went back to his room and lay down, while the world spun and he felt as if he was falling off the bed. He shut his eyes, promising inwardly, 'I'm not going to drink after today, so long as I live.' Then he fell asleep.

9

When he woke the following morning to the sound of his uncle's call to prayer, he felt as if his skull had detached itself from his body. He had a hammering headache, and when he tried to move the fluid in his brain seemed to swell and shift about as if it could ebb and flow like the sea. This was no headache, but something else he had never known or suffered in his life before, and to top it all he was suffering from continual and wretched nausea. He attended prayers with his uncle without performing his ablutions. He could have excused himself the trip to the mosque, but really he wanted to go. Afterwards he went back to his room and made himself tea and a cheese-and-melon-jam sandwich. The tea made him feel a little better, but he only took one bite of the sandwich. He had completely lost his appetite.

He went to college and listened to the morning lectures, but the hammering wouldn't stop; nor would the sickness, although it was less violent. He didn't go to the afternoon lecture on Islamic civilisation, but instead sat in the canteen with a glass of strong tea with lemon juice. He felt nauseous whenever images of the previous day's outing entered his mind, and the very thought of *arak* provoked in him a violent urge to vomit. It was only with crippling twinges of conscience that he could remember what he had done with Raqiyya, and when he recalled how he had wanted to slap the image of his mother he was horrified. But the strange thing was that all these painful emotions mingled with the extraordinarily pleasurable recollection of his orgasm.

He lived that whole day waiting for the next, in the hope that when a new day dawned the hammering would stop and the nausea disappear. He went home and tried to relax, but the slightest movement started off the hammering and the tidal movements in his head. He didn't eat lunch with his housemates. Abd al-Rahman came looking for him because he hadn't slept with them on the roof the night before, and now he didn't want his lunch. Something was up. Hisham reassured him that everything was okay, but that he wasn't hungry because he'd had a sandwich at college. Abd al-Rahman left and then Hamad arrived, evidently very worried. He asked him how he was and when Hisham told him that he'd been drinking *arak* Hamad laughed. 'Welcome to the Friendly Club,' he said. Then he explained that what he was feeling was quite natural for someone who'd been drinking for the first time, and that he'd get used to it and after a while it wouldn't have any effect. At this Hisham shouted, 'The first and last time, by your father's head!' But he couldn't finish the sentence; the hammering had started again. Hamad went out laughing after giving Hisham a look that he thought a little strange. 'Okay … we'll see,' was all he said.

Moudhi came in several times that day to check how he was, as there was obviously something wrong. Each time he told her he was fine, though he was stretched out stiff on the bed like a lifeless corpse. Whenever she came in he tried to smile and get up, although he knew that the hammering would start again. Every time she asked him if he needed anything, he said no. Finally she brought him a pot of hot mint and a lemon chopped in two. She put the tray on the desk, squeezed half a lemon and poured the juice.

'It must be a touch of cold,' she said. 'Sleeping on the roof isn't safe these days. You must drink it all,' she added as she handed him the glass of mint. 'God willing, you'll get your health back quicker than you think. Come on, drink!' She pushed the glass towards him, her smile visible behind the veil. He got up slowly and drank the mint without really wanting it, while Moudhi stood beside the bed, refusing to leave before he had drunk it all. He finished the glass and lay down again while Moudhi wiped his brow with the other half of the lemon. He actually did feel a little better. He imagined he could see the face of his mother smiling from behind Moudhi's veil, but he felt a little embarrassed at Moudhi being in his room even though he had begun to feel familiar with her. He got up from the bed and walked over to his desk, where he picked up a book at random, sat down and pretended to read.

'I feel completely recovered,' he said. 'I don't know how to thank you.' Moudhi smiled and made to leave.

'Praise be to God,' she said. 'I'll make you a glass of hot milk that will make you sleep like a little lamb.' She rushed off without waiting for a reply. Hisham smiled as the image of his mother teased him again. He had no idea why Taha Hussein's story of Oedipus* came into his mind at that moment. He wished that he had brought it with him to read. Not that he needed to, as he had read it more than once and listened to it as a radio serial on 'Voice of the Arabs', so he could remember it perfectly. Right now he saw himself as Taha Hussein's friend. He felt like a shattered marble statue whose parts he was trying to reassemble, but he didn't know how, because the pieces were tiny and there were fragments scattered everywhere. Even if he succeeded, would it be the same old statue? Something that is smashed can be gathered up and put

---

*   Taha Hussein (1889–1973), leading Egyptian writer and intellectual.

back together, but would it be the same thing? If his mother knew that he had tasted forbidden fruit, that he had known politics, women and the curse of drink, what would she do? Would she expel him from her tenderness and affection, or would she forgive him his lapses? Would she forgive his mistakes, or would he be cursed? Would he end as Adam or Satan, or neither, as a previously unimaginable mixture of the two? Or maybe even in nothing at all?

Moudhi brought in the hot milk. He didn't want it, but she gently cajoled him. He sipped the milk quietly, now and then stealing a glance at Moudhi standing in front of the desk, unwilling to move until he had drunk the last drop.

10

He was awake when the voice of the *muezzin* sang out its sweet melody, calling the faithful to dawn prayers. For the first time he realised how beautiful the voice of a *muezzin* could be, though the voice of *their muezzin* was usually hoarse and unpleasant. He was in a great mood – his thumping headache and that awful feeling of nausea had gone – although now and then his conscience still stabbed him. He went to the bathroom and took a cold shower, watching the cold water mingle with soap and run off his body on its way to the drain, as if he were seeing the foul residue of his evil deed leave his soul, never to return.

At the mosque he prayed as he had never prayed before, and stayed on long after prayers were over. He needed to talk to someone, but not just anyone. Taking a copy of the Qur'an, Hisham leaned back against the wall and prepared to open the holy book just as his uncle was finishing his prayers (including extra devotions and invocations) and preparing to leave the mosque. When he saw Hisham holding the Qur'an, he gave a broad, contented smile (something he'd seldom seen before on his uncle's face), and left without addressing him, though Hisham heard him murmur, 'God bless you, my son. God bless you, my son.' Hisham opened the Qur'an and began to read: *By the star when it sets, your friend has not strayed or fallen into error, nor does he speak from desire ...*

When he got back from the mosque, Moudhi had made breakfast. She looked pleased when she saw that Hisham was in the best of health. But Hisham knew, as he sat at the table, that she would spit on him had she any idea what he had done. They all sat and ate, in silence, the small plates of beans with warm, dry, Afghan bread, and drank their milky tea. Hisham's uncle ate contentedly, looking at him with a generous smile that never left his face. Before getting up, he looked at his sons. 'I wish you were more like Hisham,' he said, 'a young man like no other.' Then he got up and looked at Hisham, saying, 'God bless you, my son, and may He make many like you.' He left for his room, murmuring some of his favourite prayers. As usual, a silent Muhammad followed immediately after him.

Abd al-Rahman looked at Hisham and smiled, stuffing more food into his mouth. Hamad got up and leaned against the wall with a glass in his hand, asking quietly, 'What's up? What's all this flirting between you and father?'

'It's very strange,' said Ahmad. 'Father rarely praises anyone. What *have* you been up to?' Eyes stared at him from every side; Hisham was mortified.

'Nothing,' he said. 'Nothing at all. He just spotted me as he left the mosque ... reading the Qur'an. That's all.'

'Does anyone stay in the mosque after father?' asked Ahmad, open-mouthed. 'This is indeed a true miracle.'

'Yes. What *is* going on in Hisham's soul?' asked Hamad. 'Since when has he been addicted to the mosque?' He drank the rest of his milky tea and poured another. 'Anyway,' he said, laughing. 'It's a good thing. Now we can sit chatting in the evening in your room without arousing anyone's suspicions. Congratulations, my friend, you have become one of God's trusty saints, and now you can come to no harm.'

Hisham was excruciatingly embarrassed by his cousins' comments, and was suffering fresh pangs of conscience and stomach cramps, but still they showed no sign of stopping. Hamad went on in the same sarcastic vein: 'I had no idea you could be so cunning. Anyone would think you were a weak and innocent dove, but it seems there's a snake lurking in the grass.' When he had finished, he gave a loud laugh, but Abd al-Rahman stopped him.

'You're being unfair to Hisham, my friends,' he said. 'He's not guilty of your charges. He really is just an innocent lamb.'

As Abd al-Rahman spoke he glanced at Hisham from the corner of his eye, winking and smirking as if to say, 'There you are, I've testified for you, and made you an example in this house. No one will have any suspicions about us after today.' This was exactly what Hamad had been implying, though in a different way.

Everyone left; Abd al-Rahman to go to school, and the others to work. Hisham stayed where he was, thinking, while Moudhi and Said collected the leftovers and cleaned up. Moudhi was muttering angrily to herself. He had no idea what she was saying, but he could be pretty sure that she was cursing her brother Muhammad's wife, Anoud – or poor Said, who was often the butt of Moudhi's wrath. Hisham ignored them and reflected on his current situation. Why didn't his cousins believe that what he had done in the mosque was no hypocrisy or blasphemous trick, but a real genuine feeling? He smiled as he thought of his uncle; such a good man, just deceived by appearances like most people. When he really had been innocent, his uncle hadn't praised him at all, and now that he had faltered, he praised him excessively. But he couldn't be blamed; he had nothing to go on except appearances. He saw Hisham praying and judged him to be virtuous, although the worst of God's creatures prayed along with everyone else.

Moudhi's voice woke him from his reverie. She had stopped cleaning. 'Aren't you going to the mosque today?' she asked. He smiled at her. Then he got up, still meditating, though his thumping headache and violent nausea had vanished.

11

During the days that followed, he tried to go straight. He went from home to college, from college to home or sometimes to his friends' house, but nowhere else. It comforted him to behave like this. His conscience eased and he felt peace and contentment return. Now, when he pictured his mother's face, it was clearly smiling. But despite the pangs it caused him, there was one thing he could not get out of his mind: Raqiyya's body, and its wild, tangled triangle. Whenever images of that soft brown body flickered across his mind, the exciting feeling of pleasure returned, and he felt lust creep into every part of his body, blotting out all painful feelings of remorse.

These images began to frighten him. He saw them whenever he walked to his friends' house and caught sight of Muhaysin's window in the distance. When he was alone in his own room, Raqiyya's image forced itself upon him and every limb in his body stiffened. He went looking for Abd al-Rahman in the hope that he could make another date with her, but stopped himself at the last moment. He would go straight whatever the sacrifices.

But whenever he talked to Abd al-Rahman he felt his resistance waning. His cousin had seen Raqiyya several times and reported that she was always asking after him. Abd al-Rahman laughed and added, 'I don't know what you did for her ... or *to* her. She never stops asking about you – she's quite insistent.' He winked and laughed. Hisham didn't know whether Abd al-Rahman was exaggerating or telling the truth, but he still felt proud and elated by this lavish praise. Every cell in his body yearned for Raqiyya; her damp, wild triangle never left his mind, despite all the painful remorse it caused him merely to picture the ugly thing. And he had felt deeply ashamed since picturing his mother's face framed by Raqiyya's triangle in a dream.

One night he was revising for his first formal examination. The whole place was in total silence; everyone was asleep. This late at night, all he could hear was the sound of wild dogs patrolling the streets. They got nearer, then further away. He couldn't concentrate; Raqiyya commandeered his thoughts. He was supposed to be memorising the fluctuations of supply and demand, and how they varied with any change of circumstance, but the graphs made him think of things entirely unconnected with economics. He was boiling hot, though the weather in Riyadh was quite moderate for that time in July and his fan was revolving quietly and slowly. He needed some fresh air, so he got up from his chair, drew it under the window and looked out at the empty street. He watched the dogs chasing one another, competing for food and bitches. Shutting his eyes, he filled his lungs with air – wishing it were as fresh to breathe as the desert air in Nejd. He felt pleasantly intoxicated – though he'd drunk nothing – and utterly tranquil. He was about to collapse into bed, when something in the window of the house opposite caught his eye. It was half-closed, and a curious pale light filtered through its transparent shutters. It surprised him that anyone should be awake at this late hour of the night. The principles of economics beckoned, but a movement through the shutters made him stay where he was and look more closely. What he saw made his heart beat faster, and his whole body stiffen and drip with sweat: a man and a woman, completely naked, having sex. He was transfixed by the sight, and watched, spellbound, until the man was spent. Hisham watched as he got up and left the room while the woman lay motionless, her eyes fixed on the window. For one terrifying moment he thought she was looking straight at him. She had seen him spying on her. He turned his face from the window, but the temptation was too strong, and he gazed out again. She was still lying there, looking at the window, but now she seemed to be smiling. He couldn't move. He was paralysed. Then the man came back, at which point the woman got up and left the room, then came back and turned off the light so that Hisham could no longer see anything. He got down from the window and threw himself on the bed, extremely aroused. He saw nothing but the woman's buttocks and breasts. Then, suddenly, he was afraid. What if the woman had seen him spying on their most intimate and private act? They were neighbours, and would know his uncle and his family. Would they complain about him to his uncle? That would be a disaster. His perfect record would collapse in front of his uncle and Moudhi – his uncle might even tell Hisham's family! It would break his mother's heart and destroy his father's trust.

But the woman hadn't moved or looked embarrassed when she saw him spying from the window ... perhaps she hadn't seen him, and he had just imagined it. After all she'd done nothing to hide her naked body – she'd just lain there. And how could she let herself perform this most intimate of acts with the window as good as open, since their shutters hid nothing? Perhaps they had wanted the fresh evening breezes and were sure the street would be empty at this time of night. But why had she stayed there when she saw him? Perhaps she hadn't seen him. No. She had definitely seen him; their eyes had met. Hisham was lost in confusion. He forgot all about economics; forgot the fluctuations of supply and demand and the balance between the producer and the consumer, when suddenly he was overcome by weariness. He got up from his bed and went up onto the roof where everyone was snoring deeply except for Hamad, whose bed was still empty.

12

The whole next day he was terrified, anxious in case something happened – in case his uncle summoned him, or Moudhi came in looking upset. But the day passed without incident. His uncle smiled when he saw him, and Moudhi busied herself with her daily routine, muttering and grumbling as usual. When darkness came and everything fell quiet, the dogs were soon back on the scene, scratching themselves and barking at each other, while Hisham found himself tormented by a burning curiosity. He tried to get a grip on himself so as not to give in to every little whim, but a fire he could not put out was eating him from within. He took up his position of the night before and began to watch …

This time the window opposite was shut tight. There wasn't a glimmer of light within. He was greatly frustrated, and then his fear returned. They must have realised what had happened last night but were avoiding a scandal, for fear of the neighbours. From now on they would have a powerful hold over him.

His fear and frustration made him restless, and he wanted to go out, but something on the roof of the one-storey house caught his eye. Everything was steeped in darkness, but for a faint glimmer of light coming from the stars, or perhaps it came from the street light in the distance ... it wasn't significant. What mattered was what kept Hisham rooted to the spot, eyes as wide as they would open. He watched a shadowy figure come from the direction of the stairwell and make for the other side of the roof, returning to the area above the window with a large bundle on its shoulder. The figure threw the bundle onto the floor, spread it out, then covered it with a light blanket and put down two small pillows. Then it went back to the house.

It was the shadow of a woman; it had to be the same woman he had seen yesterday.

In only a few moments the shadow returned, and this time it was clear that it was the same woman. She was wearing a flimsy dress that revealed every bulge on her curvaceous body – those undulations impossible to hide. She looked around, and then shot a glance at Hisham's small window. He ducked his head, though this time he had no doubt that she had seen him. Down he got from his chair, heart pounding, and tried to pull himself together. He put out the light, trying to calm down and get back his breath, but his sense that something was taking place on the rooftop opposite made him leap up madly and go back to the window, feeling a little safer now that he had put out the light.

The woman lay on her bed. Hisham tried to imagine the details of the body stretched out before him in the dark, but two dogs snapped at each other in the street below, their loud barking destroying the night's silence. Then the fighting suddenly stopped. The two dogs began to chase a third, and the barking moved further away.

He turned his attention back to the rooftop opposite. Nothing had changed, but after a while another shadow appeared and climbed onto the bed ... the man from last night. He was wearing a white *tob* and a white skullcap. He took off the *tob* but left the skullcap. Still wearing his underclothes (long white pants and a white short-sleeved vest) he slipped in beside the woman. Hisham's imagination filled in what happened next.

When he slept that night, his dreams featured naked men and women in a parched desert. They were laughing and chasing each other about under the burning rays of the sun. But somehow the men and women never touched.

13

One afternoon Hisham was sitting in the canteen munching a sandwich of boiled eggs with tomatoes and hot peppers. He was looking quickly through his notes on legal principles – he was going to be tested on them in less than an hour. He was engrossed in his revision, but deep down he was extremely agitated: spying on the house opposite had become a nightly habit that distracted him from revising as he ought to have. He started when he felt a hand patting his shoulder. 'Hisham,' said a voice. He stopped chewing and turned round. What a surprise! It was Adnan al-Ali, looking just the same, his face as pale as a mummy's and wreathed in smiles. Hisham leapt up and embraced his childhood friend warmly, his mind full of memories. His stomach shrank as he remembered the organisation. He invited Adnan to sit down, and examined him closely. He hadn't changed much, though he had got thinner, and he had left the downy hair on his chin to grow as it pleased. Hisham quizzed him about Dammam and Adama and everything else. Then, as if the question had just occurred to him, he asked, 'What brings you to Riyadh? How long have you been here? And how did you know where I was –?'

'Slowly! Slowly, my brother!' said Adnan, stopping him with a wave of his hand and smiling. 'Slowly!'

'I've been here for five days,' he said quietly, once he had caught his breath.

'Five days? Five days, and you only looked for me today! You're a fine friend!'

'Didn't I say "take it easy", my brother?' Adnan caught his breath again and continued. 'I've been here for five days. I gave my papers in to the College of Agriculture. They only accepted me after a lot of pleading and beard-kissing – and the intervention of some high-up people. They're right, of course – I am very late. The important thing is, I've been staying with some relatives who are students, and here I am ... that's all there is to it.'

'But what about Rome and the arts? Why are you entering the College of Agriculture when you loathe applied sciences?'

Adnan smiled and crossed his hands in his lap. 'Father was right,' he said. 'Art is a waste of time. Working in a secondary school has no real future and my marks won't qualify me to enter medicine or engineering. So there you have it.' Adnan spoke in his usual calm, quiet voice, but with a strange new confidence Hisham didn't recognise. Could people change in less than two months? He couldn't stop himself from objecting.

'But you are talented, Adnan. God forbid that you should waste your talent!'

Adnan smiled and said nonchalantly, with no obvious emotion, 'No talent, no nothing. Everyone will find his own destiny. God's choice is best.'

'Anyway,' he added, after an interval of silence, 'I've thought seriously about this question of art. What's the point of art, really? It's a waste of time God doesn't approve of. And I don't want to waste time that I shall be held accountable for on the Day of Judgment.'

Hisham was so staggered he was struck dumb. Was this the

same Adnan he had left less than two months ago? Adnan, who had once found his only refuge in drawing, now refused to draw! Almost everything about him seemed changed, except for his pale face and that expression of his that was more like the expression of the dead, even if his eyes sparkled more than before. Then again, what was this constant talk about God and the Day of Judgment? Even their friend Salim, the most religious of them all, didn't mention these things much.

'That's not true,' said Hisham, trying to escape his questionings. 'Art isn't a waste of time. It's an expression of all that is sublime in our lives and our souls; a philosophical expression, if you want. Art is an expression of the absolute in us: the poet in his poem; the artist on his canvas; the musician in his composition. All of these are expressing the sublime aspect of human existence, far removed from the details of deadly mundanity. You yourself only discovered your true nature with brush and paints when life was choking you. Why? Because that is where you found yourself. And I believe,' he added, after a short pause, 'that you are still like that, but I don't know what has happened to you. I haven't been away for more than a couple of months, but, I don't know ...' He tailed off hopelessly.

Adnan seemed confused but tried to smile, while looking into the distance. 'You haven't changed, Hisham,' he said. 'All your life you have liked to argue and keep certainty at arm's length. As for me, I've settled things.' He was silent for a little as he gazed straight ahead. 'Yes,' he continued firmly. 'I've left things to the Master to do as He wishes. We are only weak creatures, and this world is only a passing station. We have forgotten God. We have forgotten Him.'

He stopped speaking. Hisham's eyes nearly started from their sockets. This wasn't Adnan, even if it looked like Adnan. His face took on the expression of a simpleton.

'My God, how you have changed, Adnan! I don't recognise you!' Adnan gave a short laugh.

'No, my friend,' he said. 'I haven't changed, but I've reached the sort of stability from which there can be no future change.' There was another short silence. The two friends gazed at each other. Then Hisham looked at his watch and began to gather his books together.

'You must excuse me,' he said. 'I've got an exam in less than five minutes. Tell me ... where do you live?'

'In Halla,' came the answer.

Adnan described the place to him as they walked towards the college building, where they parted as Hisham prepared for the cold bath in which Doctor Najar al-Shatartun would soon be drowning him.

14

Later that afternoon, Hisham went to Halla for the first time since coming to Riyadh. It wasn't far from al-Batha Street, but he got lost in some alleys before arriving at Adnan's house. He knocked on the narrow, pale-green iron door for some time without anyone answering, and was just on the point of leaving when a voice came from inside indicating that someone was there. The door opened and a man wearing a pair of long flowing white trousers, a short-sleeved shirt and a white skullcap peered out. He was rather similar to Adnan, but taller and plumper, with a light beard that covered his chin and cheeks.

'Good evening,' said Hisham. 'Is brother Adnan around?'

'Peace be upon you, and the mercy and blessings of God. Yes, come on in.' The young man opened the door as far as it would go, and Hisham entered. The man closed the door, looked at Hisham, smiled, and then led him to a room on the right of the entrance. 'Come in,' he said again with a smile. 'I'll tell Adnan you're here. Your name, sir?'

'Hisham ... Hisham al-Abir.'

'Pleased to meet you.'

'And you.'

The young man disappeared into the interior of the house. The room Hisham waited in was clean and simple. A green carpet covered the floor. Yellow armchairs and sofas lined the walls. He sat in the first chair he found. A smell of damp filled the place – a dampness you wouldn't find in the Nejd air, but which reminded him of Dammam.

He didn't have to wait long. Adnan appeared quickly, echoing Hisham's greeting and looking the spitting image of his housemate. The two sat down beside each other. Then the person who had opened the door came in, carrying a tea tray with a small silver pot on it and two glasses, which he set in front of Adnan. 'Please excuse me, brother Adnan,' he said, the smile never leaving his face. 'I have some work that has to be done.' He added, 'Blessings be upon you, brother Adnan,' looking at Adnan and smiling, then quietly walked off.

They drank the tea in silence, then Adnan suddenly leapt up as if a snake had bitten him. 'I've forgotten something!' He rushed out, and came back with a wad of banknotes in his hand, which he thrust at Hisham. 'God curse forgetfulness,' he said. 'This is some money that my father gave me to give you. It's from your father.' Hisham smiled, took the money and slipped it quietly into his pocket. He went back to the glass of tea he was sipping, thinking of the money. It was clearly a large sum: not less than two hundred *riyal*s – he'd spotted several 'tenners'. After a short silence Hisham spoke, screwing his eyes up nervously, 'What's the news about the arrests?'

This was a crafty question on Hisham's part. He was looking for further reassurance, on top of the comfort he derived from all the time that had passed. He also wanted to frighten Adnan. But Adnan continued to sip his tea.

'Nothing new,' he said quietly, looking at the wooden ceiling.

'Some defectors in Qatif and Ahsa ... Anyway, I don't care any more.'

'Some defectors?' This was a new expression Hisham hadn't heard before. But the biggest surprise was that Adnan no longer cared. 'You don't care any more? How come?'

'I told you earlier, I've left everything to the Almighty.'

There was a short silence, then Adnan said, as if performing a duty, 'Would you like to see the house?' Without waiting for an answer, he got up. 'You'll love it,' he said. 'It's better than our house in Dammam, and my housemates are a great improvement on Majid and his brothers ... Yusuf's brothers ....' He gave a short laugh. Hisham got up slowly and followed Adnan, who walked with a firm step Hisham had never noticed before.

'This is the courtyard ... we don't use it much although it's very spacious.' Around the courtyard were three rooms spread out along the sides, as well as a bathroom and the entrance to a stairway. Adnan led him to the first room on the left of the entrance, a smile covering his face. 'This is my room ...' He took a deep breath. 'Come in,' he said. 'Make yourself at home.' He gave a short, abrupt laugh, then quickly entered the room. There was a carpet striped with yellow and green covering the length of the room, and an orange blanket on the floor in the far corner, under the only window to the left of the door. There was also a metal clothes rack, like the one Hisham had, and a black bag thrown down carelessly beside the door, as well as some books scattered on the floor beside the blanket.

'So. What do you think of my room?'

'Not bad, not bad.'

Hisham went over to examine the books. *The Fatwas of Ibn Taymiyya, Signposts on the Way, My Journey from Doubt to Certainty, God Reveals Himself in the Scientific Age, Rescuing the Sorrowful from Satan's Snares, The Revival of the Religious Sciences, The Steps of the Travellers, The Future of This Religion.*

He finished flicking through the books and said, 'Indeed, art *is* a waste of time.' His tone was sarcastic, although he had intended it to sound funny. Adnan, however, reacted in a way he hadn't anticipated.

'This is useful knowledge. I regret all those years that I spent on useless things. Drawing, and sterile debate.' Hisham saw what Adnan meant and was cut to the quick, but he only said, 'Steady on, my friend ... I meant it as a joke.' But Adnan was extremely angry.

'No jokes, no rubbish,' he said. 'You shouldn't joke about such matters.'

'Too much joking and laughter kills the heart and weakens one's manhood,' he continued, resuming his composure. 'As the Prophet, on whom be peace, said.' For the first time in his life, Hisham felt disconcerted by Adnan.

'On Him be blessings and peace,' said Hisham, trying to be diplomatic. 'Anyway, these are all useful books. They cultivate goodness and increase the sublime.' Adnan relaxed and the calm returned to his eyes.

'What a crafty old dodger you are. You have an extraordinary gift. I wish you could be part of Islam and its people.'

'What am I, a *Buddhist*?' replied Hisham, open-mouthed. 'Am I Muhammad's opponent?'

'No, you are worse than all of those,' replied Adnan calmly. 'Aren't you a Marxist? A Baathist? I know you better than yourself. That's enough to expel you from the community.' *Expel? Community? Was this Adnan?*

'But I believe in God and his Prophet and –'

'Stop talking rubbish. I know you. Faith is a matter of words *and* deeds. You have neither. I am sorry, I don't mean to insult you, but this is the truth. God is not ashamed of the truth, so why should we, his servants, be ashamed of it or pretend not to know it?'

Hisham was livid. *I'm neither words nor deeds*. It made him sick. But he stifled his anger, pulled himself together and got up, saying, 'You must excuse me, I have to leave.'

Adnan tried to stop him, but it was obviously out of politeness and Hisham insisted on going. Adnan accompanied him to the outer door. Before he left, Adnan asked him to wait for a moment, then disappeared inside and returned with a little book that he pushed towards Hisham. 'I am sure that you will like it,' he said smiling. 'And perhaps God will help you and guide you.' Hisham reluctantly took the book, gave his friend a quick look, then went off hearing the door close behind him.

15

All the way from the station to al-Batha Street, where he could board the local bus, he thought about Adnan and the extraordinary change in his life and personality. In the bus heading towards Usarat Street, by way of al-Khazzan Street, he flipped through the book Adnan had given him: al-Ghazali's *Al-Munqidh min al-Dalal* ('Deliverance from Error'). He loathed this sort of book, but he was determined to read it, in the hope of finding some explanation for the revolution in Adnan's life; until now Adnan had always been so predictable.

When he shut the door of his room that evening, he was delighted by the sum his father had sent him: two hundred and fifty *riyal*s. He slipped them into a book in his little study, made himself some tea, leaned back against the wall and began to read *Al-Munqidh min al-Dalal*. It really was an amazing book, despite its diminutive size – very thought-provoking, even though its ending didn't satisfy Hisham. It concluded that faith was nothing but light which God poured into the heart, and that the intellect and will had nothing to do with it. Its conclusion was pure fatalism, though perhaps it was this fatalism that had affected Adnan so quickly and powerfully. Hisham compared it with historical materialism. Wasn't that also a sort of fate? But he rejected the idea, and returned to the topic of Adnan again.

The Adnan Hisham knew was almost pacifist in nature – so mild-mannered it could be seen as a flaw in his character. He was sensitive, with extremely refined feelings. It would never have occurred to Hisham that he could have been turned head-over-heels so quickly. Finding an explanation was really bugging him. He had always dealt with Adnan on the basis that he was just a friend; he had never before tried to make him the object of serious contemplation. But when he started to look at the full picture of Adnan's life, certain things stood out which hadn't seemed significant before.

A person like Adnan could only thrive in an atmosphere of certainty and security; protected by an environment that constantly shielded and directed him. Because he was a person of sensitive feelings, he was often anxious and was easily upset. The intricate details of life that his brother Majid could deal with so well worried and upset Adnan because he couldn't handle them. So for Adnan, drawing had become a sort of retreat from these annoying details; a solitary refuge in which he could find a way of proving himself superior to his brother and his brother's success in the eyes of his father and people in general. Hisham smiled wryly at this idea, thinking of Jean-Paul Sartre's remark – he couldn't remember where he had read or heard it – that people were their own worst enemies.

Drawing was an expression of anxiety and a search for absolute certainty at the same time. Adnan resorted to it when he was upset, finding in it the security that his soul craved. But it was only a temporary solace, which ended as soon as he emerged from his studio. Adnan wanted perfect security and never-ending certainty. He wanted someone to be responsible for him the whole time so that he would never suffer the tormenting anxiety of having to deal with choice. Even opting for the Agricultural College had not been a choice so much as a submission to his father's will ... so as to make his father responsible for it.

It was at this point that Hisham remembered how Adnan's artistic efforts had lessened considerably once he became involved in the organisation. The organisation had become a substitute father-figure, taking decisions for him in the absence of his own father. And now, today, here he was handing all responsibility for his life to the True Father.

Memories and forgotten details crowded Hisham's mind; things he had paid no attention to, but which were now proving to be remarkably significant. He realised that his relationship with Adnan had been very one-sided. Although the two friends were both fond of peace and quiet, Adnan was so meek and mild about everything that it sometimes got on Hisham's nerves, even though in other ways it suited him for his friend to be like this. Adnan made him feel powerful, and even though he was his best friend, that was a pleasant sensation. Then an old incident leapt into Hisham's mind. He had no idea why at this precise moment he should remember something that had happened such a long time ago .

They had been in the fourth grade of elementary school. The Qur'an and Qur'anic recitation were the two most difficult and unpopular subjects with the pupils. Both were taught by the school director, Abd al-Salam al-Faq'awi, who was very strict with the pupils, and never let the stick leave his right hand. This stick would descend on their tender bodies whenever they stumbled over a word when reciting a verse, or when they failed to apply the principles of *tajwid* to their recitation. They trembled at the mere mention of *idgham* and *ghanna* and *iqlab*.* That meant being beaten with the

---

* Technical terms referring to detailed points of pronunciation in Qur'anic recitation (*tajwid*).

stick, and being kept at school at the end of the day. They couldn't appeal to anyone. Al-Faq'awi was the director, and their families approved of this harsh treatment, which they hoped would make men of them in the end. But it was inevitable that they would make mistakes, because the teacher stood right in front of them as they recited, amusing himself by striking his left hand gently with the stick in a way that struck terror into their hearts.

Al-Faq'awi never smiled, and his face was a terrifying spectacle: one-eyed and pockmarked, with a thick, straggling moustache and beard. Even the schoolteachers feared him, because he could sack them or write bad reports about them. He often came into their classes unannounced, stick in hand, and in front of the class mocked any teacher he thought was failing in his duties – and, of course, they were always failing.

In one of al-Faq'awi's classes, the pupils were required to recite some verses of the Holy Qur'an, making clear the letters that needed *idgham, ghanna* and *iqlab*. Before Adnan's turn came, he raised his finger to ask permission to go to the toilet. The teacher reprimanded him sternly. Adnan sat hunched in his seat staring at the Holy Qur'an in front of him, shaking terribly. Hisham's turn to recite came and went. As usual, the stick had its share of him that day though, thank goodness, he had not made so many mistakes that he was laid out on the floor and beaten with a whip, then given a detention. The teacher told Adnan to stand up and recite, but he stayed silent, shaking. Then he began to cry. The teacher noticed a patch of urine under Adnan's chair. He grabbed him violently by his shoulder and examined his wet clothes. He hit Adnan with the stick, then dragged him to the front of the class, put his legs in the whipping seat and ordered the nearest two pupils to lift it up. The stick came down again, hard and savagely, as Adnan continued to scream, and the teacher cursed, with the saliva flying from his mouth, as he repeated, 'Cursed children ... if your families don't know how to bring you up, I'll do it myself ... I'll do it myself!' The cane continued to rise and fall. When the teacher finished, he spat at Adnan, cursing, then left the class after ordering Adnan to stay for an hour after the end of the teaching day when the other pupils had left.

Classes finished. Hisham had not yet left, but stayed with Adnan. Tears still hung in the corners of his eyes. 'Why didn't you go to the toilet?' Hisham asked.

'The teacher was in a temper, and I was absolutely desperate. What do you expect me to do?' replied Adnan innocently, wiping away a tear with his sleeve.

'You should have gone, come what may. He would only beat you and give you detention ... What's it matter?' said Hisham.

Hisham smiled as he remembered scenes he had long since thought lost from his mind. He decided to read Freud and the psychoanalytical school more carefully, hoping they would give some answers to the questions that he couldn't find answers to in Marxism.

When he had gone to the mosque at dawn that time after his sexual experience with Raqiyya, he had prayed deeply and pleasurably for the first time in his life, and had experienced some kind of profound spiritual revelation. Before that, his prayers had been mere physical movements, devoid of spirit, and really just a recognition of social conventions. Although he felt insignificant when he observed such conventions, he couldn't abandon them altogether, for God was merciful and forgiving, even though his creatures knew no mercy or forgiveness. But after that violent experience with Raqiyya, when he'd suffered an unbearable pyschological split, he needed a merciful and forgiving Father on whom he could throw his burdens. A Father not like other fathers; a Father who would forgive his errors and mistakes, take him by the hand and lead him to rest after suffering; to release from all the guilt and pain inside him.

But what a difference there was between his state of mind after Raqiyya and this strange upset in the case of Adnan. In a crisis it was quite normal to look for a merciful, powerful father and a gentle mother. Everyone looked for a shoulder to cry on and someone to throw one's burdens onto. But few people wanted to stay crying on that shoulder. It might be comforting, but much better was to learn from one's mistakes and then go out and get it right. Pleasure lay in the existence of pleasure's opposite, not only in pleasure itself. And though it might be nice to find someone willing to take on all your responsibilities, the price was extremely high: freedom itself. Only a child could afford this price, and who wanted to remain a child forever? We all find warmth in our mother's embrace, and strength on our father's shoulder, but few people want to stay forever in her embrace or on his shoulder. Nevertheless, it seemed that Adnan was one of them.

Religion was an urgent requirement. God existed, but it was also necessary for Him to exist. If He didn't exist, there would have been no need for Him. And if there had been no need for Him, He would not have existed. Need and existence complemented themselves at this point. Personal experience was the best proof. To hell with Marx, Feuerbach and al-Rawandi. They saw in religion nothing but ritual and form. But the essence of religion was this essential need, without which one just could not live. Without God, it was inevitable that existence became an absurdity, and an unbearable burden. Perhaps life was like this! But it was up to us not to let it be so, otherwise what was the meaning of life? A saying of Voltaire's came to Hisham's mind again: *If God had not existed, it would have been necessary to invent Him.* And he recalled a saying of Ivan Karamazov's, that everything became permitted and justifiable when there was no God.

The street dogs were barking. Hisham was still leaning against the wall, oblivious to the cold tea he was still drinking.. He threw down *Al-Munqidh min al-Dalal*. He took the chair and put it under the window, then turned out the lights, and began to follow what was happening on the opposite bank of the silent river of the road.

16

How pleasant the weather always was in Nejd at this time of year!
It was neither too hot nor too cold, neither damp nor dry, just
pleasant, like the descriptions of paradise. These days he hung
around the canteen with his new friends, sometimes gossiping
about the teachers or the news, while on other occasions they
would just chatter aimlessly, mostly about 'girls'. He seemed the
least experienced of them, indeed not experienced at all. They
would be talking about Mizna and Badriyya, Hayla and Aisha,
Awatif, Ibtisam and Muna, and he couldn't find anything to say.
He wanted to talk about Noura and about Raqiyya and tell them
about the stories he was writing about Moudhi, but something
stopped him. So he remained silent, immersing himself in the
principles of law and economics, until he was called a 'bookworm'
and 'Four Eyes'. Even though he disliked this description, he was
trusted and loved by everyone. His friends would seek him out to
help them with subjects they didn't understand, or to solve their
emotional problems. They would consult him on the beauty of
their girls, bringing photographs in their pockets. He liked this and

hated it at the same time. To be trusted meant that one was not an object of fear, and this annoyed him, for he didn't want to seem 'safe' all the time.

He took many trips out on the Kharis Road, sometimes with Abd al-Rahman, but usually with Muhammad and Muhaysin, when they made one of their frequent visits to the house and had a spare car. On those days, Nejd became something else. It reverted to the days that had seen Qays and Leila, Antara and Abla, and that transparent poetry which you can only find in Nejd. Everything was beautiful; even men's behaviour became finer and more transparent, after being coarse and tasteless. The sun and land of Nejd knew no mercy when they were given the chance, and how many were the chances!

He started to sleep in his room. The cold on the roof was unbearable in the early hours of the morning. This also gave him a better opportunity to observe the street opposite, and to follow the activity of the husband and wife who had now moved back down to the lower floor. The roof had been transformed into a barren area of red and yellow dust on which the winds played at midday. His relationship with the 'new' Adnan was now nothing more than a meaningless social convention. He would sometimes meet him in the canteen, when he ate one of Amm Wardan's sandwiches after noon – just a passing greeting, a conventional question about how each of them was, then everything would return to normal. It was obvious that Adnan didn't want to continue their friendship, and Hisham wasn't enthusiastic either. Adnan didn't usually come to the canteen alone. There were usually two colleagues with him, both wearing unkempt beards. Sometimes there were as many as five, drinking tea and speaking out of earshot in a whisper. The thing that most surprised Hisham was that they hardly ever smiled. If one of them actually did smile, he covered his face with the sleeve of his gown as if to apologise, then reverted to those impenetrable features, and Adnan would do the same. He couldn't remember

72

him ever doing that before. The thing that disturbed Adnan and his friends most was when Hisham and his friends were sitting at an adjacent table letting rip dirty jokes and laughing at the top of their voices, then talking and shouting. Despite the fact that Hisham only occasionally took part in this rowdy talk, he liked to sit among these colleagues and steal a glance at Adnan and his friends. He would see Adnan stealing a glance at him, and then the pair of them would look at the table again as if they hadn't seen each other. Adnan's group looked down on Hisham's group; they would soon get up, repeating, 'There is no power or might except with God ... there is no power or might except with God,' while the others carried on laughing and shouting. Hisham didn't take much notice of the 'new' Adnan's style, or his new personality, yet he felt that he had lost something indefinable. And Hisham also felt that life was concealing something from him; something new he couldn't put his finger on.

One day he was coming back from college, after having a snack with his friends at their house. He had been doing that a lot recently in spite of Muhanna, whose eyes betrayed anger quite clearly even though he didn't express it openly. That didn't bother Hisham much, so long as Muhammad, Muahysin and Dais showed him genuine affection and so long as he frequently brought with him fresh milk for lunch, or beans and fresh bread, and sometimes *mutabbaq* with eggs or bananas many evenings for supper. The strange thing was that Muhanna was politer to him when Hisham bought the supper.

One day, burping the whole way from the effect of the milk he had drunk at lunch, he reached home just before the call to afternoon prayers. He knew that this uncle would be in the mosque, that Ahmad was probably doing 'overtime', and that Abd al-Rahman was either taking a siesta in his room or wandering the alleyways of Riyadh in search of amusement, and God only knew where Hamad might be! – so he felt free to stop and belch as he pleased. The street was deserted – there weren't even any dogs or boys, so when he reached the corner of his uncle's house he stopped for a moment to look at the house opposite. Mentally he replayed what he had seen in the room and on the roof – then suddenly stiffened. He felt a strong desire to disappear, but the door had opened. A woman looked out. She wore a black scarf round her neck that hung to the ends of her hair, except for some fine strands that glinted in the golden sun. She was carrying a bucket of rubbish, which she threw out before suddenly noticing him. She didn't react, just clasped the bucket to her chest and stayed standing beside the door. Hisham had no idea how long the two of them exchanged feverish glances; on these occasions time is not measured in minutes and hours. He shivered. It was quite definitely the woman on the roof. A sort of terrible embarrassment overwhelmed him. He couldn't meet her gaze, but retreated, cringing like a dog, and shut himself into his room. His heart thumped, sweat dripped from every pore in his body and he seethed with shame. But when he had calmed down a little he drew his chair up to the window and peered out.

Her door was shut, but her window was wide open and she was sweeping the room, with her bottom to the window. He almost exploded when he glimpsed the cleft between her buttocks. The room was spotless, but still she continued sweeping. He was loving this. Suddenly she spun round and smiled at him before slamming the window shut. She had seen him! She had known he was there from the first moment. Perhaps she also knew of his nocturnal spying. He felt happy and terrified all at once, and he craved a cigarette. Shouting for Said, he ran down the stairs.

Moudhi got to him first, trying to cover her face with her veil, and saying in a clearly agitated voice, 'OK, OK! What's the matter? God willing nothing is wrong!'

'No, no, nothing's wrong. I'm wanting Abd al-Rahman. Where's Abd al-Rahman?' asked Hisham. Moudhi calmed down.

'Enough of this,' she said. 'You're driving me mad. All this commotion for a dimwit! You're always going on like this!' Hisham pulled himself together and calmed down.

'I need him for something important,' he said. 'Where is he?'

'One moment, and I'll fetch him, said Moudhi, going back inside. It was only a few moments before Abd al-Rahman entered, his hair straggly and uncombed. He was clearly anxious. 'It's not like you to shout for me. I hope to God there's nothing wrong?'

'No, nothing's wrong. I just needed a cigarette. Do you have one?' Abd al-Rahman looked startled, then shouted with laughter. 'God confound you, *sheikh*! All this for a cigarette! Take one. No! Take the whole packet!' He threw Hisham a packet of Marlboro Reds and made for the door, still laughing. Before he shut it behind him, he turned and looked quizzically at Hisham, asking, 'Since when have you smoked?' Hisham just smiled and took out a cigarette. He lit it as Abd al-Rahman went out, yawning, 'God curse you, you've caused enough trouble this afternoon.'

The cigarette was fantastic. He experienced the usual pleasant queasiness and that delicious erotic tension. How he longed for Raqiyya. In fact, right now he was ready to take any woman – so what about the woman over the road? He climbed back onto the chair, but saw nothing. The door and the window were shut. He stepped down onto the ground, lit another cigarette, which he smoked right down to the filter, then went to his little stove and made tea, arguing with himself all the while: *There's no doubt that she saw me. And there's no doubt that she wants what I want. But wait. How can I be sure? It's perfectly obvious. How can I be sure?*

He dragged on another cigarette and looked out of the window again: *Nothing ... I'm dreaming. No ... Yes! What about her husband? He's the wealthiest man around – but is life just possessions? No. But neither is it just my precious metaphysics! – She saw me and smiled ... perhaps. But then, does everyone who smiles at you want to fuck you?*

He smiled ... *fuck* ... what a harsh, dreadful word, expressing nothing pleasurable sounding. There's no doubt that we Arabs are not just harsh in our way of life, Hisham thought, but also harsh in our hearts and feelings. *Fucking*. But if that is so, where do Ibn al-Muluh and Kuthayyir and the others get their finer feelings from? They were just the exceptions to the rule. And what does my life have to do with the poetry of Majnun and Kuthayyir? But *fuck* remains a harsh, ugly word, making the whole concept of sex seem more mechanical than sensuous. He dozed off, smiling pleasurably to himself.

17

From then on Hisham slowed down as he approached the house on his way back from college, his eyes glued to the door of the house opposite. Every time he came back the door would open, and the woman would appear and give him the same smile. Hisham would dive inside, hiding the excitement bubbling up inside him. She was obviously watching for him from the window that overlooked their street. Otherwise, how could she see when he was coming home? He was certain that she wanted him. He had no idea why. But she definitely wanted him. He was confused, torn between the promise of pleasure and the prospect of huge embarrassment. But after several of these encounters, he screwed up enough courage to smile back at her, then dashed inside, feeling like he'd achieved something major. He went up to his room, lit a cigarette, and drew heavily on it until his nerves had calmed a little. (Cigarettes no longer induced that delicious headache, the salivation in his mouth or any of the sexual feelings he had derived from them in the past. Now smoking was a need he was compelled to satisy. So now he bought his own cigarettes – a development that pleased Abd al-Rahman, who had begun to grumble about Hisham's consumption of his own.

One day, he came back from college before noon. Doctor Said Ghadban had taken the day off, Doctor Mutawalli Shahtuti had – as usual – disappeared, and there was no one at his friends' house. As he approached his uncle's house, the door opposite opened and the woman appeared, smiling. He smiled back. This time, though, after quickly checking the alley to her left and right, she beckoned him over. The street was empty but for a few dogs crouching and yawning in corners. Hisham's heart was in his mouth. He almost tripped over his cloak as he ran inside. He raced up to his room, slamming the door behind him, and immediately lit a cigarette which he smoked with a trembling hand. But despite his terror, he was very aroused. When he had calmed down a bit, he drew the chair across to the window and looked out.

She was in the usual room, sitting on the floor with her eyes trained on his window. She smiled again, as if she had been waiting for him. Pain shot through his head and he almost fell off his chair. He got down, soaked with sweat, and lit another cigarette, but it didn't bring him the calm he hoped for. Unconsciously he made for his wooden box, taking out a plastic bottle one-quarter full of *arak*. He unscrewed its cap, then immediately screwed it on again and put the bottle back in the box. He lit another cigarette. Then he went back to the wooden box and hesitantly drew out the bottle again. He remembered his promise to keep away from drink forever. But he craved that delicious headache, that state of abandonment and carelessness he had felt the last time he drank. Then he thought of all the nausea and terrible pyschological torment afterwards. For several minutes he stood, paralysed, holding the bottle. At last he opened it, then took a teacup and poured a quarter measure into it, which he topped up to the brim with water. He stared at the cup for a few moments, then swallowed its contents in a single gulp, like a man removing his own chains. Fire burnt his throat and his stomach heaved, but he got a grip on himself as his mouth began to water. It was only a few minutes before his stomach settled and that pleasurable ache began to fill his head with confident feelings of lust and bravery. He went back to the chair and looked out … She was still there. Their eyes met and they both smiled. He gestured to her, asking if he should come. She nodded assent, then got up and shut the window.

Hisham poured himself another cup of *arak* and drank it slowly as he smoked. He no longer felt any fear or embarrassment, or anything painful at all. Everything in his mind focused on the pleasure that lay in store. He downed the last of the *arak*, ground out his cigarette in the ashtray and hurried downstairs, aware of nothing until he stood at the door of her house. Then he looked around him, made certain that the alley was empty, and pushed wide the half-open door, shutting it quickly behind him. He was inside, and the woman was standing there waiting for him.

She grabbed him by the hand and pulled him into the room in which he had first seen her. Without any preliminaries, she threw herself at him and kissed him passionately, as if she had known him for a long time. In a few moments they were stretched out together on the floor. Their embraces were more passionate than any he had experienced with Raqiyya, because this time it was him taking the lead. But as the effects of the *arak* began to wear off, he started to feel nervous again. He was terrified about the scandal there would be if her husband came back without any warning. He wanted to leave, but she persuaded him to stay, convincing him that it was impossible that her husband would show up now. She asked him to drink tea with her, and he accepted despite himself. She went to get the tea ready, wearing nothing but a short blue, see-through dress with no underclothes. Her whole body quivered as she walked. She brought the tea, put it in front of him and poured a cup which she handed him, laughing, showing her pure white teeth. 'By the way, my name is Sarah. But my friends call me Suwayr.'

'And I'm –'

'I know. Hisham, isn't it?'

'Yes ... but how did you know?' She laughed mischievously. Her dress had slipped, revealing her belly. He glimpsed her shaven triangle.

'Aren't we neighbours?' she said. 'I made discreet inquiries about you.' She looked at him out of the corner of her eye as she calmly sipped her tea, smiling cryptically. She had her legs tucked under her bottom, so that the skin on her knees and thighs was taut, and glowed in the light filtering through the window.

'I knew that you spied on us on the roof from your room,' she said. 'I knew that you were there. I knew that I would get you. I wanted you from the moment I saw you, though you didn't know it. I started to look for you there, watching from the window, when you were coming back home ...'

Hisham felt feverishly hot, though the temperature was quite moderate. His cheeks were flushed, and beads of sweat had collected on his wide brow. Suwayr saw his embarrassment, and leaned forward to kiss his cheeks. Then she sat back down, saying with obvious tenderness, smiling clearly, 'Ever since I first saw you, I felt something strange drawing me to you. I felt that I had known you for ages. I felt that we were bound together by something like fate that couldn't be repelled or resisted. Call it what you like, but this is what I felt.'

Silence descended, broken only by the sound of their tea-drinking, until she said, 'Your face spoke of everything that I needed: innocence, love and compassion. This is what I have always looked for.' Then, without any warning, she suddenly broke into silent tears. They streamed down her face. She was forced to raise her legs to hide her face between them. Her dress came off completely, but for the first time he saw her body without that overpowering lust. Instead his throat ached, and his whole body prickled. He stretched out his hand and put it on her bare knee, feeling many different sensations, none of which was lust. When she felt his hand on her knee, she covered it with her's and looked up at him submissively. Then she drew his face to hers and planted a kiss deep on his lips. Her salty tears ran onto his lips as they embraced. They became one flesh again.

when he was suddenly aware of Suwayr, her voluptuous body and distinctive smell of lemon perfume, her broad smile and her provocative eyes, standing right in front of him. Her cloak had fallen from her head and lay on her shoulders; her thick hair fell to just below her bottom, and she had wrapped its ends around her waist. When he saw her he leapt up instinctively and locked his door shut. Then he retraced his steps while Suwayr watched him, laughing irrepressibly as she covered her mouth with her sleeve. Her eyes were fixed on him, radiating childish glee.

'You're mad,' he said. 'You're completely mad.' He stared at her, transfixed, every particle of his body on edge. His hands shook, and he spoke in a whisper, looking nervously at the door. Suwayr laughed, taking off her gown to reveal a flowing, gaily-patterned dress, the front open halfway down her rebellious breasts. She threw herself on him and dragged him towards the bed. Then she sat him on it and planted a deep kiss on his mouth. Her eyes melted and she said, 'Yes, I'm mad for you. Ever since I saw you, I've been mad.'

She kissed him again, then glanced round the room. 'This is lovely ...' She broke off, then said passionately, 'It's enough for you to be breathing in it for the room to be nice.' At this Hisham felt a glorious burst of self-importance, despite his considerable fear that they would be discovered. He lit a cigarette and dragged greedily on it, blowing the smoke into Suwayr's face, as if to challenge her, or exercise his inflated ego by humiliating her. He knew that she didn't like smoking; she had told him so before. But she just closed her eyes and breathed in the smoke, saying, 'Even the smoke you exhale is different from other smoke. It's enough for it to be mixed with your breath for me to like it.'

She kissed him again. He felt a surge of pleasure; he was almost bursting from pride. She came closer to him and their bodies met. He felt the warmth of her body mingled with a feminine smell and the smell of lemon. They spoke in a whisper, which stopped when Suwayr closed his mouth with hers. He asked her how she had managed to come to his room. Laughing with happiness and pride, she hugged him and whispered in his ear:

'My love, my love! Don't you know that Moudhi is my friend? We are neighbours. I visit her when I'm in the mood. It seems that visiting her will cross my mind quite often from now on!' She laughed tenderly. But Hisham was confused.

'Aren't you afraid that Moudhi will suspect something?' Suwayr laughed again.

'My love, Moudhi is always busy, I even leave without her saying goodbye to me at the door. If I wanted to burgle the whole house, there'd be no one to stop me.' She was silent for a bit, smiling and gazing at Hisham. Then she said, 'Moudhi is convinced you are the purest being on earth.' He felt a sharp pain in his stomach as she said that, and flushed deep purple. Suwayr noticed and stopped laughing. She hugged him, whispering in an excited voice, 'And you *are* the purest being on earth ... but Moudhi doesn't believe you are capable of anything except reading and studying. She doesn't know about the tender heart inside you, or your pure spirit. You are my beloved, and will remain my beloved forever.' She pulled away from him, her eyes bathed in tears that refused to fall. He felt pain in his stomach again, but it was a different kind of pain. Gently he pulled her head onto his shoulder. Suwayr began to cry, sobbing, 'I'm sorry, I'm sorry. I didn't mean to hurt your feelings. I know them better than anyone, even though I have only got to know you recently. No. I have known you for a long time, and I knew that it was you I had been waiting for the first time we met.'

She continued to weep. Hisham waited for her to calm down, then raised her head from his shoulder. Her eyes and cheeks were completely soaked in tears. She took her veil and started to wipe them away, smiling and apologising, 'I'm being so cruel.' Hisham felt that he really loved her. His throat hurt, and tears filled his eyes. They stayed for a moment without speaking, looking at each other, then she suddenly stood up and took her cloak, saying, 'It's time to go. Alyan will arrive soon, and I haven't got supper ready yet.' She hurried to the door. Before she left, she blew him a kiss, and smiled. Then he sat alone, the scent of lemon filling the room.

After that, Suwayr came to him three times a week. Whenever she left, he felt loathsome and small. He was betraying the trust of the Prophet's family and stabbing them in the back, just as long ago he had shattered the image his mother had of him. Had he turned into such a despicable creature so quickly and so utterly? He began to frequent the mosque, but he could not attain the same fervour that he had felt the time he went after his experience with Raqiyya. And he was winning the admiration and absolute trust of his uncle, which made him loathe himself even more. So the last time Suwayr visited him, he asked her not to come back. She protested at first, but he threatened to break off the relationship once and for all. Reluctantly, she accepted. In actual fact he was determined to break the relationship with her anyway, but he couldn't. He carried on going to her in her house. Lust, love, fear, anxiety and loathing enveloped him every visit. Love for her, like the love he felt for Noura, began to grow within him. He desired her more than Raqiyya, and treasured her, but not like Moudhi. To him, she had almost come to represent all three of these women, but he kept hidden powerful feelings of hate and disgust for her. These feelings clung to him, and nothing he could do could rid him of them.

19

Then something happened that made him forget himself, forget Suwayr, forget his studies, forget everything else. Fighting broke out between the Jordanian army and the Palestinian resistance organisations in Amman. Everyone huddled around their radios to listen for the latest news and details of the battles. Everyone was obsessed by what was happening in 'Wahdat', 'Marka', 'al-Mahatta' and 'Jabal Hussein', which they took to calling 'Revolutionary Jabal', just as the *fedayeen* themselves did. Hisham would leave college and head straight for his friends' house, where they would gather in the hall around a radio and a large pot of tea, drinking it by force of habit and listening in a silence occasionally punctuated by quick, angry comments:

'Hussein has confirmed that he is a collaborator; there's absolutely no room for doubt.'

'Didn't he say we are all *fedayeen*?'

'What a traitor!'

'How happy Israel must be!'

'Nasser* won't stand with his hands tied in the face of this bloodbath and this treachery!'

'The hope is that Syria will intervene'

'How could the Iraqi army not intervene in Jordan?'

'It's a conspiracy, a conspiracy!'

Shrieks of joy would ring out whenever news came that a division of the Jordanian army had joined the resistance, or that a military commander had rebelled against the army and joined the ranks of the *fedayeen*. There was an overwhelming feeling that the resistance would persevere and that the *fedayeen* would triumph despite the conspiracies and treachery of Jordan's King Hussein, of Israel, and of America, who lurked behind it all.

The needle on the radio jumped from station to station: from 'London' to the 'Voice of America' to the 'Voice of the Arabs' and the 'Voice of the Revolution' – where it usually stayed. When the needle fell by chance on Radio Amman or the Israeli Broadcasting Authority they would fumble to change it, cursing and swearing. Muhanna wanted to keep the needle the whole time on 'Voice of the Arabs', but the others wanted 'Voice of the Revolution'. He would give in, huffing and puffing and muttering incomprehensibly, then slip away to his room where the transistor radio was permanently tuned to his favourite station. He would shut the door, having already made himself a pot of tea.

Their thirst for knowledge could not be quenched by the news from 'London', the 'Voice of America' or any other station. The young people believed that America and the imperialist powers were behind the conspiracy. They trusted only the 'Voice of

---

*   Gamal Abdel-Nasser (1918–70) led the Free Officers' Movement that brought an end to the Egyptian monarchy on 23 July 1952, becoming President of Egypt (1954–70). Events alluded to in chapters 19 and 20 include the war over Suez (1956); the union of Egypt with Syria in the United Arab Republic (1958–62); the 1967 Six Day War with Israel; and the Palestinian-Jordanian clashes of 'Black September', 1970.

the Revolution' and only felt happy when it gave them news of resistance victories.

Their excitement reached fever pitch when a delegation from the Arab League managed to smuggle Abu Ammar (Yasser Arafat) out of Amman to Cairo, in preparation for the Arab summit conference called by Gamal Abdel-Nasser to address the situation. The story of his departure sounded more like a fantasy from the traditional stories of the 'Days of the Arabs'.* The delegation managed to smuggle him out in traditional Arab dress, and the stock of the Kuwaiti Sheikh Sa'd al-'Abdallah al-Sabah rose considerably, after his role in this extraordinary operation became known. Muhanna was exasperated by this summit story; he would have preferred Nasser to intervene directly and finish King Hussein off. Despite this, he kept repeating, 'Didn't I tell you ... only Nasser can solve it.' As much as they were agreed on loathing King Hussein, they harboured a deep admiration for Mu'ammar al-Gaddafi, especially when he drew his revolver on King Hussein at the conference. It was enough for Nasser to have described al-Gaddafi as the 'guardian of the nation', and to say that al-Gaddafi reminded him of his youth, for Muhanna to admire him. In fact, this was reason enough for everyone to admire Mu'ammar al-Gaddafi, regardless of anything else.

---

*   Stories of inter-tribal conflicts among the pre-Islamic Arabs.

20

Gamal Abdel-Nasser died ... and they all suffered a kind of paralysis – a stupefaction. Was he really dead? No one believed that he could die. They knew that he was human and therefore mortal, yet ... he wouldn't actually *die*. But die he did, and with him died many dreams and hopes. He died carrying the cares of the nation; the nation that he loved had killed him. He died after bidding farewell to Sheikh Sabah al-Salim al-Sabah, the Emir of Kuwait, the last of his fellow Arabs to see him. He died after stopping the bloodshed in Jordan, but he killed himself to do it. The nation killed him. They had all killed him. Everyone grieved with the poet Nizar Qabbani:

> *We killed you, last of the Prophets,*
> *We killed you.*
> It is nothing new for us
> To murder the Companions and the Saints.
> How many Prophets have we killed?

How many *imams* have we slaughtered as they said the evening
prayer?
All our history is suffering;
All our days are Karbala.*

Hisham's cousin Ahmad brought him the news on a morning
Hisham would never forget as long as he lived. He was getting ready
to go to college, when suddenly, to Hisham's surprise, Ahmad burst
into his room. He poured himself a glass of tea, took a large gulp,
then said calmly, 'Have you heard the news? Your friend has died.
Gamal has died, and may God never bring him back.' Hisham was
combing his hair. His hands started to tremble, the comb fell from
his grip and he stared in horror at Ahmad.

'What ... what did you say?'

'Gamal has died ... or did you think he was immortal?' Ahmad
sniggered. Hisham felt an enormous hatred for his cousin, and at
the same time a dagger plunged itself deep inside him. He wanted
to cry, but a lump in his throat prevented him. His eyes stung with
tears, but he couldn't weep. Ahmad walked out, oblivious to the
pain he had caused, and Hisham did not go to college that day.

Gamal Abdel-Nasser was a symbol; a universal father-figure.
They hated him, they loathed him, they argued with him, they
fought with him, but they could not live without him or bear the
thought of losing him. You may hate your father intensely, deep
down you may wish he would vanish so that you can be free,
but as soon as he dies you are confronted by the void he has left.
Pain tears you apart, and your conscience tortures you, because
you once wished him dead. When your father dies, you feel that
something of yourself has also died; that the wall you leaned upon
has collapsed. Until its collapse you hadn't even noticed you were

---

* Karbala, a city in Iraq, is where Hussein ibn Ali was martyred in AD 680. The place
subsequently became a sacred rallying point for Shi'ite Muslims.

leaning on it, now you long for it with all your heart. But can what is past return? Nasser meant all this to Hisham.

He was in a state of confusion and considerable distress. Had Nasser really died, or was it just a rumour? He set off for his friends' house in a daze. The door was open, so he walked straight in and found everyone sitting around the radio in the hall, grief-stricken. Muhanna and Muhammad were weeping, hunched over with their heads in their arms. So it was true. Hisham sat beside Muhaysin, feeling an almost unbearably painful swelling in his throat. He was overwhelmed by the need to cry, like the day long past when he heard of his aunt Hila's death. Since then, he had rarely cried: once when he had said goodbye to his mother as he left for Beirut; and on another occasion when he heard that his aunt Sharifa had died. Now he rested his head on his knees and began to cry quietly.

As he wept, he felt that he was not grieving for someone else, but for himself. He had been born the year Nasser launched his revolution. He was not yet three months old when the 23rd of July Movement came into being. Nasser's heroics in Port Said and Suez were the backdrop against which he lived his early childhood. Like a dream, he still remembered the day his mother had picked him up and danced him around the room following the withdrawal of the Tripartite Forces. He could remember perfectly his mother's subsequent accounts of courageous deeds in Port Said and Suez, and his father's tales of heroes like Gawal Gamal – his father never stopped telling him how Gawal Gamal filled his aeroplane with explosives and plunged it, and himself, into the heart of an enemy destroyer, thereby putting an end to the supposedly indestructible ship.

As he grew up Hisham became increasingly conscious of Abdel-Nasser's achievements. Nasser was implementing the union with Syria as Hisham was beginning to take in the world around him, and to this day he could remember his father and father's friends' cheers when the union was announced. They were sitting in a circle around the big radio in the sitting room. His father had bought a massive aerial for the occasion so that he could tune into stations all over the world. An image of Nasser standing amidst the crowds in Damascus still stuck in Hisham's memory. That was also the year he went to primary school. For all the years of primary school Arab life rang with one name: Gamal Abdel-Nasser. For Arabs, every political event was linked to Nasser: the union, its dissolution, the revolution and war in Yemen, the Socialist Union, Socialist laws, Algerian independence, the revolution in Iraq, the resistance to the Baghdad Pact and the Arab Union ... Nasser was in the very air they breathed.

By the time Hisham left primary school, Nasser was the Arabs' only leader, still unrivalled, despite the disaster of the breakup of the union. By the time he left middle school Nasser's star had fallen, but as a symbol he endured in people's hearts. Can symbols fall? June 1967 came, and with it the transforming moment of simultaneous death and awakening. Politically, Gamal Abdel-Nasser died that June, three years before his body died, and with the death of Nasser many other dreams died.

Hisham clearly remembered the day he awoke to the disaster. For many, the previous day held the promise of a stroll on the shores of Haifa, Jaffa and Tel Aviv; now, suddenly, Zionists were promenading on the banks of the Suez Canal and praying in the ancient city of Jerusalem, drinking beer in al-Bireh and the golden *arak* of Ramallah in Tulkarm, bathing in olive oil in Nablus and filling their lungs with the air of the Golan and Jabal al-Sheikh. Their souls died within them as their eyes opened to the huge illusion they had been living – but no one blamed Nasser; they blamed everything and everyone except Nasser. The father could do no wrong, even when he was mistaken. When he resigned they wept; when he revoked his resignation, they rejoiced and said that perhaps it was a new dawn. Deep inside themselves they feared that it might be a new illusion, but they trusted Nasser in spite of everything; they wanted to trust him.

Hisham remembered those gloomy days well. Everything about them was tasteless, colourless, without smell. The songs of Abd al-Wahhab, Abd al-Halim, Farid and Umm Kulthumm were whetted blades and burning whips, and there was nothing but sorrow and dejection. *The songs in our mouths are salty, the women's locks are salty ... our skins are dead to feeling, and our souls complain of their ruin.* That's how Nizar Qabbani put it, transformed by the disaster from a poet of love and melancholy into a poet who 'writes with a knife'.

Nasser was dying while Hisham was at university – and with Nasser, a part of Hisham was also dying; a phase of his life was over, and a new phase was beginning. How couldn't he be deeply affected by Nasser's death, when his life had been linked with the great man's since birth? In the organisation, they'd tried to teach him to hate Nasser. Even at a time when he had been dazzled by the scientific methodology of Marxism, when Nasser was anyway unpopular in his own country after the revolution and civil war in Yemen, Hisham had still tried to defend him. He was incapable of hating him ... and his soul blamed him for hating him a single moment.

21

December came. The cold and frost penetrated the bones before the flesh. There is nothing worse than the heat of Riyadh except its cold, and nothing worse than its cold except its heat. Five months had gone by in this new city of his, or rather this new world of his. In that time he had become someone completely different from the person who, what now seemed like an age ago, drove into Riyadh in a hot tin box on a hot, windy day in August. He had changed so much in those five months. He was now a regular smoker and drank from time to time. He had actually started asking his cousin Hamad to buy drink for him in exchange for money. He had a steady girlfriend, and although her love for him had recently become unbearably exaggerated, it still flattered him. For his part, he certainly felt a sort of love for her, despite the twinges of conscience he felt whenever he had been with her, or when he heard someone mention her husband, whom he couldn't seem to escape no matter how hard he tried. He wasn't particularly attached to Suwayr even though he loved her, but she was besotted with him – to the extent that she was becoming over-protective. Once, when she accused him of having a relationship with his cousin Moudhi, they quarrelled and he threatened not to come back, and she wept and wept and begged him for forgiveness, which made him even more pleased with himself.

Despite his relationship with Suwayr, he couldn't forget Noura, and deep down inside he continued to love her. Sometimes he went back to meet Raqiyya, although sex with her was no longer such a preoccupation since he had got to know Suwayr. For him, his love for Noura was of a precious, indescribable kind. It gave him a lovely, pleasurable feeling that he didn't get from his relationship with Suwayr. As for Raqiyya, he found that sex with her had become more passionate since he had met Suwayr. It was a strange thing, sex. The flavour of it varied though the act was the same. Sometimes he would make a date with Raqiyya through Abd al-Rahman, and they would go into the desert as they had done before, but once the weather got colder he took to meeting her where she lived under cover of darkness, without anyone in the house the wiser.

When Hisham was alone, reflecting on his exploits, it struck him how much he had changed. It saddened him, but only briefly, and he soon forgot his sadness and returned to his illicit pleasures. Once Raqiyya tried to persuade him to meet her in his room, but he adamantly refused and she never returned to the subject again. She took to murmuring words of love to him, but he never felt love for her. Neither did he hate her. She aroused a powerful lust in him that he never experienced with Suwayr, and sometimes a feeling of inescapable sorrow. There were three women in his life now: one he loved, but would never allow himself to lust after; another he only lusted after; and a third he loved and lusted after at the same time. But his feelings for Suwayr never reached as far as his love for Noura, and his lust for never extended as far as his lust for Raqiyya; Suwayr was like an incomplete mixture of them both.

How those first five months in Riyadh had changed him!

Cigarettes, drink, women ... and income enough to afford all these pleasures. He was no longer saving most of it, as he had done in the past, but there was enough over, even if he hadn't got quite so much to spare. It made him smile to remember the day he'd received the first instalment from college. He had immediately felt like a real man, with no need to wait for pocket money from his father. He had become completely independent, and he derived enormous pleasure from feeling such power. The first thing he did when he received his grant was buy an expensive bottle of perfume for Suwayr (twenty-five *riyal*s all at one go!) because he was tired of the cheap lemon smell that clung to her. Suwayr was as pleased as a child who has been given a nice toy. She told him it was the first time anyone had given her anything. She opened the perfume bottle and savoured its scent with her eyes closed. He smiled, reminded of Raqiyya smelling the *arak* in Khashm al-An. Suwayr dabbed some on her neck and under her ears, then gave generously of herself when they made love that day. He was afraid that her husband would smell the perfume, but she assured him that Alyan never noticed such things. He would come home exhausted, just about able to eat, make love and go to sleep. She wouldn't wear this perfume for anyone except Hisham; as for Alyan, even the scent of lemon was too much for him. She laughed tenderly, while he concentrated on the hand that was tightly squeezing his stomach ...

Yes, he had indeed changed, even in his appearance – he had grown a moustache, to the delight of the women he knew: Moudhi squealed with pleasure, Suwayr gave him lots of love, and Raqiyya said that now she considered him a real man. Pride filled his heart; he felt capable of anything.

Only one aspect of his former life remained unchanged: his love of reading and his devotion to his studies, most of which he loathed. His parents were constantly on his mind. He tried to atone for his new lifestyle with the academic achievements that meant the world to his father. In fact, his grades were always high, although he was studying fewer hours than before. But though he had once allowed the organisation to divert him from academic achievement, he would not let his current pastimes distract him from achieving the highest possible marks. His professors and his fellow students both admired him equally; he was outstanding in every subject. Despite this, he could not conquer his growing self-hatred. He knew exactly why it was, but he could do nothing about it – or lacked the inclination to do anything about it. He told himself he was just doing what every young man of his age did, but still he couldn't shift that despicable feeling within.

It was now almost the end of December, and the end-of-term exams were approaching. The biting cold penetrated everywhere. His coal heater was no longer powerful enough to heat the room. He shivered like a soaked bird, despite the fire that was always burning, and despite the heavy blanket that he wore wrapped around himself the whole time, while he tried to solve the mysteries of accounting – a subject he hated with all his heart. The Nejd weather, which knows no mercy or moderation ... like its people! Or were the people like the weather? Who knows? Either way, it was as cold as death in winter, and as hot as hell in summer. There were only a few days in between which vanished as soon as they arrived, like apricots in season.

He wrapped himself in his blanket, rubbing his hands before the stove. He had thrown the accounting book across the room and was now revising some terms from *Principles of Law*. Suddenly the door of his room burst open and Muhaysin's face appeared, followed rapidly by the rest of his person. He made for the stove and rubbed his hands vigorously over the burning embers, savouring their heat. Hisham threw off his blanket, feeling a fresh blast of cold, and made for the other side of the room where he turned on the electric stove, put on a saucepan of water, then hurried back to the heater and began to rub his hands over the embers in turn. Something important must have brought Muhaysin out unnanounced at this time of night. Could it be something to do with the organisation? Hisham shivered and took to his blanket again, waiting anxiously for Muhaysin to say something. He did not have to wait long.

'I had an argument today with Muhanna,' said Muhaysin, looking closely at Hisham. Enormously relieved, Hisham continued to look at his friend, seeking some further explanation.

'We had some friends round today, as usual, and they had supper with us. After they left, Muhanna criticised us for having so many visitors, and for spending too much of the kitty. He said that the house had become a sort of 'refuge for everyone', even though supper didn't come out of the kitty.' Muhaysin was silent for a moment, as he ran his two warm hands over his face.

'No one said anything,' he continued. 'but Muhanna went further, calling us a bunch of spongers with no future. At this point, I completely lost my temper and defended myself with such uncharacteristic force that Muhanna exploded with rage and accused me in particular of turning the house into a free-for-all. Then I lost it completely and punched him.'

They were interupted by the whistling kettle. Hisham got up and made tea, coming back with it on a tray. The two of them took quick, appreciative gulps of their hot drinks, and soon a delicious warmth began to flood through them.

'Muhanna couldn't handle this,' continued Muhaysin. 'He got up, stormed off to his room and came back a bit later carrying a bag full of clothes and books. Our friends tried to stop him from leaving, but he was as stubborn as ever and left, saying he'd be back later to settle up.' Muhaysin paused while he poured himself another glass of tea. 'Muhammad and Dais rounded on me,' he went on, 'and criticised me for my treatment of Muhanna, but I was furious and told them I was leaving too.'

'I told them,' he said, eyes wide and taking a large gulp of tea,

22

The following day, the two of them went looking for a new place to live in a suitable location and at a reasonable price. They started immediately after the afternoon prayers, calling on numerous small estate agents in the quarters near the district of Alisha – Alisha itself being too expensive for them. They wandered around until the call came to evening prayers and the shops began shutting their doors. They waited until prayers had finished, then made for a *ful* (beans) and *mutabbaq* (casserole) restaurant where they snatched a quick supper. They made do with an egg and tomato sandwich before going home. They'd seen a lot of houses and flats, including some in good locations at good prices, but each time they met with a refusal when the landlord or broker found out they were bachelors.

It's hellish to be a bachelor in Riyadh, Hisham thought. No one trusts you, everyone avoids you, as if you were a rat on the move. You're guilty until you prove your innocence; most people take it for granted you're some kind of criminal. While he was house-hunting, Hisham learnt a lot. He became convinced that all this fear of bachelors was actually a lack of trust in women, who crouched behind walls built to separate them from the nearest man. The virtuous woman would remain virtuous even if she was alone among a thousand men, and a man can only take from a woman what she wants to give him. You cannot, Hisham reasoned, force a woman to give something she doesn't want to, but if a woman wants to give something, no power can stop her. Take the girl who was shut up in a box by a devil, who then threw it to the bottom of the sea, only ever bringing it up and opening it when he wanted her. Despite that, the girl was able to make love to more than five hundred people, the last of them being Shahriyar, as the famous story in the *Thousand and One Nights* tells us. The people of Riyadh persecute men because they do not trust women.

They looked everywhere: in Shumaisi, the Umm Salim roundabout, Asir Street, Manfuha, Zahrat al-Badi'a, Ujailiyya and in Alisha itself on the off-chance, but without success. After they had almost given up, they found a house in an alley branching off a dirt road leading from Asir Street. It was a pleasant surprise by any standard when the broker didn't object to their bachelor status. His only comment was that their behaviour when they moved in would determine whether they could stay or not – an unusual position for a broker like him to take. They didn't haggle much about the rent. They were so happy that they forgot about the rent being high, at five thousand *riyal*s a year. When they saw the house they were even more pleased, because it was airy and spacious. It wasn't a mudbrick house, but a modern house built of reinforced concrete, with four living rooms, two bathrooms, a kitchen and a small paved courtyard open to the sky. Two of the living rooms directly overlooked the courtyard, as did the kitchen, and a room next to the front door. This had a bathroom opposite, with a small door separating it from the courtyard. The fourth room was on the roof. This was actually the most spacious room of all, with two windows – one of which overlooked the alley – while the other

18

After this, his relationship with Suwayr strengthened. He visited her a lot. They would talk a great deal, and often they would make love. He started to skip the occasional morning lecture, especially Shahtuti's and al-Ghadban's, so as to see her. Sometimes, when he reflected that he had betrayed his entire upbringing, he felt sick with self-loathing. But he was unable to stop himself spinning round and round in a wheel he'd set rolling himself – and, indeed, he didn't really want to stop.

He stopped spying on her when one night, creeping up to the window, he saw her making love to her husband. The sight enraged him. But although he stopped spying on them, anger and lust still gripped him whenever he heard the dogs barking outside, because they conjured images of Suwayr moaning under her husband. He would feel a great loathing for her, and a fierce loathing for himself, before lust quickly took the place of anger.

He discovered she was foolhardy. One day, around noon, he was flicking through magazines in his room, leaning against the wall, and listening to Umm Kulthumm singing, *Ask the golden cups,* opened onto the wide roof. There were no windows in any of the other rooms except for one in the outermost room overlooking the alley. Hisham bagged the upper room for himself. It would give him the seclusion and quiet he wanted, especially knowing that Muhaysin had a lot of friends and acquaintances. Hisham wanted to mix with people when he chose, not when the others wanted to. Muhaysin chose the bigger of the two rooms opening onto the courtyard, and they turned the other room next to the kitchen into a storeroom for food. The outer room they turned into a reception room.

When they signed the rental agreement in the afternoon – a historic day for Hisham – they paid the broker half the rent in advance. Hisham, after some persuasion and the signing of various agreements and contracts, had already borrowed eight hundred *riyal*s from his cousin Ahmad. Swept along with enthusiasm, they went straight to an auction and bought a small fridge, a gas stove complete with chimney pipe and some essential kitchen utensils. They put off furnishing the reception room until the half-year holiday, when they would move in permanently.

During the days leading up to the holiday they went to their new home every afternoon to explore their new neighbourhood. Hisham could feel a delightful glee within him, whose source was an almost alarming sense of freedom and independence; this was the first time he had ever been truly self-sufficient.

Their new neighbourhood was like much of Riyadh: alleys and narrow dirt streets with houses on both sides, most of them built of mudbrick but some built of reinforced concrete. Their neighbourhood was near one of the scientific institutes and the general government hospital, so it was full of students, teachers and low-grade officials, with services like bakeries, small groceries and laundries scattered about. Not far away lay Asir Street, with its butcher shops, *ful* restaurants, dry bread bakeries and fast sandwich and *mutabbaq* shops. Everything about the new quarter, with its great location and its abundant services, seemed relaxing. It was possible to get everywhere on foot. Alisha, where the college was, was not more than half an hour's walk away, and the local bus went from Asir Street to every part of Riyadh for four *piastres* a ride.

As for the neighbours, they knew nothing about them. All they knew was that they were family people. There were no bachelors apart from themselves in the alley. Their house adjoined three others on one side, four on the other and two houses at the back. After that, there were several empty plots of land dividing other clusters of houses. Opposite theirs were more houses built together on the other side of the alley, which resounded with the shouts of children that started after the afternoon prayers and only stopped just before the evening prayers, to be replaced by the howling and scrapping of stray dogs.

They noticed, from the dubious glances directed at them when they came to the house every afternoon, that their presence worried the neighbours. Even when they greeted one of the neighbours who happened to be there, he returned the greeting with some incomprehensible grunt, looking at them distrustfully. If the Prophet had not said, 'Greeting is a custom, but returning it is a duty,' he would probably not have responded at all. They decided to be as disciplined and upright as possible in order to win the trust of these neighbours; but how would this be possible when they could sense hidden eyes following their every movement from behind closed doors and windows …?

23

When he told Suwayr of his determination to move house after the holiday, she went mad. He didn't dare tell her the news until he had given her as much of his physical love as he could muster, and she seemed happy and contented. He himself hadn't realised he was capable of giving so much love all at once, but deep down he felt that this might be their last meeting. Her blind jealousy had lately become annoying, and the twinge he felt whenever he left her place was more insistent than ever, especially when he passed in front of Alyan's shop and saw him busy chopping meat, trusting in the goodness of the whole world, completely oblivious to what was going on almost under his eyes.

They were sipping milk with ginger when he told her he had decided upon the move. She put the glass nervously on the tray and looked at him with wide eyes that had lost none of their sharpness though filled with tears.

'Now I know what this vast quantity of love was for,' she said bitterly. 'I was wondering what had come over you today. I told myself that at last you had fallen in love with me. How stupid I am

…' She couldn't finish but burst into tears, resting her head on her bare knees. He tried to calm her, but she snatched her hand away with unexpected force. 'Take your hand away, you deceiver,' she said in a quavering voice. 'Do you want to leave me now that I've found you?'

'Who told you that? I'll be a bit further away, but I'm not leaving you.'

'You liar!'

He left her to cry for as long as she needed. Eventually she calmed down a little and stared at him through bloodshot eyes, still weeping. Then she wiped her tears away with her hand. 'I knew that the end was coming,' she said, her voice cracking. 'But I wasn't expecting it so soon. It was all too good. There I was swimming in a lake of happiness, and now I'm drowning in the Devil's lake. Here I am returning to darkness once again …'

She paused to wipe away a falling tear, then smiled sadly and said, 'I was madly in love with you from the first time I saw you. I didn't know the meaning of love before you. I know that you have never loved me, you have only loved my body. I don't mind, so long as you are with me and near me. But for you now to leave me … I wish I had never known you … I wish I had never known you.' She started to cry again, and could not continue. He felt at that moment as if a sharp blade was piercing his body from inside, cutting through everything it found in its way. Without thinking he pulled her to him, burying her head in his breast, this time without any resistance on her part. He left her to cry as he ran his hand through her freshly perfumed hair.

'I love you,' he said. 'Believe me, I love you, I cannot live without you.' She dragged her head from his breast.

'You love me?' she said in a broken voice, the tears still welling up in her eyes. 'Liar! Does a lover desert his beloved?'

'Who told you that I am going to leave you? It's just that I am moving to a new house.' For the first time since he had told her the news of his move, she smiled.

'Really?' she asked, looking at him miserably. 'But you'll be a long way away from me.'

'Don't they say that absence kindles the fire of love?' He smiled as he said this, while she laughed timidly.

'My love for you has been burning ever since I knew you,' she said, now weeping less violently. 'It doesn't need anything else to kindle it. Have you ever seen anyone blowing on a fire on a stormy day?'

'Our relationship will be stronger, believe me.'

At that moment, he meant what he said, while she was silent and a little calmer. He looked at her flushed face and the wavy hair that had fallen chaotically about her bare shoulders. She dried her tears, then said in a voice tinged with doubt, 'I hope you are telling the truth ... do I have any choice but to believe you? You will show me your new house, won't you?'

'No, don't think about that. But you'll always be seeing me, believe me!' He smiled, then pulled her towards him. She threw herself on him with her whole body, and they became one flesh.

24

The half-year examinations finally finished, and he passed them with excellent marks. He was eager to see his family, friends and Noura in Dammam, after the long months of separation that seemed to him like an age. Indeed, it had been an age, judging by the events and changes he had experienced. He was desperate with longing for his mother's face, his father's brow, for Noura's scent and for the gang at Abd al-Karim's house. He packed his travelling bag several days before he was due to leave. The day before he set off, he visited Suwayr to say goodbye. She didn't stop crying the whole time. 'I have a feeling that this is our last meeting,' she said, and he wasn't prepared to set her mind at rest. He was so anxious for Dammam that he cared about nothing else. He said goodbye to her abruptly while she squatted in the room, sobbing. Then he passed by his friends' house and said goodbye to Muhammad and Dais.

On the eve of his departure, he met up with Muhaysin and his two cousins Hamad and Abd al-Rahman in his room. Hamad presented them with a bottle of Haig's whisky to celebrate Hisham's departure. They poured some of it into a teapot, added ice and water, and had a leisurely drink from small tea glasses – except for Abd al-Rahman, who contented himself with smoking. Hisham saw that Muhaysin was drinking. He called him on it, surprised. The reply was a quick smile and a whispered comment, 'We're not such peasants ...' He smiled back, not bothered about the reason, just pleased that his friend was drinking. Everyone was in a great mood, especially Hisham, who couldn't wait for the following day, and clouds of smoke steeped in alcohol gathered in the room from all the Marlboros and Abu Bass. Their snacks were simple – yellow cheese, tuna and some nuts and dry cheese. They didn't think that they needed anything more, especially given that Umm Kulthumm was singing on the 'Voice of the Arabs' that evening.

Hisham was drinking, smoking and musing to himself. The alcohol gave him a clarity of mind he had never known before, while at the same time, with each glass that he drank, he felt desire overpowering his entire being. Suwayr came into his mind. He longed to be with her at that moment, to say goodbye to her properly. He almost jumped up to his window to she what she was doing. He imagined her making love to Alyan, and felt the heat of arousal pulse through his veins. But with the fourth glass his desire became less intense, and he began to think objectively of his relationship with this woman. Did he really love her, as he had told her, or was it simply lust? If it was simply lust, then why didn't he miss Raqiyya as he missed Suwayr, despite the fact that he had become annoyed lately at his relationship with her, and despite sometimes feeling that he didn't want her? Was loathing a sort of love? But what was love? He loved Noura, but he didn't have the same feeling for Suwayr that he had when he thought of Noura. He neither loved nor hated Raqiyya, but he was consumed with lust for her when her wild triangle came into his mind and he imagined her soft, cruel body. What was love, then? He couldn't stop thinking about Suwayr. He really wanted her physically, but sometimes he thought about her without feeling any arousal at all. With Raqiyya it was the opposite; he could never think about her without growing tense with longing. Perhaps it was the sympathy and pity he'd felt for Suwayr ever since she told him the story of her marriage to Alyan.

She'd been very young, about sixteen, when she was betrothed to Alyan, who was even then over forty-five. When they told her, she was overwhelmed with happiness. She saw it as a chance to escape the tyranny of her father, the cruelty of her mother and her brothers' orders. She would have her own house and her own garden. She would finally be free and independent. She imagined herself as a bride with a man at her side to protect her and provide her with a fatherly presence and the warmth of a home. But this happiness was short-lasting. She soon wished she had never left her father's house. It was clear what the marriage would be like from the first night. She was penetrated by a sullen man whose appearance made her miserable from the moment she saw him. She had none of the usual romantic dreams for a girl of her age at that time; instead, she had to slave in the house from morning to night. She had even had to leave school after the sixth year.

Suwayr had never imagined her husband could be such a lout. She couldn't care less whether he was young or old, she was just looking for a warm heart. But that first night, Alyan threw himself straight on her without any preliminaries. She was paralysed with terror, incapable of doing anything. He ripped off her clothes and penetrated her, forcefully and painfully, oblivious to her screams or her suffering under his heavy body. She felt no pleasure or happiness that night. All she was conscious of was the pain, and the blood that stained her white sheet. When he had got what he wanted from her, he turned on his back and snored loudly, leaving her traumatised in a way that had affected her ever since. Even her tears were too terrified to fall that night.

But she knew the value of her blood the following day, when

her mother came and turned over the stained sheet, laughing and shrieking with joy, then kissing her daughter and congratulating her on such a fortunate marriage. Then her father came in with a smile on his face, congratulating her in his turn. She knew that those drops of blood were the most precious thing she possessed; they were her holy of holies, the only part of her precious to her family. And now those drops had gone, had she retained any sanctity or value? The sheep were sacrificed, and that was the end of it all.

In the end, she submitted to her fate 'for better or worse', as she used to say. Her new life was no different from her old one, except that the master of the house now had claims on her actual body, which was one up on those in charge of the old house. When two years went by without her becoming pregnant, Alyan first started to wonder, then to upbraid her, threatening to take another wife who would give him a son to bear his name. With all her heart she wished that he would marry again and give her some peace, but he didn't, and her life continued as before.

When she saw Hisham spying on her from his window, and took to watching out for his daily return from college, some hidden feelings of femininity began to stir, and she felt something shift within her, the nature of which she could not comprehend even though she was knew it was there. That was what she told him. Hisham remembered now that he had asked her whether there wasn't anyone else who had stirred those hidden emotions, but she reacted furiously, bursting into tears which he'd quickly calmed with soothing kisses and apologies. From that time on, however, doubts plagued him despite his attempts to make light of them, though they contradicted the unadulterated, unconditional love he could see she offered him.

He tried to persuade himself that they were not bound to each other in any way, that whether he doubted her loyalty or not he did not have the right to hold her to account for what she did.

Nonetheless, jealousy consumed him whenever he wondered about her other lovers. And when he heard the dogs bark at the end of the night, he would even feel jealous of her husband – the sight of him made him feel both insignificant and jealous. Yes, he loved Suwayr in a way that he just could not fathom. But did love need understanding or philosophy? It's just a feeling. And if what he felt for Suwayr wasn't love, what was it? It was impossible to get to the bottom of emotions.

Hisham was dragged from his musings by a light knocking on the door. Everyone jumped, and there was a sudden hush. Who could it be? Perhaps his uncle had smelled the smoke and heard their loud laughter (God forbid, they all prayed to themselves!). They hastily put out their cigarettes and hid the ashtrays and the whisky bottle under the bed. Then Hisham, trying to walk straight, got up to open the door. The effect of all the glasses he had drunk rapidly wore off. His skin prickled from the cold. His mind was working feverishly to devise a suitable excuse for their being together if it was his uncle. As soon as he opened the door, however, he felt huge relief. It was only his cousin Ahmad, with a paper bag. Ahmad walked in and ostentatiously sniffed the air in the room, while everyone grinned and swore, 'God confound you, *sheikh*!'

Ahmad sat down, his narrow eyes contracting still further. 'God confound me?' he said. 'What are you doing, you lot, causing such a disturbance?'

'You're always confounding us, so may God reward you in the same way, *sheikh*!' said Hamad, pouring himself another glass of whisky, while Ahmad laughed, sniffing again.

'For God's sake,' he said. 'You've turned this room into a chimney! But there's another strange smell,' he said, sniffing more thoroughly. He looked at the teapot, then at the company, his eyes screwed up. 'What's this?' he asked. 'Tea? It's nice, is it, cold like this?' He reached for the pot, and as soon as he touched it, said,

'As I thought, you bunch of sinners. Cold tea!' He lifted the lid of the teapot and hurriedly smelled it, then said with a sigh, moving it away from his face, 'Curse you! Whisky in al-Mubaraki's house! God's servants beware!'

'Give us a break from your meddling and hypocrisy today!' said one of them, as another added, 'If you want to drink, that's fine, but if you want to make life difficult for us as usual, there's the door!'

Ahmad laughed. 'You have your religion and I have mine,' he said. 'Don't make life difficult for me and I won't make life difficult for you!' He smiled round at them. 'But you are welcome to this gift.' He took a package wrapped in silver paper from his paper bag and unwrapped it. The smell of roast meat spread through the room. 'A kilo of roast leg of lamb that I bought to eat with Hisham to celebrate his departure, though God knows how you will divide it!'

They cheered, then set on the lamb. In a few seconds all trace of it had gone.

When they left the room just after midnight, the bottle of Haig's was completely empty. Hamad took it with him to dispose of in his special way. Some liquid remained in the pot, but no more than a single glass. Hisham's head was spinning as he thought of these last life-changing months. He poured the rest for himself, and began to drink and muse ... Suwayr ... He couldn't resist it. He dragged the chair below the window and looked out. Everything was quiet. No movement, not a glimmer of light could be seen from there, while dogs could be heard barking everywhere. The biting December winds stung him. He went back to drink the rest of the glass; the room spun round and round.

He came to the following morning with a knocking on the door. He found himself on the bed fully clothed, with a violent headache tearing his skull apart. But he was as happy as could be, for today he would see his loved ones in Dammam. He got up and opened the door, after putting the pot in its proper place beside the door. Moudhi was there, carrying a tea tray and some loaves of dry bread and a plate of fried tomatoes. She put it all down in the middle of the room, then went out, saying, 'Forgive us for being so inadequate … Don't go before we've seen you.' He nodded his head, in which waves were clashing and hammers beating, and followed her to the bathroom.

25

The railway station was extremely crowded. The half-year examinations had finished, and everyone wanted to spend the vacation with their families. He saw several faces that he recognised from secondary school. He exchanged hasty greetings with them, then joined the crowd, first to get a ticket and then to get a decent seat. The crowd didn't annoy him or get him down, because he knew that at the end of it lay Dammam, his family, his loved ones and the sea ... How he yearned for the sea after so many months in a city without a sea! When the train finally moved off he had already started *Al-Tariq*, by Naguib Mahfouz. Soon the red hills of sand passed quickly on either side of the train.

About halfway between Riyadh and Dammam, he started to feel extremely hungry. He hadn't eaten any of Moudhi's breakfast, except for drinking the tea. At the time he hadn't wanted anything, not with that splitting headache. It was still very painful, even if it was now less intense. He put *Al-Tariq* to one side and went to the restaurant at the rear of the train. There he sat at a table beside the window, ordered chicken, rice and cola, and began to eat quietly.

The chicken tasted nothing like chicken but more like cooked fibre, and the rice didn't taste like rice. The smell from it was distinctly unappetising, but despite that he ate the whole lot. The restaurant car wasn't crowded; most of the passengers had brought their own food and drink, but there were a few people sitting down. Some were drinking tea or juice, others were eating sandwiches and some were doing nothing at all except watching the sand dunes, which had turned yellow beyond Dahna, passing by like the years of one's life.

He finished his meal and ordered a glass of tea which he drank quietly as he smoked, inhaling deeply and blowing the smoke upwards, watching it disperse across the roof of the carriage. He was deep in thought about nothing in particular when he felt a hand placed on his shoulder and a familiar voice saying, 'hello'. He looked to see whose voice it was and there was Adnan, standing behind him wearing the trace of a smile. He had grown thinner, although his face was less pallid – what one could see of his face, that is; his hair sprawled over most of it, completely unkempt. His large beard was untrimmed, while his moustache was extremely neat and obviously clipped. He was wearing a short brown woollen *tob* and a red headdress with no headband. You could see the front of his head and the edge of his white skullcap. The trace of a smell of aloe oil wafted gently from him.

Hisham got up at once, smiling broadly, and held out his hand in his friend's direction. 'Greetings to you too,' he said, trying to make his voice sound deep. 'God bless you.' The pair shook hands and Hisham pulled his friend into a spare seat opposite him at the table. For a short time they examined each other – they hadn't met for around two months. Even in the college canteen, Adnan had avoided him recently. Hisham finally brought the silence to an end by asking his friend if he wanted to eat or drink anything, but he refused. Adnan looked at him intently. 'Wow!' he said. 'It's your moustache. You seem older than you really are, but more handsome!' Hisham smiled and thanked him for the compliment. 'But wouldn't it have been better to let your beard grow?' added Adnan. 'That is nearer to the love of God and obedience to the Prophet, and the beard is one of the signs of true manhood.' Hisham didn't want to get involved in an argument of any sort, so he smiled, nodding his head in agreement. 'The moustache is a first step,' he said. 'Perhaps the beard will come next, God willing.' Adnan knew his friend better than anyone else. He realised that Hisham did not want to embark on a conversation of this sort. He quickly made ready to get up, saying quickly, 'God willing, God willing. And by the way, you will quit smoking, which injures the health and angers God. God will always reward the man who does good.' Hisham tried to stop him leaving, but he insisted, saying that he was with some other friends, then left, heading for a table at the end of the restaurant where two people looking just like Adnan sat drinking tea. Hisham ordered another glass of tea. Blowing smoke into the air he stole a glance in Adnan's direction, trying to rationalise the change that had come over his oldest friend.

There was no one waiting for him at the station. He hadn't told anyone he was coming. This was deliberate, despite the fact that he knew they would be expecting him. He left the train hurriedly, found his case, then took the first taxi he saw without even asking about the fare. He gave the driver the address, and the taxi sped off down the main road in the direction of Eighteenth Street.

He missed everything about Dammam. Even the ugly municipal architecture seemed beautiful this time, as he passed it on his way home. In less than ten minutes the taxi was standing in front of their house. How beautiful and how comfortingly familiar it was right then! He jumped out and gave the driver two *riyal*s without any haggling. Then he pounded on the door and rang the bell at the same time, his heart beating hard. A few moments later, he heard a voice he knew well. It seemed to be coming from a long way away, as it repeated, 'Okay … okay!' Then it came closer, asking, 'Who is it? Who is at the door?'

'It's me … it's me, Mother!' The door opened wide and he immediately found himself savouring his mother's delightful scent. She kissed him several times, and he kissed her brow, then surrendered to her warm embrace. His father wasn't in. He was at one of the evening gatherings he often went to in the winter. They sat in the television room, with all the familiar memories it aroused, as his mother scrutinised him from top to bottom, smiling. The joy shone in her eyes.

'Goodness me … You've become a man, Hisham … and handsome with it!' She gestured to his dark moustache. He smiled back, stroking it.

'The monkey is a gazelle in the eyes of its mother!' he said. His mother laughed, revealing the distinctive gaps between her teeth, then said, 'Monkey or gazelle, the important thing is that God gives you health and happiness, with a long life and salvation!' Then she got up, promising him a special supper of his favourite dishes, and left him on his own.

He looked at the room around him. Nothing in it had changed at all, everything was exactly as it had been. He laughed at himself. He'd only been away five or six months at most. What could change in a house that had been accustomed to so much order and stability? If only his mother knew how much he'd changed in those few short months. He wasn't as innocent nowadays. He had tried every despicable vice in her book: he had drunk alcohol, he had made love to women and he was a regular smoker. What would his mother think if she knew what he had done in Riyadh? She wouldn't hate him, of course; he would remain her son whatever happened, but she would be wounded in a way that would never heal.

'You must be starving!' his mother cried as she returned, carrying the tea tray and a small plate containing round *ma'mul*, pistachio pastries, and *ghurayyiba*, sweet butter pastries. Beside the tea, there was some green mint. She put the tray in front of him without sitting down, then turned and went back to the kitchen, saying, 'I'll finish cooking while you enjoy your tea.' He tried to make her stay and forget the cooking – it was already eight in the evening – but she refused. 'How many Hishams do I have to take pleasure in?' she said, her whole face turning into a broad, unadulterated smile. 'Anyway, the winter nights are long, don't worry!' Then she disappeared into the kitchen. There was nothing more delicious than his mother's tea and sweetmeats on a winter's night. He drank the tea as if he had not tasted it in years, and ate her date cakes as if he were seeing and tasting them for the first time in his life. Moudhi's tea had no flavour, and he couldn't remember Suwayr's tea at all, despite having drunk so much of it.

He finished the tea and cake, with his mother still in the kitchen. The smell of boiled onions wafted all through the house. He got up and switched on the television. Hiyam Younis was singing *My Heart's Devotion*. He turned it off and went to his room … everything was as it had been. The bed, the books, the table, everything. He sat on the bed and smiled, the memories tumbling about in his head. Here was the first kiss in his life with Noura. It had been sweeter than honey (never mind that he didn't like honey), and hotter than fire. He had kissed others since, and for far longer, but the taste of that kiss still burned his lips.

There was his small library, every book with its own story and its own memories. Here was the book in which Adnan had found the leaflet that had been the beginning of the rift between him and his lifelong friend. And here was the book through which he had discovered Marxism for the first time. The night he finished reading it he hadn't slept at all, but instead lay burning with thoughts and ideas. It was the story that had fanned the political flames inside him when he read it for the first time.

He left his room and went towards the courtyard at the rear. There was the money he had buried for the organisation. He lit a cigarette and took a huge drag as he gazed at the spot where the money was. Now the organisation had vanished, and six months had passed without anyone asking about it. It was all over and he was beginning a new life – so why shouldn't he take the money? He had a right to it. He was about to dig it up, but something made him shrink away at the last moment. He threw the cigarette over the wall of the house and went back inside.

His mother was still in the kitchen, and he was watching a local show – crass, there was no other word for it – when his father came in. He leapt up, kissed his brow and embraced him. His father's face showed obvious joy, despite his efforts not to, for like every traditional Nejdi, the most important thing for his father to preserve, whatever life threw at him, was his absolute composure. Hisham was used to his father behaving like this. He knew that his father would like to hug him tight, but that he stopped himself. Before sitting down, his father shouted to his mother at the top of his voice, 'Be happy, Umm Hisham ... Hisham has arrived safely, thank God!' His mother's voice could be heard in the distance, repeating, 'By the Prophet, by the Prophet, God willing! God grant you salvation!'

Then his father sat down in his favourite corner of the room, while Hisham found a place beside him. His father began to ask him about his studies, about his uncle and cousins, about his new moustache and the other usual things, until his mother appeared carrying the tablecloth that heralded the arrival of supper. The three of them arranged themselves around the tray of meat and potatoes and tucked in happily. 'God bless Hisham,' said his father. 'At last a reason for a decent supper.' Then he laughed contentedly, while his mother retorted in a mock angry tone, teasing him gently, 'Goodness ... It's as if you went to bed hungry every night. Have we forgotten how to eat?' And they all laughed, as mother and father looked happily at Hisham. My God! How he loved these two people ...

When he went to bed that night, he felt he had at last returned to his roots, to a place that he loved and where he belonged, especially after his mother's kiss that took him back to those childhood days. He went to sleep with a contented smile on his lips, and slept as if he had never tasted sleep until that day.

26

He got up early the following morning to the special sound of his mother's kindly voice. He was desperate to see Dammam and its people. He couldn't believe he'd only been away five months; it felt like ages since he'd left. He ate the *shakshouka* that his mother had prepared for breakfast quickly – his father had left for work some time beforehand – then he went out, his mother praying that God would keep evil people out of his way.

He walked straight down to the sea where he sat, enjoying the seasonal weather and the peculiar smell of the ocean, heavy with the scent of decay. Even the noticeable smell of sewage was pleasantly nostalgic, and for a time he lost himself in the sea and his memories. Then he wandered off down al-Hubb Street for a while. He turned towards his old school-monitor Rashid's house, seized by a desire to knock on the door and ask for him, but he thrust the idea out of his head and walked quickly in the other direction as if trying to get away from himself. He passed the house of his former cell commander Farid al-Midrasi. He was struck by the same desire to knock on the door, but again he hurried away and went back to wander around al-Hubb Street again. He went into the café he had once sat in with his comrades in the organisation Zaki and Marzuq, ordered tea with milk, which he drank quickly, smoked a cigarette, then returned to loafing around the street. The street was empty at that time of day, except for a few women wandering around, and some unemployed workmen. One of the women caught his attention, walking slowly, wrapped in an *abaya*, her face covered by a veil so fine that it hid nothing. She didn't have a pretty face. She was plump, almost fat, with enormous thighs separated by a deep and obvious slit that showed their constant quivering. The sight of her swaying bottom aroused Hisham. Growing excited, he stared at her lustfully, drawing deeply on a cigarette. The woman became aware of his hot looks and stared back at him, smiling seductively, but at the last moment he quit flirting and walked quickly on. How much Riyadh had changed him! He'd lived in Dammam all his life and more than once come to al-Hubb Street, but never before had he seen what he had just seen or had the ideas he had had today.

He got fed up walking around and decided to go to Abd al-Karim's house. He must have woken up by now, Hisham thought, it was nearly ten o'clock. On his way there he passed the Municipal Park, and immediately thought of Rashid and Mansur, the men responsible for his entry into the organisation. He was dying of curiosity to know what had become of them and of Farid, but he wasn't prepared to ask about any of them. The alley where Abd al-Karim's house lay was as quiet as death, except for a council worker who was lazily sweeping the street with a tatty broom that collected nothing. He knocked on the door. After a few moments, he could hear the harsh voice of Abd al-Karim's mother screeching, 'Who is it? Who's knocking?'

'It's me ... Hisham, Hisham al-Abir.'

The small metal door quickly opened to reveal the face of Abd al-Karim's mother, her veil lowered.

'Hello, thank God you have arrived safely,' she said. 'Come on in. Abd al-Karim is still asleep. It's a holiday, as you know.' And in he walked, into the sitting room that he knew so well.

He chose a seat near the door and took a look around. Everything was exactly the same. It was as if he had only left it yesterday. He smiled at himself again – he'd only been away five months, not five years. What could happen in five months in a town as quiet as Dammam? Abd al-Karim's mother brought tea and put it down in front of him, saying, 'I've woken Abd al-Karim. He's just coming.' She had hardly finished speaking when Abd al-Karim appeared at the door, wiping his face with a small towel that he then threw over his shoulder. He was still in his nightclothes, which also served as his underclothes: a white, short-sleeved vest and white, knee-length pants. His mother looked at him. 'It's chilly, Abd al-Karim,' she scolded. 'Put something on, or you'll catch cold.' Abd al-Karim nodded in agreement, but grinned and hurried towards Hisham to greet him. The pair embraced, then sat down beside each other. Even before they had settled, Abd al-Karim's mother returned with a brown woollen *tob* in her hand which she threw to Abd al-Karim, telling him to put it on. When she was satisfied that he was doing as he was told, she left, praying for health and happiness for them both, and asking God to keep them safe from the companions of evil.

Hisham was eager to know the news; news of anything and everything. He asked about his schoolfriends Saud, Abd al-Aziz and Salim; for news of school, and what Abd al-Karim was intending to do after his leaving exams – there was nothing new to learn. At last, Hisham plucked up courage and, with an air of feigned indifference, asked about Rashid. Abd al-Karim laughed at the mention of 'Goatface' and told Hisham they'd appointed a new school-monitor, better looking than Goatface – who'd disappeared without trace a while ago. Hisham concluded that Rashid had either run off to Bahrain, then on to somewhere else, as he had told

Hisham he planned to, or else he'd been imprisoned. Fear gripped him once more, and for the first time he felt a strange loathing for Dammam.

The conversation continued between the two friends in a routine fashion: Abd al-Karim commented on his friend's new moustache; then Hisham told him about some of his adventures in Riyadh. But when he saw the excitement on his friend's face, he exaggerated his descriptions, inventing totally fictitious stories and mentioning the smallest details. He took his inspiration from those smuggled stories they used to read on their day trips together. He was beginning to realise the distance that now divided him not only from his friends in Dammam, but also from the time when he didn't really know Dammam itself, or what lay hidden behind its innocent face. They were still living in a dimension he had left behind, and which had left him behind – when he enrolled in the organisation, when he smoked his first cigarette, when he drank his first glass of alcohol and slept with his first woman. Abd al-Karim asked about the last thing he had read. Hisham told him he was reading *Anna Karenina*, and they began to discuss the novel. The two friends talked until after midday, when Hisham got up to leave despite Abd al-Karim's pleas to stay and share their lunch. Hisham made the excuse that his mother was waiting for him with lunch, but asked Abd al-Karim to gather together some friends later in the afternoon. He also told him that Adnan was in Dammam and that they'd travelled together on the same train.

On the way back home, Hisham passed Noura's house. He resolved to see her that night.

27

When he went back to Abd al-Karim's house in the afternoon, all his old friends were there except Adnan. They embraced warmly. The chat centred on Hisham's moustache, with a lot of ribald comments about why he'd suddenly decided to grow it. He thought at first that Abd al-Karim must have passed on some of what he'd told him that morning – Abd al-Karim had been known to be indiscreet in the past. But he soon realised that his suspicions were unfounded and that it was just a bit of fun. He asked after Adnan, and Abd al-Karim told him he'd sent his younger brother out to get everyone, but Adnan hadn't appeared.

Nothing about the group had changed. The topics of conversation were the same and the repartee almost the same. He felt a new kind of boredom creep over him. Was this what he had been pining for all that time in Riyadh? Spending time with this gang had once been the most delightful thing in Hisham's world. So why was he so bored today, when he'd hardly been with them for ten minutes? He felt deathly silent in the midst of this group of people who seemed strangers to him. Was this the 'world of innocence' he had felt guilty about, when he had smashed its ideals and ripped off the veils of its innocence? He looked around at his friends all sipping their tea and laughing, envying them their composure and innocence. But he didn't want to go back to their world – and couldn't even if he wanted to. He had discovered new worlds of excitement – worlds of fear, unease and pleasure – and it wouldn't be easy for him to return to the innocent world his friends still lived in. These worlds might be wicked by his mother's standards and the standards of the innocent world in which this gang lived, but they'd become an indispensable part of his life. Without them, his life would be tasteless, colourless, devoid of smell. These guys hadn't tasted women, their heads hadn't known drink, they had not experienced the thrill of adventure and the fear of the unknown. Was anyone who hadn't passed through this tunnel of pleasure and fear really living life? It might all be a mistake, but what was life's pleasure without mistakes? A mistake meant experience, and experience meant freedom of choice, and the whole of life consisted of moments of choice and rebellion. Those beautiful, innocent days in the past might have been blameless, they might have been pure happiness, but it was a routine happiness, a tune played on one string. How could one know pleasure without pain, or know error without the sharp bite of sin and the lashes of guilt? How could one feel life's warmth without the restlessness of adventure and the desire to plunge into the unknown? Hisham had uncovered new worlds, making it impossible for him to return to his old world. A learned man could not become ignorant again, even should he want to. An ignorant man might be happier than a learned one, but the happiness of a learned man, steeped in the restlessness of the universe, is more exciting and more pleasurable. Could this be his situation today? He didn't know. All he knew was that boredom was almost stifling him.

He had decided to leave when Adnan suddenly appeared, greeting everyone with, 'Peace be upon you.'

'And on you be peace, and the mercy and blessings of God,' everyone replied, as if with one voice. They all stood up to embrace him.

'Where have you been, man?'

'What's this beard ... a real one or a false one?'

'What's with beards and moustaches these days?'

Adnan sat down at the edge of the room near the door, ignoring Abd al-Karim's protestations that he sit near Hisham in the middle of the gathering. Saud asked Adnan lightheartedly about the new beard and why he'd grown it, and Adnan answered him with unexpected force, 'It would be better to ask why we shave our beards rather than why we let them grow. Letting them grow, not shaving them, is the normal thing. Isn't that so, Salim?' he added, turning towards Salim. But Salim said nothing. His eyes, like everyone's, showed surprise at Adnan's strange fervour. They were all silent for a moment, finishing their tea, then Abd al-Aziz shouted, 'Goodbye, everyone!' Saud, Salim and Abd al-Karim surrounded him, while Adnan got up and made his excuses for leaving. Hisham used this moment to escape from his boredom and got up. 'Take me with you, Adnan,' he said. They left despite Abd al-Karim's insistence that they stay, while the others watched them go in astonishment. At the front door, they looked briefly at each other without speaking, then each went his own separate way.

28

He was with his parents in the television room, sipping milk and ginger, while his father listened to the news from London on a small radio. His mother was busying herself with some crochet. In the middle of the floor was a portable coal stove. Hisham, however, was feeling hotter than even the coals in the stove, in anticipation of the moment when Noura arrived with the milk as she always did. His heart beat faster when he heard the doorbell and his fervour increased just as it had in those days long gone, when he had been a small boy. Umm Hisham threw down her crochet and got up. 'It's time for Umm Muhammad's milk delivery,' she said. Hisham stayed where he was for a few moments, in a state of great excitement, then got up and went into the corridor, pretending to need the bathroom, while his mother came in followed by a girl of about twelve, carrying a churn of milk. The pair went into the kitchen. Hisham went in to the bathroom and came out again quickly, as his mother was saying goodbye to the girl. 'Say hello to your mother for me, Badriyya,' she said, then went back to the TV room, wiping her hands on the edge of her veil.

Assuming a calm he did not feel, he asked his mother about the girl. His mother told him she was called Badriyya, and was Umm Muhammad's daughter ... Noura's sister, then. Still calm, he questioned her further, 'Umm Muhammad's daughter ... so, she's the sister of the girl who used to bring the milk ... what was her name?'

'Noura. That was Noura ... You've forgotten quickly, my son,' replied his mother, casually. A cryptic smile crossed his face as they both went back to the television room, where his father was now getting ready to go out to his usual evening gathering. Hisham was desperate to know what had become of Noura. When he was sure that his father had left the house, he moved nearer to the stove and held his hands over the coals. With pretended spontaneity, he mused, 'Oh, yes, I remember Noura, Mother. But why doesn't she still bring the milk?' His mother looked at him with eyes that he thought knew everything, then looked again at the crochet work in her hand. 'Noura's grown up and wears a veil now,' she said calmly. 'She can't go out on her own at a time like this! Besides,' she went on after a short pause, 'she was engaged two months ago, and she can't go around the houses any more. How I wanted her for you ... manners, money, beauty and above everything, patience. But everyone must be content with their lot!' She sighed quietly as she said this.

The news hit Hisham like a thunderbolt. Noura engaged? He wasn't actually thinking of marrying her, or anyone else – the idea of marriage hadn't entered his mind. But he hadn't imagined anyone else sharing his interest in Noura; indeed, he couldn't imagine Noura being anyone else's, and he couldn't imagine Noura marrying and becoming like Suwayr. She was made for something else, not marriage. He couldn't stay any longer in the room, so he went out into the street and hovered at a distance from her house, determined to see her somehow. But first he had to let her know he was there. Could he send a note with Badriyya? That was risky, and the outcome very uncertain. Should he knock on their door on the pretext of saying hello to her father? But that wasn't the customary way of doing things. Finally, he had an idea. There was one way, and one way only. He smiled and walked back to his house.

When he got back, he was surprised to find his father there. The biting cold that night had stopped many people from turning up to his gathering, and those that did had elected to go home to enjoy some warmth and an early bed.

When the *muezzin* at their local mosque started the call to prayer Hisham sprang up, much to his father's surprise. 'Where are you going?' he asked. Hisham explained that he wanted to go to the mosque. His father was astonished. Hisham hadn't been in the habit of performing prayer duties. His parents had been relaxed about this. Though they urged him to obey God's commands, at least occasionally, they believed that being too strict in these matters would turn him off prayer completely. But to pray in the mosque with the community – that was a radical change in his behaviour! Even Abu Hisham didn't go to the mosque to say his prayers. Like most people in Dammam, Hisham's father usually said his prayers at home, unlike people in Riyadh or Qusaim, who thought prayers should be performed in the mosque unless they had some particular reason to say them at home, either alone or in a group. His father looked at him and smiled. 'I see you've become religious,' he said. 'I'm coming with you. Wait for me until I've washed.'

On the way to the mosque, his father jokingly asked him, 'I didn't know you'd turned religious and now prayed with the community in the mosque. Has Riyadh turned you into a real Nejdi?' Abu Hisham gave a rare laugh, then became his usual stern, calm self again, as he added rather firmly, 'Listen, my son … God is present everywhere. Piety lies in good intentions and in behaving well towards other people, not just in the actions of prayer. Prayer has no value unless it stops you being wicked and behaving badly. God does not need ritual. Pray in the mosque, at home, or anywhere you like: the place is not important. God has given us his whole earth as a mosque in which to purify ourselves, but the urgent thing is to be sincere in everything you do. This is the true service of God ...' They reached the mosque as his father finished.

The *muezzin* had already given the call to prayer and now everyone was lining up behind the *imam*, who intoned monotonously, 'Line up, make your rows straight. God does not look at a crooked line.' Then he recited, 'God is most high', and started on the opening *sura* of the Qur'an in a soft, melodious voice.

When prayers were over Hisham looked around for Abu Muhammad, until he spotted him sitting directly behind the *imam*. As soon as the congregation started to leave, Hisham stood up to perform the two customary extra *rak'as*, his eyes never leaving Abu Muhammad, who was also performing these ritual bows, a prescribed part of the Islamic prayer ritual. Hisham's father was amazed at the piety that had suddenly come over his son. Hisham could see that he wasn't very pleased by it. Abu Hisham thought that performing the obligatory prayers with sincerity, and dealing properly with God's people, was all that a man needed for happiness in this life and the next. However, he could see no alternative but to keep his son company, so he quickly prayed the two extra *rak'as* then sat down, muttering the customary Arabic words of praise for the Almighty. Hisham, however, carried on praying, so as to keep up with Abu Muhammad, stopping only when he saw Abu Muhammad stop. Then he looked at his astonished father, saying, 'Isn't that Abu Muhammad? I think I should say hello.' Without waiting for an answer, he rushed up to Abu Muhammad, greeting him with a kiss to the head. 'Good evening, uncle!' he said. Abu Muhammad immediately recognised him and asked him how he was and how his father was. Hisham gestured towards his father who was standing, ready to leave. The two men approached each other and embraced, reproaching one another for failing to stay in touch, then they all three left together. When they were all in front of Noura's house, her father invited them in. Hisham's father made an excuse, but Abu Muhammad insisted on their having supper with him the following evening. After much persuasion, Hisham's father agreed, and Abu Muhammad bade them farewell. They walked home in silence – one man's eyes filled with puzzlement, the other with a cunning smile on his lips.

29

It was the first time he had been into Noura's house openly without fear, and the first time he had gone beyond the garden into the house itself. Everything whispered of her presence: the palm tree in the far corner had observed their first meeting; the grass here and there in the garden sighed, *Noura was here ... she sat here ... she stood here ...* He was now in her house, united with her in a single place, where her breath moved back and forth. Those innocent days began to tug at his heart again.

There were not many people there for supper: himself and his father, Abu Muhammad and his eldest son Muhammad, two people he did not know and Noura's fiancé, whom Hisham scrutinised with jealousy gnawing at his heart. He was a handsome young man of about twenty-four, tall and slenderly built, almost swarthy, with sharp features, a wispy moustache and a small, square, dark beard covering the edges of his chin. Hisham felt an enormous loathing for him, eespecially when the young man proved to be extremely polite and courteous.

They sat round a large bowl of rice, on top of which rested a whole lamb, still with its head, and with the liver, stomach and innards arranged around it. The rice was decorated with raisins and pine nuts, with a few boiled eggs planted in it. Several small plates were arranged around the large dish, containing sopped bread and meat, or crushed wheat and salad, and there were two large dishes of fruit at the edges of the table. One of Abu Muhammad's sons stood at the head of the gathering holding fresh yoghurt, waiting for a signal from anyone sitting down. During the meal, Abu Muhammad teased his future son-in-law, saying, 'Have some *qursan*, Fahd. Your future wife made it. Perhaps once you've tasted it you'll see sense and cancel the wedding!' Everyone laughed, then someone said, 'Weddings and marriage are all trouble! God be praised, women are all trouble, a free man is the happiest!'

'The problem is that one can't live with them, and one can't live without them! But God will do what is best!' joined in another. The quips and laughter continued as they tore into the lamb with their bare hands, kneading the meat with the rice then popping it into their mouths. Hisham ate nothing but sopped bread – and some pieces of meat Abu Muhammad put before him. To him it was the tastiest sopped bread dish he had tasted in his life, because Noura's hands had touched it.

Hisham's father was the first to finish eating, but he didn't get up. He stayed where he sat, licking the remains of food from his hand, and occupied himself peeling an orange until he was sure that everyone had finished. Then he got up, saying, 'God bless you, Abu Muhammad, God grant you blessings!' Then everyone rose as one, repeating the same sentence. Cups of bitter coffee with saffron were passed round, then incense, after which everyone began to leave, again offering the blessing to Abu Muhammad that they had given when they'd finished eating. One of the guests tried to invite them all to supper in his turn, but they refused and he didn't insist, so everything finished with Abu Muhammad's supper. When he lay down on his bed that night, Hisham felt tremendously happy and excited, because he knew that Noura knew he was in town, and could devise a plan to meet him if she still loved him. It was up to her now; he had done what he could. He closed his eyes contentedly, waiting for whatever the next day might bring.

30

He was in the sitting room browsing through a few magazines the next afternoon, when he heard the front doorbell. A few moments later his mother came in, saying hurriedly, 'You must leave the room at once, Hisham, guests have arrived unexpectedly – Umm Muhammad and Noura, and the women's room isn't tidy.' His heart beat faster when he heard Noura's name. He slipped into his room and shut the door behind him. It was only a few moments before he heard his mother's voice uttering expressions of greeting and praise to God, mingled with the voice of Umm Muhammad congratulating her on Hisham's return. He could hear her laughing as she said, 'Goodness, we only heard yesterday from Abu Muhammad, forgive us for being so remiss ...' Then he heard his mother's voice, 'There's no need to apologise among friends, Umm Muhammad.' His plan had succeeded, then. He guessed that Noura had insisted that this visit was a duty. He knew that Umm Muhammad, like his own mother, was reluctant to leave the house unless it was really necessary. He opened the door a little and glanced into the hall. There was Noura's back; he knew that figure well. She went into the sitting room behind her mother and his mother – it was enough to start the heat coursing through his body despite the biting February cold.

He stayed in his room leafing through another magazine, his ears straining for sounds from the other side of the house. He thought he caught the noise of a *tob* rustling near his room. He dropped his magazine and made for the door. Under it he found a meticulously folded piece of paper. He snatched the note, yanked opened the door, and saw Noura walking back to the sitting room. Before she disappeared into it, she snatched a surprisingly bold glance at him, giving him a smile that made him certain she still loved him. She had powdered her face. He unfolded the paper and read, 'Tonight, same time, same place.' Smiling, he tore it to pieces; she had understood his plan and fallen in with it. Hisham went out into the street and lit a cigarette, which he smoked feeling overwhelmed with happiness, then he went back into the house to count the minutes until evening should finally come.

31

As soon as the call to evening prayers was over, he left and made
for Noura's house. He thanked God that his father hadn't been at
home. He might have assumed Hisham was going to the mosque
and accompanied him. Hisham could hardly contain himself,
thought it wasn't yet time for his meeting. He chose a dark corner
in an alley opposite the house and waited, smoking nervously. After
about half an hour, Abu Muhammad came back from the mosque,
went into the house and shut the door behind him. After another
quarter of an hour, the door reopened a fraction, the gap so small
it could hardly be seen. Hisham stamped out his cigarette and went
hesitantly towards the door, taut with nerves. He glanced around
cautiously, then pushed at the door and found himself inside. He
was struck immediately by Noura's smell, which reached him
through a powerful scent of perfume. She pulled him quickly by
the shoulder as she always did, and dragged him to their usual
corner under the palm tree. Before they sat down, she threw herself
at him and kissed him with a passion and warmth he hadn't known
in her before.

When they separated, he used the dim light available to study her; to see what effect five months had had on her. Had she changed or was she immune to change, like everything else here in Dammam? She seemed more vivacious, and she was plumper. Everything in her that could had become fuller and rounder. Her hair, which she had always worn combed into two long pigtails, was now left to flow freely, falling down over her back and the tops of her thighs. Everything about her spoke of a new maturity; she had become a real woman, capable of arousing every desire. Only one thing about her annoyed him, for a reason he couldn't understand: she had put lipstick and makeup on her face, and sprayed perfume behind her ears. Noura had changed a lot while he had been away, and Hisham did not like the ways she had changed. Isn't it strange , he thought, how things we love change when we don't want them to, while the things we want to change stay the same? This was not the Noura he had kissed for the first time in his room. She was more like Suwayr now – in fact, she *was* Suwayr. But he didn't want Suwayr now, he wanted Noura.

When they sat down she threw her head on his breast and kissed every part of his face within reach of her lips. She was murmuring about love and desire, and the days that had vanished from her life while he was away. He said nothing the whole time. Then she pulled away from him, laughing in a whisper, not covering her mouth with her sleeve as she would have done once, but leaving the whites of her small parted teeth to gleam in the darkness.

'When I saw you today with your new looks,' she said, 'I almost threw myself on you and to hell with the consequences. I didn't know that a moustache could make you so beautiful.'

He smiled at this comment, seized by the urge to flatter her.

'Beauty is for women,' he said. 'Men are just handsome.'

'Call it what you like … You *are* beautiful. You are exciting, in fact.'

Again she threw herself at him and kissed him passionately.

How you have changed, Noura! he said to himself as her lips continued to rove across his face. *Where did you learn how to kiss like this?*

'I wish I could stay with you forever,' she said breathlessly when their embrace eased for a few seconds.

'What about Fahd, your fiancé?' he said, frowning.

For the first time since they had met, the smile disappeared from her face. She bowed her head towards the ground and played with some grass between her fingers.

'You know, then,' she said, extremely quietly.

'Can things like that be hidden?'

There was a short silence. He looked at her as she continued to play with the grass, head bowed.

'I have to get married,' she said. 'I'm almost seventeen now. I can't wait for you to graduate from university to get married. And even if I wanted to, my father won't wait for me. There have been several suitors, and if he knew about our relationship, he would kill me.'

She was silent for a moment, then went on, 'The fact is that Fahd is an excellent young man, kind and gentle, with an excellent job, and he will let me finish my education. I couldn't have found a better man for a husband – except for you, of course,' she added, 'but we can't get married.'

Her last sentence wounded Hisham terribly; from nowhere, he was overwhelmed by a feeling of insignificance. But she was right in what she said. Noura had really matured; no longer was she Noura the Milkmaid. It was true that her fate really wasn't in her hands, and even he was not complete master of his own fate. Were he to want to get married, he would not be completely free to choose whomever he wanted. There were customs and practices, people you could marry and people you couldn't. If he were to rebel against all that, his fate would be total isolation. Not only would he be cut off from all his relations, he would inflict terrible pain on everyone. He didn't want to hurt anyone, least of all his parents. As he and Noura spoke, he suddenly recalled a conversation from his distant childhood.

He had been almost twelve years old, on a trip one Friday with his parents and some other families to one of the date palm plantations scattered around Dammam. The men were playing cards and discussing the news, hot from Syria and Iraq at the time, and what Nasser would do. The radio never left their side. The women were in another part of the plantation, singing and dancing and laughing, while the children played between the men and the women. Hisham remembered that he had abandoned the other children to play with Mayyada, the daughter of his father's friend, Hammud al-Shahham. She was about ten and extremely pretty, like one of those expensive dolls he had seen in the luxury shops in Emir Khalid Street in the city of Khubar. She had long, chestnut-coloured hair, honey eyes and pale skin, with touches of red on her cheeks that glowed at the least movement. She had crimson lips and extremely fine features, and two prominent dimples that stood out whenever she laughed or smiled. On the way back to the house, the girl came up by chance in conversation when his mother asked him whether he had enjoyed himself. He mentioned that he'd been playing with Mayyada the whole time. His mother smiled and said, 'God preserve her, she'll be a paragon of beauty when she grows up. She's taken on the best of both her parents – Syrian beauty and the slim build of the Nejdis.'

'I'll marry her when I grow up,' Hisham said, innocently.

At this point his father interjected, saying, 'No, my son … she's not one of ours.' Hisham didn't understand. 'What do you mean?' he asked.

'There are people you can marry and people you can't,' explained his father. 'Two entirely different sets of people.'

He still didn't understand. 'But her father Hammud al-Shahham is one of your best friends, and her mother is one of your dearest acquaintances, Mother.'

'If only ...' said his father. 'But these are two different things. Marriage is one thing and friendship quite another.'

Still Hisham didn't understand. 'But our relative, Jar Allah al-Abir, married an American girl when he was in America ...'

'To marry an American isn't the same ... That's one thing, and we're talking about another.' But he still didn't understand. Years later, when he was older and understood most things, it still didn't make any sense to him.

The fact was that Noura was 'available', but he couldn't and didn't want to marry him now, and her father couldn't wait for Hisham's family to see if Hisham graduated before they asked for her hand. She was quite right, but still he felt an overpowering sense of his own worthlessness.

'Hisham ... Hisham! Where have you gone?'

Noura's voice brought him back to reality. He turned to her with a smile. 'Where could I possibly go when you are with me?' he said. He planted a quick kiss on her lips. 'It's late,' he said, getting up. 'Time to go.'

'Incidentally,' he said, by way of a parting shot. 'You're far more beautiful without makeup.' He made for the front door leaving Noura sitting on the freezing ground, looking at him with astonishment and shivering with cold.

32

He headed straight for the bathroom after entering the house, wiped the traces of lipstick from his face, then made for his room, where he lay down on the bed to think. A strange thing, the world ... Was this the meeting he had waited for for so long? He felt no happiness; in fact he didn't feel anything at all. He felt as though all the love that had been motivating him had suddenly disappeared. No ... he still loved her, but not in the same way. Something had changed and he couldn't explain it. She was prettier and more mature now, and he wanted her passionately, just as he wanted Suwayr and Raqiyya and others, but he wouldn't do with her what he had done with Suwayr and Raqiyya, whatever happened, for she was neither Suwayr nor Raqiyya. Was that because she was engaged? Perhaps. But she couldn't be blamed for getting engaged, for marriage did not signify love just as love did not necessarily lead to marriage. Love was a feeling and marriage was an arrangement, and they did not necessarily go together. Had he fallen out of love with her? No, he loved her, but in a different way, and now he also desired her. What was the difference between lust and love, and could they come together? He didn't know. No, he did know. Love was a feeling and lust was a desire. But what was the difference between feeling and desire? He couldn't go on thinking. He got up and joined his parents in the TV room where Umm Kulthumm was singing, *Is love's sight drunk? Drunk? Drunk like us?*

33

The days of the vacation went by in their boring way, exactly the opposite of what he had been expecting. The strange thing was that he missed Riyadh a lot – again something he hadn't expected while he was there. The friends' get-togethers were a tedium he could no longer bear. Noura, who had aroused his desire – the Noura he had once feared for because of this desire – did not return. He seemed to be inhaling the putrid smells from the sea for the first time and he loathed them, he found them unbearable. What had happened? Can we only appreciate things when we have lost them? Are they valueless when they are within our grasp? Perhaps, perhaps ... Hisham didn't know.

Very occasionally he would go to the get-togethers, but he would soon leave to hang around al-Hubb Street, eyeing the girls' plump, swaying buttocks, or Emir Khalid Street in Khubar, where he would follow the small, rounded bottoms of the American girls stuffed into tight trousers. His breath came faster when he saw their bare red thighs thrusting from their tiny shorts, which they wore despite the coldness of the weather. Then he severed his connections with the group entirely. Adnan's absence encouraged Hisham to stay away as well. Once he called on Adnan but didn't find him at home. Instead he spent some time with Adnan's brother Majid, who complained about the ways in which Adnan had changed, wishing he had stayed as he was when he used to paint. He told Hisham that Adnan had burned all his pictures, that he spent hours at the mosque and no longer watched television, and that their father didn't know what to do in the face of his peculiar behaviour. He'd tried to get to the bottom of the change in his son, but Adnan had replied with unaccustomed anger, 'We were on the side of the Devil and you didn't like it. Now we've taken God's side and you still don't like it. What do you want? Do you forbid one of God's servants to say "My Lord God"?' Hisham drank tea with Majid, then left before Adnan came home and never went back again.

Once he found himself in front of the Bank of the Netherlands, where his friends Zaki and Marzuq had worked. He thought of asking for them, but stopped himself at the last moment. Perhaps it was his soul that was afraid and prevented him. He only visited Noura once – at her insistence – after their first encounter. He feared for her in case he lost control of himself. On this occasion, she let him roam over her body at will and do things that she hadn't previously allowed. At times she seemed ready to give him everything ... but at the last moment he wouldn't let himself cross certain boundaries, despite his overwhelming, burning desire. Deep down, he felt responsible for her, and for transporting her from her world of innocence. He didn't feel anything like that with Raqiyya. With Suwayr he felt certain pangs within, but he only really struggled with himself over Noura. This was in spite of the voice inside him that advised him to seize the opportunity before somebody else did – but such thoughts filled him with self-loathing. He was unsure of himself. Perhaps he would do it if he were to meet her once more, so he decided to keep away from her completely, which is what he did for the rest of the vacation. She sent him notes under the door or with her sister Badriyya, but he did not respond. The last day of holidays, she sent him a letter imploring him in the name of the love between them to tell her the reason for his reticence but he ignored her plea, counting the hours before he travelled, when he would be relieved of this torment.

34

Riyadh felt different on his return. Even its fine red dust had a special flavour; it was beautiful and evocative, like the white snows of Moscow which the Russian writers have so often praised. But the dust of Riyadh is warmer, and right then it was in fairly short supply. In fact it had almost disappeared, dampened down by the rain before it could blow about. It would return with the first rays of the sun. The sun in Riyadh is scorching, winter and summer alike, yet pleasant in either season. In fact, just now everything about Riyadh seemed pleasant and enjoyable.

The first thing he did the evening he arrived was to pay off his debt to Ahmad. Then he went to his friends' house. He and Muhaysin agreed to move to their new lodgings the following day. Then Hisham returned to the room in his uncle's house and gathered together his simple belongings, taking a last furtive look at Suwayr and Alyan's house. The place was shrouded in darkness; there wasn't a glimmer of light in the house to suggest that anyone was there … where could they be? The roof was now a swamp of accumulated rainwater. He was tempted to go and knock on the door to see if anyone was in, but he stopped himself – then forgot the subject completely in a wave of enthusiasm for the move to the new house.

The following afternoon, after taking a last lunch with his uncle and cousins, he left with Abd al-Rahman. They hired a taxi, which they loaded with Hisham's personal possessions, making a detour to Muhaysin's to pick up his things. Then they all headed to the new place, where they were met by a group of children in the street while furtive eyes followed their every movement from behind closed doors and windows. Though the neighbourhood women were invisible, the young men were acutely conscious of the intensity of their looks.

While they were busy moving their things, one of the neighbours came up to them. The hostility was clear on his thin face eaten away by smallpox. Without even greeting them, he gave them a warning and a piece of advice, very direct and sharp: 'You should know that the people living here are families ... I hope we shall see nothing of you but good, and hear nothing but good, and may the warner be excused, as the saying goes!' He uttered this last sentence wagging his finger in their faces. Muhaysin approached him with a smile, saying in a friendly tone:

'God willing, you will see nothing but good. We are family people too, and we also have women we are anxious about.' The man's anger subsided, and he walked back to his house, muttering, 'It will be OK, God willing.' Then he disappeared behind the small iron door.

They only finished unloading their things and getting them into the house just before the evening prayers. They were eager to perform the sunset prayers in the local mosque, keen that their neighbours in the alley see them worship. Then they went to buy pots and pans and other essentials. Once they were back in their new lodgings, Muhaysin prepared their first pot of tea, which everyone drank with unusual relish.

35

It soon became clear to Hisham how wise he had been in choosing the upper room, for Muhaysin's friends and acquaintances were more numerous than he had expected. They came almost every day, almost all the time and without any prior warning: at noon, after the afternoon prayers, after sunset, after the evening prayers, and at the end of the evening. This made it almost impossible for Muhaysin to study seriously. Muhaysin discovered that in his heart of hearts he didn't like studying engineering, but preferred economics or business management. His friends' presence at every hour of the day provided an excuse not to study the subjects he hated. After a while, he decided to leave the College of Engineering completely. He didn't think of enrolling at another college, but decided to look for a scholarship in America in any field. Indeed, America became Muhaysin's new obsession. He was inspired by the stories he heard from his friends and acquaintances who had come back from America, where the people were rich and the world was rich and varied. Muhaysin abandoned everything connected with study and devoted his time to socialising. He started trying to get to know people who could fulfil his dream of going to America.

They had not yet put furniture in the sitting room, so the visitors spent their time in Muhaysin's room, playing cards and gossiping about politics, sex and religion. Hisham sometimes joined them, but he would come and go as he pleased. That was the advantage of his secluded room; it gave him freedom of choice. The most frequent visitors to the new place were Muhammad and Dais from the old house. In fact, they visited and stayed so much they were almost like lodgers. Once, they suggested moving in with Hisham and Muhaysin, especially as the house was big enough for them all. They also weren't happy with the pair who had taken the place of Muhaysin and Muhanna in their own house. They were practically strangers, but the high rent had forced them to join up with people they knew nothing about except that they were from the same area. Hisham, however, refused completely, despite being fond of Muhammad and Dais. He wanted to study, however much it cost him, and having more people in the house might prove a distraction. Besides, they were being watched by the neighbours and he didn't want any trouble. Muhaysin was inclined to accept the proposal but Hisham had made up his mind about it and wouldn't allow any argument.

36

His new room was not as comfortable as his old one. It was actually quite cramped, but it was warmer, and it was cosier because it was his own room in his own house and not the house of his uncle. It was enough that he could completely relax in this room. On the walls he had pinned pictures of Marx, Engels, Lenin, Guevara, Ho Chi Minh, Marilyn Monroe, Jayne Mansfield, Brigitte Bardot, Suad Husni, Shadia, Hind Rustam and Nadia Lutfi. But the most striking pictures in the room were those of Abu Ali, the name he had given Adolf Hitler after being told that was what people called him during the Second World War. He had a strange, hidden admiration for Hitler – although he had absolutely no faith in his ideas – and in a vague sort of way he loved him. He'd read *Mein Kampf* several times, and even though he disliked the ideas expressed in it he continued to dip into it occasionally. Did he actually believe any of it – although he did not want to admit to it – or was he finding that a leftist like himself could not be persuaded by Fascist ideas? He didn't know, and perhaps he didn't want to know. It was enough for him to love Abu Ali, believe Karl Marx and support Ernesto Che Guevara ... and die of desire for Jayne Mansfield ...

The days passed in the new lodgings in the usual way. Little had changed, apart from a few chores that Hisham wasn't used to. They followed the same routine in the new lodgings as they had in the old: Muhaysin would look after the house one day, and Hisham the next. So far as provisions and other essentials were concerned, they both contributed to the weekly shop on Friday afternoon from the supermarket, where prices were cheaper. Attending to household matters was a novelty for Hisham. But there were no particular problems apart from the cooking, which was a burden despite the fact that they only cooked *kabsa* stew for lunch and had boiled eggs or tuna for supper. Still, with the help of Muhaysin, he believed he might become quite a good cook. The two of them developed a routine of going every Thursday after evening prayers to the elegant Wazir Street in the middle of town, where they would eat in a classy restaurant. Usually they had lentil soup, roast meat and plates of *hummous* and *mutabbal*, with a couple of bottles of cola. They would round off the meal with two cups of Turkish coffee. Then they would pace up and down the street, looking in the elegant shops and following the prettiest women in Riyadh; they would fill their nostrils with alluring perfumes and carefully scrutinise the details of slim bodies wrapped in translucent *abayas* that hid nothing. They would gaze into the most beautiful faces one could find, made even more so by the women's transparent veils, wondering how such slender hips, such fleshy thighs and such rebellious breasts could be brought together in a single body. Once they tired of wandering around and following women, they would make for a big bookstore, buy any newspapers and magazines they could find, then take the local bus back home where they would spend the rest of the night drinking tea, smoking cigarettes and listening to songs. Then they would go to their separate rooms, each of them dreaming of the women of Wazir Street, and feeling that he owned the whole world.

This Thursday routine could vary if there was a better alternative. At first infrequently, and then more often than not, Muhaysin's friends would come round for the evening, and they would play cards and chat. That didn't stop them going to Wazir Street, however. They would simply go and come back early in time to meet their friends. Hisham only joined them when Muhammad, Dais and Abd al-Rahman were among the visitors. He remained wary of too many people, and was amazed that Muhaysin could stand all these gatherings and all these friends. The only thing that actually stopped them going to Wazir Street at all was when Hamad paid them a delicious surprise visit, carrying a paper bag containing a bottle of best quality *arak*. Then they would shut the door and refuse to allow anyone in, no matter who, until eventually they took to letting Muhammad and Dais join the group. Hisham was surprised to find that Muhammad and Dais also drank. 'My God, you *have* got surprises in store!' he exclaimed when he saw them drinking for the first time. Muhammad's reaction was to pour his half-full glass into his mouth all in one go, then to laugh merrily, looking at Hisham. Hamad didn't always sit with them, for he had his own group of friends, but these days he supplied them with *arak* once they'd all got the money together.

Hisham was responsible for the ice and snacks, which were never more than a few cucumbers, tomatoes and nuts, while Muhaysin's job was to prepare the *kabsa* stew, at which he was reckoned to be an expert. They sat in Muhaysin's room, where they drank and listened to Talal Maddah, Muhammad Abduh and Tariq Abd al-Hakim. They would listen and then gradually grow deaf to the music as the intensity of the political discussions increased with the first few glasses. After the fourth glass, they listened to Umm Kulthumm, Abd al-Wahhab, Abd al-Halim or Farid, swaying with pleasure to *The Remains*, *Cleopatra*, *Mister Bold Eyes* or *Spring*. They all talked at the same time, though in reality everyone was talking to himself. Dais talked about the heroes of the novels he was reading, all of them wronged or oppressed; Muhammad talked about his plans for travel and the places he wanted to see; while Muhaysin talked only of America and the good life there. When Hamad was there, he would discuss his problems at work and home, and his hopes for a place of his own.

Drink made Hisham extremely amorous. He would fantasise about Raqiyya, Suwayr and even Noura, and sometimes imagine arousing scenes from films he had seen in cinema clubs. He wished Suwayr or Noura were there so that he could show them things they would never dream of, or else that the room was full of naked women and he the only man among them. At the same time, he would talk about Marxism, Existentialism, Sufism, God and the Devil. The closed room became full of smoke, the smell of *arak*, the sighs of Umm Kulthumm, Abd al-Wahhab's tears, Farid's groaning and Abd al-Wahhab's imprecations. But it was an expansive universe, limitless for those that were in it.

The evening would conclude with a meal of Muhaysin's *kabsa*, then – if he was there – Hamad would leave at the end of the evening, while Dais and Muhammad would stay and sleep where they were. In the morning, everyone would get up, their heads horribly transformed into seas of clashing waves. They would find the leftovers from yesterday's *kabsa* (God knows how they ate it!) and drink an enormous pot of thick tea, then Dais and Muhammad would leave. Hisham would take a long shower, then go to Friday prayers with his uncle, and have lunch in the big house. Muhaysin sometimes accompanied him but sometimes stayed home, smoking, drinking tea and eating whatever food happened to be there, which was usually boiled eggs or leftover *kabsa*, if there was any.

One Thursday evening, Hisham and Muhaysin were getting ready to go out to Wazir Street. They hadn't any *arak* yet, although they'd asked Hamad to buy some, because Dais and Muhammad had come round unusually early. Dais was carrying a large plastic bag, which looked like it had something heavy in it. Everyone went to Muhaysin's room, where Dais took out the contents of the bag, which consisted of four bottled water containers filled with a clear reddish liquid. He took one of the bottles and raised it in the air, saying with a proud smile, 'Here's my latest invention ... local wine, not Bordeaux!'

'He's been preparing this surprise for three weeks,' said Muhammad. 'He's turned his room into a secret wine factory for you!' They all laughed. 'Even our two colleagues at home have begun to complain about the strange smell coming from Dais's room,' continued Muhammad, laughing, 'but he persuaded them that this was what his room always smelled like at this time of the year.' There was fresh laughter, then Muhaysin got up and went to the kitchen. He came back with four glasses, unusually clean and sparkling. Dais filled them roughly halfway, then raised his own glass, saying, 'Cheers!'. He took a great gulp, and everyone copied him.

It wasn't a good taste: there was a strong smell and taste of yeast, and the acidity of the vinegar had not been absorbed at all. But Dais still stared round anxiously, seeking their opinion of his handiwork. Hisham was the first to comment.

'Good wine,' he said. 'Better than *arak*, anyway.' He was being polite, afraid of hurting Dais's sensitive feelings. He preferred *arak*, which had a more immediate effect, and always reminded him of his first outing to the Kharis road.

'At least it doesn't cost as much as *arak*,' said Muhaysin. 'Or am I wrong?' he asked, looking at Dais.

Dais smiled proudly and said, 'Not at all ... a little grape juice, a tin of yeast, and lots of water and sugar. That's all there is to it. Isn't chemistry one of the blessings of the age?'

Everyone laughed. 'And of every age!' they said, emptying the remains of their glasses into their mouths and holding them out for more, which made Dais very proud. After the second glass, Muhaysin got up.

'It looks as though we're not going out this evening,' he said, looking at Hisham. 'I'll shut the doors and start getting the *kabsa* ready.'

Meanwhile, Dais was sifting through the tapes. He sighed loudly as he took one of them and put it on the small tape recorder. It was only a few seconds before the sound of Nazim al-Ghazali's singing resounded round the room: *Camel driver, the people who were here have gone ... A dark, Christian girl, I saw her ring a bell, and I said, 'Who taught that beauty bell-ringing?'* The smell of vetch filled the entire place.

37

Their days in the new lodgings went by without incident. The dubious looks cast at the two young friends and their endless visitors by the local men as they came and went were all that disturbed their tranquillity. They were very careful not to upset the neighbours with any behaviour that might count against them. Even when they spent the evening chatting with their friends, one of their most important rituals was to shut the door of the room where they were meeting and to shut the inner door between the front door and the rest of the house. They were careful not to laugh louder than necessary, or to turn up the volume on the radio or cassette player more than they had to. They wanted to win the trust of this hostile environment by any means and to avoid trouble at all costs. They even pretended to ignore the furtive looks of certain women of the quarter from behind half-closed doors and windows – enticing looks that implied all sorts of seductive adventure. This was despite the blazing passions lit within them both instantly, whenever here or there their glances met the twinkle of a half-hidden eye.

With time, by praying frequently with the congregation in the mosque and walking there and back with their eyes fixed on the ground, they were able to win the trust and respect of everyone. And they returned the greetings of some of the residents with better, more polite ones. In fact, they always tried to get their greetings in first. Sometimes they discussed those furtive looks. They would get so carried away by the passion of their conversation and the fiery lust ignited within them both that they felt driven to start something with one of the women concerned. The best time was the late morning, when the houses were full of women looking for some adventure to relieve them from their agonising routine of total boredom. But the two friends would soon switch to some other plan in order to preserve their excellent reputation.

On one occasion their resolve was severely tested. They were coming back from university earlier than usual and the alley was completely deserted. As they unlocked the door of their house, the door of the house opposite suddenly opened to reveal two faces – girls in the prime of life wearing nothing on their heads, their long, jet-black hair gleaming with oil and hanging loose over their shoulders, their eyes huge and dark as moonless desert nights, and their skin the colour of ripening dates. The girls smiled seductively at them. The two young men stood where they were, paralysed with surprise and overcome by indecision. Then they ran inside, as if pursued by wild animals. They stood for a short time recovering their breath, then made for the deserted sitting room and peered out the window overlooking the alley. The two girls were still crouching behind the door. Their eyes met – briefly – then they slammed the window shut. This incident recurred several times, and on each occasion their inclination was to start on an adventure and to hell with the consequences, but they backed off at the last moment to preserve their hard-won reputation. If they were to have an adventure, there were plenty of streets and alleys in Riyadh, so they resolved to let it be far away from their own quarter.

Their reputation was like pure gold, so much so that the women of the quarter stopped spying on them. They became freer after gaining the trust of their neighbours, so that eventually Hisham and Abd al-Rahman felt able to bring Raqiyya to the house; then another time she came with one of her friends; then the visits became more frequent without anyone suspecting anything. The first time Raqiyya came with Abd al-Rahman, it was in the afternoon. Their neighbour opposite knocked on the door and inquired politely about the guests inside. Hisham answered that they were his sister and brother-in-law who had come to visit and clean the house. The neighbour believed him and went back to his house, repeating, 'God bless you … God bless you,' and never asked again about anyone entering or leaving the house. What a fine veil it was, this blameless reputation of theirs: it protected them from all suspicion, and even concealed facts that were clear as the sun in broad daylight, as the expression goes. They no doubt meant the sun of the East, not the sun of the West.

Nonetheless, an uneasy sense of worthlessness continued to haunt Hisham. Despite the pleasure of his adventures with Raqiyya and her like, despite the new friendships that he had made and despite the intensity of his sense of adventure, the blade of his conscience continued to pierce him; it would not leave him to rest. After any exciting sexual adventure, or the day after any drunken evening, the ghost of his mother would invade his mind and his conscience would start on its sadistic diversions. He would pledge not to drink again or make love to women, indeed he would resolve to remain in complete seclusion and not to mix with anyone. However, he soon forgot all that when he'd drunk a little *arak* or wine, or tasted one of those smooth bodies. His marks in college began to plummet, to the surprise of his professors. This made him feel more and more anguish. He would rush back to his books with great enthusiasm, but soon his thoughts became preoccupied again by the softness of some particular body, or the fun he'd had the last time he'd got drunk with his friends. Then the letters would dance in front of his eyes, and despite his best efforts he would no longer be reading.

He no longer felt at ease with himself, except for the odd afternoon when he went out with Muhaysin to a date plantation near their quarter. There they would sit on the damp ground and watch the early spring breeze play with the palm trees around them, as the disk of the sun grew larger and turned crimson on its way to its journey's end in the sea by Jabal Qaf. They would say anything that came into their minds. They had conversations about God and existence, fate, destiny and chance; about heaven and hell, Adam and the Devil; Existentialism and Marxism; Islam and Christianity, Muhammad and Christ; about Riyadh, Qusaim and Dammam. They would talk about everything except their own personal lives. They would carry on talking and smoking until darkness let down its cloak and the grasshoppers started to sing; until the croaking of the frogs rose to a fevered prayer of desire, when, with the pale light of the stars, loneliness would pierce them and they would leave, feeling that they were nothing in this universe, that it had nothing to do with them. Then they would feel both contentment and hidden anxiety. Hisham's uncertainties would die; the spectre of his mother would disappear from his mind and he would sleep soundly that night, resolving to abandon his sinful life and devote himself to study and study alone ... but the curse of mankind is forgetfulness.

38

Two months had passed since his return from vacation. He had only occasionally thought of Suwayr, and only ever when he was drunk. One Friday afternoon, he was alone in his uncle's sitting room drinking tea. They had eaten lunch, and everyone had gone for their siesta when Moudhi came in and began to chat to him. Moudhi talked a lot about everything, and he wasn't really listening, although he was nodding his head and smiling. However, he couldn't help hearing when Moudhi said:

'It's strange about our neighbour Sarah … She's always asking about you, so much so that I've begun to suspect there's something between you.'

She said this laughing quietly and sharply like a mouse. He was holding his glass and smiling, but his smile immediately vanished and his hand began to shake uncontrollably. He felt as though his head was boiling inside. He put the glass down on the tray and his hands in his lap, trying to hide their trembling. He tried to get a grip on himself, summoning all his self-control to appear calm.

'Something between me and Sarah? What nonsense is this?' he

said. He was sure she had guessed, and it would only be a few moments before he collapsed completely. He would be forced to ask Moudhi to cover it up and keep it a secret between them. He was preparing himself for a full confession, when Moudhi said calmly:

'Why are you so agitated? You must be annoyed that I've pulled your leg. Would it make sense for there to be anything between the sensible Hisham and a woman like Sarah?' She put her hand on his. 'You are definitely annoyed,' she said, snatching it back quickly. 'Your hand is so cold and damp. I'm very sorry. It seems I went too far ... I, I ...' She couldn't complete the sentence. Her voice tailed off and she fell silent, looking at the floor. Hisham relaxed a little and his spirits revived. He thanked God for the beautiful masks we wear, which hide our true natures from others. But an ugly feeling of self-loathing began to spread through his soul. Of course *he* knew there was a relationship between himself and Suwayr, and that Moudhi had been correct in her suspicions, even though she herself had not believed them – or had not wanted to believe them. Really, why should Suwayr ask about him if there was nothing between them? Moudhi, however, could see nothing but the angel's mask Hisham wore, and she was not able to see behind it, or rather, she did not want to see – for we see what we want to see, not what can be seen. What made him feel even more disgusted with himself was Moudhi's pain at his reaction: she had spoken the truth in jest, while he had felt relieved when the truth had been concealed. The world is a strange place, he thought. One man can commit a sin without suffering, while another suffers at the mere suspicion of a sin. The loathing inside him grew almost unbearable, and he nearly shouted in the face of the innocent, suffering Moudhi:

'You're right about what you said ... I'm a devil wearing an angel's mask! No. I am worse than a devil: a devil expresses himself, but I have the soul of a devil and the look of an angel!'

Instead he looked at her calmly. The smile returned to his lips;

there was a wise expression on his face, and a childish innocence in his eyes. 'Don't worry,' he said. 'You don't need to be sorry. You didn't mean any offence.' As he spoke, he felt his stomach cramp with pain, but the innocent look never left his face. Moudhi fidgeted a little and tried to say something, but her mouth would not obey her. A few vague words came out, then she quickly got up and left, wiping her nose with the edge of her veil, and leaving him alone in the sitting room in a state of mounting self-disgust.

39

When he left his uncle's house that afternoon, it was in a state of weightlessness. He could not feel the ground beneath his feet, nor the world around him, nor the cigarette that burned his finger when he reached its end. He had caused Moudhi to suffer, he had forgotten Suwayr, Noura had become a ghost from the past and he had shattered the remains of his mother's image of him. My God! How could man be the cause of so much pain to those he loved? How was it that the greater the love, the greater the suffering one caused?

For the first time in a long time, Suwayr's house made him pause. It looked deserted, devoid of life. He made up his mind to see her, so he headed for the street and checked that Alyan was in his shop; he watched him trying to stay awake as he brushed away the flies that were back from their winter holidays. Then, after checking that there were no passersby in the alley, and glancing without emotion at the window of his old room, he went back and tapped lightly on the door three times. It wasn't long before a voice came from behind the door, 'Who is it?'

He said simply, 'It's me,' in a quiet voice, glancing to right and left. The door opened to reveal a face he knew well. Nothing about it had changed; it was as pretty as ever, but for a pallor that had spread over it, like the pallor of consumption. He quickly went in; she shut the door quietly, then they went to the usual room. Suwayr was smiling cryptically the whole time in a way that reminded him of the Mona Lisa; devoid of any excitement, but somehow brimming with excitement too.

Before they sat down, she clasped him quietly to her breast and tried to smell every part of his body her nose could reach, then she kissed his mouth tenderly and lovingly; her lips were deathly cold. Hisham was determined to break off his relationship with her once and for all, now that Moudhi suspected something (and now that he no longer needed her body). When she opened the door, he'd been struck by a powerful wave of desire. He had expected her to throw herself into his arms as soon as she saw him, then that they would slip into bed at once. But her strange behaviour stifled his desire, replacing it with a feverish curiosity. She hadn't put on any sort of makeup or scent. That was perhaps natural, as she hadn't been expecting him to come. But she stayed as she was after his arrival, smiling that same calm, cryptic smile that so disturbed him. She was wearing an old, pale nightdress that left her shoulders bare. He stretched out his hand and stroked her naked shoulder, but she remained motionless, still smiling, so that the last spark of desire inside him was extinguished and he was overcome with apprehension. This was not the Suwayr he knew. Had she stopped loving him? He didn't think so, otherwise she wouldn't have let him in. What had happened, then? Was she ill? Perhaps.

Suwayr suddenly got up and left the room, coming back with a tea tray. She had put on some of the perfume he had given her all that time ago, and was wearing lipstick. And now she was wearing the blue nightdress that he liked. She still loved him, then, but why? He stopped questioning himself as she offered him a glass of tea, still smiling and looking at him without a word. The deafening silence continued, undisturbed except by the slurping of tea and the voices of some boys playing outside. He could no longer stand her cryptic smile, or her almost lethargic glances in his direction. Trying to penetrate the silence somehow, he said:

'Aren't you afraid Alyan might come home?' He knew that her husband would not come home now, and she knew that he knew it; he just wanted to speak, to say something. She said nothing, sipping her tea calmly and smiling. Silence prevailed again – even the shouting of the boys outside had stopped, as if there were a conspiracy being hatched against him. Her sleepy looks and cryptic smiles were too much for him. He finished his glass, shaking it to indicate he had drunk enough as he put it back on the tray, having made up his mind to leave. She seemed aware of his decision, saying in a voice that seemed to come from the world of the dead, or from some far-off time:

'Have I become so insignificant in your eyes? Two months without my seeing you or hearing anything about you?'

Although he was relieved she had broken the silence, he was tortured by her questions, and immediately wished she had said nothing. A murderer's killer can be crueller than the murderer himself. Hisham did not reply, but clasped his hands over his lap, a dumb smile etched on his lips. He bowed his head to the ground like an accused man waiting for the verdict on himself. She was still smiling that deadening smile, a smile that had turned into an accusing question mark interrogating every part of his body. To break the terrible silence that followed he said:

'You know … the problems of studying, and a new house. And I spent the vacation with my family … When I came back from holiday, I tried to contact you,' he added, as if he had just remembered. 'But the house was deserted, and I thought that you must have gone away … Where have you been?'

For the first time since that meeting, she laughed. 'What a

cunning one you are!' she said. 'Where have we been? Where could we have been? We're always here, and it looks as though we shall die here!'

'But only those who love us will find us,' she went on, sipping the last drop of tea and looking at him with eyes that had regained their sparkle. 'You could easily have knocked on the door and checked,' she said, pouring more tea into both their glasses. 'Just like you did this time.'

As she said that, her smile became broader, and she gave him a look that he felt stripped him completely naked. There was just this dumb smile in front of him. He surrendered utterly, bowing his head again. Suwayr knew that she had achieved her objective and instantly reverted to the Suwayr he knew. She threw herself on him and kissed him with lips that had regained their warmth.

'I was almost going mad,' she said. 'If I hadn't picked up some scraps of news from Moudhi, I really would have gone mad.' She laughed affectionately. 'I almost gave myself away to her, I was asking about you so much,' she said, her eyes sparkling strangely. 'I saw the suspicion in her eyes as I was trying to find out where you were living, though I tried to seem innocent. I was on the point of going to your new lodgings. Discovery wasn't important. Nothing was important to me anymore after you had left. If things had been entirely in my hands, I would have shouted your love to the whole population of Riyadh.' She kissed him rapidly again with burning lips. 'Every time I asked about you, I did it just to hear someone say your name,' she said. 'Even when I was on my own and overwhelmed with loneliness, I would say your name to myself and the loneliness and hopelessness would disappear.'

Suddenly she broke into floods of warm tears. He didn't know what to do. He stretched out his hand and caressed her bare shoulder gently and lovingly. She grasped his hand and put it on her wet cheek, repeating in a soft voice:

'I love you. I love you, Hisham. It is time you knew how much I love you.'

He knew that she loved him, and really he loved her ... but he loved Noura and Raqiyya and Moudhi and his mother as well. She wanted a love that it was not in his power to give, even if he had wanted to. But still he answered:

'And I love you too, Suwayr.'

She snatched his hand from her cheek. 'Liar!' she said, angrily, her voice shaking. 'Yes, liar! You don't love me, Hisham, you just want my body. You've obviously found some other body. That's why you've left me!' She burst into fresh tears. Again he caressed her gently, as she said through her tears:

'You don't know the meaning of love, otherwise you wouldn't have made me suffer so much. I love you, whether you love me or hate me!' She calmed down a little and wiped away her tears with her palm, laughing softly:

'All right, don't love me. Love my body, I don't mind ... but don't leave me ... I adore you, Hisham, and I don't want you mixed up with anyone else.'

Hisham succumbed to a sudden feeling of vanity. With no particular object or intent, he said, slightly facetiously:

'*Ishrak* only applies to God! It is forbidden to worship anyone else!'

She looked at him with moist eyes, like a wild tiger.

'Then *you* are my God!' she said, her eyes widening even further. 'You torment me and show me mercy! Everything you do is acceptable and worthy of praise!'

Now he really could not bear it. Without thinking he said, 'I seek forgiveness from God Almighty.'

As he spoke, a feeling of vanity and something he did not recognise – something like guilt – mingled inside him. Her hand clutched his. He reached out his other hand and patted and stroked her cheek, while she threw herself almost violently into his arms and began to breathe in his scent, saying again and again, 'I love you, I love you, Hisham! I adore you!'

He grabbed her roughly in his arms and bent over to smell her hair and kiss her bare neck. The fires of their lust began once more to blaze. He felt that things between them were returning to normal. He lifted her head from his chest, intending to kiss her and move towards the bed. As he was about to do so, she closed her eyes and hissed:

'May God forgive you, Hisham … don't you know that I adore every atom in your body … don't you know that I am carrying you inside me?'

He leapt up like a man who's been singed by a stray spark, pushing her head away from him. All his internal fires were abruptly extinguished, now a new fire blazed, more powerful than the others. 'What did you say?' he asked, in a trembling voice.

'I am pregnant, Hisham …'

He felt that the earth swayed beneath him and that his head had turned into a ball of fire, while she remained calm, looking at him tenderly, the dumb smile back on her face. He pulled himself together and tried to be as calm as possible.

'Congratulations … congratulations, God willing! Alyan must be very happy!'

'Yes, he's very happy. But what has Alyan got to do with it?'

'He's your husband. Doesn't he have a right to be happy after waiting so long?' Hisham said in a confused voice.

'But it's our son, Hisham!' she said, giving him a sly look. 'The fruit of our love!'

He felt as if he were about to faint, but pulled himself together.

'How do you know?'

She smiled.

'A feeling … and a woman's feeling is never wrong.' Before he could reply, she went on, 'I know that it is our son. And so do you. Don't be afraid, I won't cause you any problems. What matters to me is that I have got you forever … I am carrying you inside me and you will be part of me forever. You won't be able to leave me after today, because you are sleeping inside me and you will be with me forever!'

Before he could say anything, she planted a long kiss on his mouth. He felt the taste of salt on his lips, the bitterness of colocynth inside him, and all the misery of the world in his soul.

40

He almost abandoned his studies. If it hadn't been for his fear of failing, he wouldn't have gone to college at all. His teachers were astonished by the alarming drop in his grades, though some of them continued to give Hisham good marks because of his excellent reputation. He took to visiting Suwayr almost daily. They would just talk and relax in each other's arms, without going to bed. Suwayr sometimes tried to tempt him, but he had lost all his desire. Once he tried to make love, but couldn't do it, which just compounded his existing anxiety. He kept away from Raqiyya, whose wild triangle no longer aroused him at all. Conflicting feelings ripped him apart internally, but Suwayr seemed as calm as he was fraught; her eyes radiated happiness. She seemed happier than at any other time during her life. Whenever she opened the door to him she wore a radiant smile, and she glowed with pleasure whenever she stroked her belly, gazing at him and smiling with the happiness of a child promised a gift. They sat and talked for hour after hour about anything that came to mind. In fact, Hisham did most of the talking. Suwayr would prop her head against his shoulder, take his palm between her hands, and lie with her legs stretched out before her. From time to time she would run his palm over her belly or kiss him as she savoured the smell of his neck.

These were fleeting moments of relaxation for Hisham, the only ones granted him since discovering the new life forming inside Suwayr. When he dragged himself away, as soon as her door shut behind him, he returned to his personal hell. Even sitting and chatting with Muhaysin, Muhammad and Dais had lost its charm. However much life bustled around him, he felt lonely wherever he went. Nothing interested him any longer. He felt he had aged internally, that he was now more than a hundred years old and his life had gone on far too long. The only thing he looked forward to now was the call to afternoon prayers, which signalled that he could go to Suwayr's house afterwards. Sweat was his nightly companion, soaking him until he lost consciousness and slept without knowing how or where. Muhaysin warned him of the dangers of excess, both financially and physically, but Hisham just raised a glass in his face, cackled nervously and said:

'Your health! Cheers! A la vôtre! Who cares!'

Hamad, who supplied him with drink, also warned him of the likely consequences of excess, but Hisham made no effort to listen to either of them. Drink gave him some comfort, though by the time he woke up this had transformed into terrible sadness, with the result that he turned to alcohol again. Intoxication no longer made his veins pulsate with sexual desire, or filled his head with delicious musings. Rather, he indulged the exquisite melancholy that gripped every atom of his soul. Sometimes the first glass would stimulate desire in him, but later glasses filled his mind with a terrifying image that drove out all other thoughts: his mother's eyes, Suwayr's belly, Noura's lips, Raqiyya's bottom and Moudhi's hand merged into a weird whole that really frightened him. Suddenly, Suwayr's belly burst open and blood spilled over Raqiyya's bottom and Moudhi's hand, then Suwayr started to lick the blood from

Raqiyya's bottom and Moudhi looked at her hand and screamed. Then she licked her hand, laughing, while red tears flowed from his mother's eyes. Her face had become a lifeless waxwork, ghostly white. Noura's lips grew so bloated that her whole face became just two giant lips, and she laughed hysterically as she approached him, trying to kiss him. He would back away as she pursued him, still laughing.

With every cup he drank, his sorrow grew, and with it grew his self-indulgence. When he reached the dregs, he raised his cup in the air to shout, 'A la vôtre, Françoise Sagan! *Bonjour, Tristesse*!' Sometimes, Muhaysin would come to his room and join him in a glass or two, but he soon left, shaking his head over his friend, now living in another dimension. Several times Muhaysin tried to find out what had happened; but Hisham wouldn't speak and stayed silent, smoking and drinking. Even the tears refused to fall from his eyes, though he had a great need for them.

41

One evening, just back from Suwayr's, Hisham sat alone on the roof savouring the pleasant May breezes and forcing himself to revise a subject on which he would be tested the following day. He was trying with difficulty to resist a strong temptation to drink some *arak* when he heard a knock on the door. He didn't move, knowing Muhaysin would open it. He heard Muhaysin's greeting, then the sound of footsteps coming up the stairs. He sighed and got up, cursing Muhaysin and his never-ending visitors. Flicking away his cigarette he made for the door to the staircase, hoping that way to escape the tedium of company. But before he reached the door he was astonished to see his father's face looming over him, smiling without smiling, Abd al-Rahman and Muhaysin in tow. This was indeed a surprise.

Hisham ran to his father, kissed him on the brow and privately thanked God he'd got rid of his cigarette. Then he invited them all into his room. His father, though, preferred the roof with its pleasant May breezes. Everyone sat down on the worn-out carpet while his father looked round.

'A nice house,' he said. 'You're lucky to have found it.'

'It's a lot of rent, but worth it,' replied Muhaysin. Abu Hisham nodded understandingly. Hisham asked how everything was and what his mother was up to.

'Everything is fine. We're all fine!' replied Abu Hisham, nodding again.

'I'll make tea,' said Muhaysin, getting up. 'Abu Hisham doubtless takes his tea strong, unlike the young men of Riyadh!' Hisham's father smiled in agreement. Abd al-Rahman got up at the same time:

'Don't worry about me,' he said. 'Excuse me,' he added, addressing Hisham's father. 'I have some business. I'll have to go.'

Hisham's father gestured to him politely, 'Thanks for bringing me to Hisham's house.'

'There's no need to thank anyone for doing their duty!' replied Abd al-Rahman as he headed for the staircase. Then he stopped, as if he'd forgotten something. 'Don't forget, Abu Hisham,' he said. 'We have a lunch date tomorrow ... and we will expect you tonight, you will sleep with us, your bed is ready.' But Abu Hisham refused.

'No, I will spend the night here,' he said. 'Give my greetings to your father ... and God help us with these bachelors!'

'Goodbye, then.'

'Goodbye!' And Abd al-Rahman left.

Muhaysin brought the refreshments. 'I hope our bachelors' tea will prove favourable,' he teased. Abu Hisham said nothing, but smiled at Muhaysin in an approving way. Meanwhile Muhaysin poured the tea, offering the traditional words of welcome, and they all drank.

While Muhaysin chatted with Hisham's father about the past and the harsh lives people once suffered, often travelling miles to find work, Hisham seethed in a whirl of questions. What had brought his father to Riyadh? It was not like him to leave his work and come to Riyadh without an important reason. Was his mother all right? Hisham's mind filled with the worst possible scenarios. He shot Muhaysin a look which his friend understood perfectly.

'Excuse me, Uncle,' he said, getting up. 'Our fridge is empty. A bachelors' fridge, as you know! I'm going to buy some food for our supper. Please forgive us for being so inhospitable,' he added, turning towards the staircase. 'This house is yours, and we are your children!'

'God bless you,' replied Abu Hisham. 'You're not at all inhospitable. Bounty belongs to God!'

The time had come to put an end to this anxiety. As soon as he heard the sound of the front door being closed, Hisham turned questioningly to his father.

'Is everything all right, Father?' he asked, with obvious unease.

Abu Hisham calmly returned his look. 'Don't be anxious,' he said. 'Everything is fine.'

'Is mother all right?'

'I told you, don't be so on edge. Everything is fine.'

If everything was fine, what had brought Abu Hisham to Riyadh? Hisham could bear it no longer. His father's tranquillity disturbed him, though he knew it was characteristic.

'Do you have some business in Riyadh, then?' His father gave a short laugh as he saw how agitated Hisham was.

'I missed you,' he said. 'Isn't that excuse enough to come to Riyadh?'

No ... missing him wasn't the only reason ... he knew his father too well. A silence descended, which he took to be the calm before the crisis. His father was in Riyadh for something important, but what could it be? Hisham sipped mechanically at his tea, expecting the bomb to explode at any moment. He wished it would explode. Waiting in such agitation was terrible.

At last Abu Hisham turned to him, his face like a freshly squeezed lemon. It was clear that he was several times more agitated than his son. 'Hisham … tell me the truth,' he said. 'What have you done?'

Hisham's stomach turned upside down and his head ached; the blood pumped madly in his veins, and a sticky sweat clogged the pores of his body; black thoughts occupied his mind. Had his parents found out about his relationship with Suwayr and her pregnancy? It would be a disaster if his father had found out – and a calamity if his mother knew! But how could he know? Who would have told him? Was anyone aware of their relationship without Hisham's knowledge? If so, who? Alyan? … Abd al-Rahman? … Moudhi? … Impossible, unless … unless Suwayr had told someone about them. Moudhi, for example, or her husband. But she would be mad to have done so. Perhaps she *was* mad? Impossible that madness should have affected her to that extent. But then again, why not? Yet how would his father in Dammam know that the relationship was public knowledge before Hisham himself knew? He had seen Suwayr today, and there'd been nothing to indicate anything was wrong.

But perhaps Abu Hisham was referring to his drinking. Who could have told him? Perhaps it was Hamad. The wretch. What gave Hamad the right? It was certain that his father had found out about his drinking. With great effort Hisham pulled himself together and asked in a shaking voice:

'What do you mean, father?'

His father looked him straight in the eye. 'Don't pretend to be stupid,' he said severely. 'You know what I mean.'

Everything was out, then. The drinking *and* his relationship with Suwayr. Hisham didn't know how, but all his secrets were out.

'It's all over, Hisham. What has happened, has happened. Tell me the truth, my son, then perhaps I can help.'

Hisham's resistance crumbled before his father's severity and compassion, and he prepared to confess everything: his relationship with Suwayr, his flings with Raqiyya and her like, his relationship in Dammam with Noura, the *arak* drinking, his sessions with the gang ... everything.

He opened his mouth, trying to speak, but his father was quicker:

'Yesterday, the principal of your high school came to see me. He is one of the 'establishment', as you know. He told me that certain persons had been asking about a group of people among whom numbered yourself and Adnan. Tell me the truth, my son ... Have you acted against the government?'

So this was it, then. Hisham felt vaguely relieved, and managed a faint smile of satisfaction, though he was immediately struck by anxiety of a fresh kind. He had forgotten the organisation and his comrades; forgotten prison, and the fear of arrest. But now, here from nowhere, was the past returning in full force. If Hisham had forgotten the past, it seemed that the past had not forgotten Hisham.

He hid nothing from his father. The government knew everything now, so why shouldn't his father? The thing that oppressed the soul most was secrecy; it strangled the person with the secret. Unburdening was a great relief.

His father remained silent as he listened to Hisham's confession. It was clear that he was stunned by the shock. Abu Hisham had suffered a lot in his life, and he fully understood that trifling with the government was a matter of the utmost gravity. How could it be that his own son played around like this? It had never occurred to Abu Hisham that his quiet, introverted son could embark on an adventure so dangerous. It was a shock he had never anticipated, even in his imagination, and now here it was confronting him. Conflicting emotions flared up in Abu Hisham's mind – feelings of fear, nervousness and pride. He was fearful and anxious for the fate of his only son, and at the same time he felt hurt. He'd thought that he knew everything about Hisham's life. He had brought Hisham up to be open and not to hide anything, and here he was, suddenly revealing that what Abu Hisham didn't know about his son was more than he did know. And who was to say? Perhaps what Hisham revealed today was only a fraction of it. Doubts began to overwhelm him. Despite these, mingled with his other feelings was a secret suggestion of pride. His son, whom he had down as shy, solitary and addicted to reading, had demonstrated a rare courage: he had challenged the government. But challenging the government was the height of folly, and there was only a thin line between courage and folly. Abu Hisham didn't know that Hisham's entry into the secret organisation had been unintentional, with absolutely no planning at all; that it had no connection with either courage or folly. Appearances suggested it showed courage. But Abu Hisham thought that any trifling with the government was folly, exposing one to inevitable danger. Yet what made him at once fearful and proud, was that this folly had been undertaken by the last person on earth he would have expected: his own son Hisham. All these competing emotions crowded his thoughts as he looked silently at Hisham, still telling him things that seemed more fantasy than fact. It had never ocurred to Abu Hisham that the reader of *Superman* might have a different and more dangerous face.

'I had no idea you were a great revolutionary ...' he said, smiling, but with sorrow etched on his face. 'But you only had to meet the Baathists to become one of them,' he added, trying to sound light-hearted. 'The worst sort of people. There's no one like them except the Communists and the Brothers ... Is this the consequence of our trust in you?' he continued, after a short silence. 'How do you think your mother will react when she finds out?'

The sharp blade of guilt planted itself forcefully in Hisham's chest, as his father continued:

'I know that you haven't committed any crime impinging on our honour, but you have committed a folly to beat all follies. A stupid thing to do. Pure madness! You are our only son. Have you thought what would become of us if anything happened to you?

You work against the government! What have you got to do with the government? Do you lack for anything? Your mother and I have struggled to reach where we have for your sake, and at the end of it you put us in this position! To work against the government! Do you think you're in some sort of Arsène Lupin story,* or a game that'll soon be over? The government is a red death ... do you understand?'

His father was in an extremely emotional state and it was obvious he was having to restrain his tears. As usual, however, he kept his feelings under strict control. Meanwhile, Hisham listened in silence, though he was insulted when his father compared his actions with those in an Arsène Lupin story. He was extremely hurt to see his father so upset, and he was terrified of how his mother would react when she found out. And she would certainly find out. What could he say to self-justification? Would he say that everything had happened unintentionally? That was an excuse even worse than the mistake; it would imply he had compromised himself and his parents without any thought or feeling of responsibility. Hisham could not think of a suitable reply and opened his mouth with difficulty.

'You are quite right, father,' he said. 'If repentance and apology were any use, I would be apologising to you to the end of time, and repenting for the rest of my life. But what has happened has happened ... And no one can undo God's destiny.'

His father smiled sarcastically.

'"What has happened has happened"!' he echoed. 'No one can undo God's destiny! Is this all you have to say, Sheikh Hisham? You do something like this and then you say "God's destiny"! ... Leave God out of it! He is not a doll to play with when you want to, and abandon when you feel like it!'

---

* Arsène Lupin, French gentleman-thief turned detective, featured in more than sixty crime novels and short stories by Maurice Leblanc (1864–1941). The stories were very popular in the Arab world.

Before his father could finish, they heard the front door opening. Hisham was immediately paralysed by fear, though he knew that it was only Muhaysin coming back. He looked hurriedly at his father.

'The important thing is ... what is to be done, father?' he said, panicking.

'What is to be done? Didn't you think of that before embarking on all this?' said his father angrily. 'I don't know,' he added, quickly calming down. 'We'll think about it at leisure. Anyway, don't go to the university tomorrow. They may be waiting for you there.'

Hisham suddenly thought of Adnan.

'And what about Adnan?' he asked. 'He ought to know that they are looking for him ... I ought to go to the university. Has the principal told Adnan's father what he told you?'

'I don't know. Does Adnan or anyone else matter to me? Do what you like but don't go to the university. Listen to what I am saying this time.'

His father looked at him with a sternness Hisham had never seen before. Then he looked away and said, bitterly:

'You have been doing as you pleased, while all along we thought you were doing what pleased us ... this time, do as *we* want!'

Again Hisham felt the sharp stab of remorse. 'All right,' he agreed. 'I'll go to his house before he goes to university. He has to know!'

While they spoke, Muhaysin appeared at the door to the staircase carrying a large tray, which he put down in front of Abu Hisham.

'A blessed time,' he said. 'This is not worthy of you, but blessings come from God, may your life be long.'

'In the name of God,' said Hisham's father, as he cut the loaf of warm dry bread and dipped it in a plate of beans soaked in butter. Muhaysin was a really superb cook. He'd made beans with butter, boiled eggs, and a plate of tuna decorated with slices of tomato. They all ate in silence. His father finished quickly:

'Thank you very much, Abd al-Muhsin! May your table be full, God willing!'

'What's this? You haven't eaten anything, Uncle! Praise be to God ... no one should be shy in their own house!' Reluctantly Muhaysin made to take the tray back to the kitchen. 'I'll make tea then,' he said. 'I'm afraid we haven't got any coffee.' Hisham got up.

'Let me help,' he said. 'Excuse me, father.' They put the almost untouched plates of food in the fridge, then Muhaysin asked curiously, putting the kettle on the gas:

'Everything's all right, I hope? What's brought your father to Riyadh?'

'Oh, it's nothing ... the authorities are looking for me,' said Hisham casually, washing his hands at the kitchen sink. Muhaysin looked as if he had been struck by a thunderbolt; his eyes bulged and his mouth was wide open. He spoke like a startled idiot: 'What? ... The authorities? What do you mean?'

'I mean that the authorities want to detain me ... I was once a member of a secret organisation, and now everything has come out.'

'Everyone knows about it now,' Hisham went on, towelling his hands dry. 'The authorities, my father ... so why shouldn't you know as well? Why shouldn't everyone know? It's not as if it matters any more.'

Muhaysin was speechless. He stared dumbly at Hisham, until the kettle whistled and broke the silence. Muhaysin lifted it with a shaking hand.

'Go back to your father,' he whispered. 'I'll make the tea and join you in a moment.'

Back on the roof, Hisham found his father deep in prayer. He waited for him to finish. When Abu Hisham had completed his devotion, he looked at Hisham. Calm had returned to his face.

'I asked God for guidance,' he said. 'And with His power, He has inspired me to take the correct decision.' He sat up straight and went on,'You will travel to Beirut, and stay there until God does whatever has to be done ... you will study there, so you will have lost nothing.'

Hisham stood passively like an accused man receiving his sentence, playing no part and offering no opinion. His father, meanwhile, continued:

'I will go with you tomorrow morning to the university and retrieve your file. Then we will go to your uncle's house and in the afternoon leave for Dammam. We'll arrange your journey from there. It will allow time for your mother to see you,' he added pointedly. 'She has some rights over you too, as you know.'

Muhaysin arrived with the tea and began to pour it.

'Hisham has told me about his brush with the authorities,' he said, without any preliminaries. 'And I have an idea.' He handed Abu Hisham his tea and continued to speak, ignoring the angry looks Hisham's father directed at his son. 'Please don't be angry, Uncle. Hisham is right. If the authorities know everything now, why shouldn't everyone know? There are no secrets any longer. And anyway, I'm not just anyone, ... Or is that wrong?' He gave Hisham a glass. 'I have an idea,' he said excitedly, without waiting for them to reply. 'Why doesn't Hisham go to Qusaim and hide there ... I can arrange things. No one will be able to reach him there. What do you say?'

Muhaysin's passions were running so high that his whole body seemed to be talking, sensing an adventure on the horizon. Hisham's father smiled, and looked at Muhaysin approvingly.

'God bless you, my son,' he said. 'You are a good fellow, God be praised! But I have arranged something different. And God will do what is best ...'

'We will leave for Dammam tomorrow,' said Hisham in an resigned voice after glancing at his father. 'After that, only God knows what He will do.'

Muhaysin was startled by the speed of their decision.

'So soon?' he asked immediately. 'I didn't know that our time here would end like this, suddenly, and without warning. But you will come back, won't you?' he added, his voice shaking a little.

Hisham smiled, trying to suppress his tears and looking upwards to avoid Muhaysin's eyes. 'God knows,' he said, his sorrow plain.

There fell a heavy silence. Hisham felt as if the heavens had fallen to earth and that he was trapped between the two, unable to escape. He heard his father's voice as though it came from another dimension, or from distant aeons, across the barriers of time.

'I think that I will sleep on the roof,' said Abu Hisham. 'Hisham's room will be too crowded for both of us. There is no need for a bed, just bring me a blanket and pillow.' Muhaysin jumped up nimbly.

'At once!' he said. 'Everything will be ready.'

He left, and Hisham's father followed him with his eyes.

'God be praised, he's a good young man,' he said. Muhaysin returned with two blankets and a pillow. He spread one blanket on the carpet, placed the other, still folded, to the side of the carpet, then put the pillow beside it.

'You must be tired, uncle. It's a long way from Dammam.'

'You're right. And we have a tiring day ahead of us tomorrow.' said Abu Hisham, yawning. He took off his headdress and head cord and threw himself on the bedding.

'I'm going to talk with Muhaysin a little,' said Hisham. 'Who knows when I may see him again. *If* I see him, that is.'

He got up, his friend following. Abu Hisham's voice trailed after them:

'Don't be late. We need to get up with the morning star.'

Hisham and Muhaysin talked until just before dawn, smoking and drinking tea together. He was tempted to drink *arak*, but Muhaysin stopped him.

42

It was almost six o'clock in the morning when his father woke him. He washed his face and put on his *tob*, threw the rest of his clothes into a suitcase together with Dostoevsky's *House of the Dead*, and put on his headdress. Then he took up his bag of clothes and a small hand bag, glanced quickly around his room, sighed deeply, and left.

His father had already made tea and was sitting drinking it in the hall when Hisham came down. He was annoyed there was no bitter coffee, but he promised himself a whole pot of it at his uncle's house. Hisham's lips were desperate for a cigarette, but it was impossible to smoke with his father there. He knew that his father knew he smoked – things like that couldn't be hidden from someone as worldly as his father, but it was still impossible for Hisham to smoke openly in front of him. His father quickly finished his tea and got up.

'Come on,' he said. 'It's time to go.' He hurried out, followed by Hisham. Before shutting the door, Hisham paused thoughtfully. He put the two cases in the car, then said:

'Excuse me, father ... I must write something for Muhaysin.'
He hurried inside, pursued by his father's voice. 'Don't be long.
The first part of the day is the best!' Hisham raced up to his room,
took a pen and a piece of paper and wrote:

Dear Muhaysin,
I don't know when I will see you again, but you can be sure
that our friendship will last as long as we live, even if we are
separated by time and place. I am leaving you the room and its
contents, but please keep the books until we meet – and show
mercy to widows! I hope you get a scholarship to America,
perhaps we will meet there. Who knows? My warmest greetings
to Muhammad and Dais. I will miss you all.
Affectionately,
Hisham.

He folded the paper carefully, then went back down to
Muhaysin's room. He was sound asleep and snoring. Hisham put
the note on a small table beside the bed with his house keys, gazed
one last time on his friend's face, and hurried outside.

Hisham got out of the car at the intersection of al-Khazzan
and al-Usarat Streets. He explained to his father how to get to
the university, and they agreed to meet at his uncle's house. Then
he boarded the local bus to al-Batha. The whole way to Halla,
he prayed God that Adnan would not already have left. He was
fairly confident of this, as it was still only a few minutes after seven
o'clock. The small street was full of life. Most people there started
their day immediately after the dawn prayers. He knocked quietly
on the door several times. When he didn't get an answer, he knocked
again harder, worried. The door finally opened to reveal the face
of one of Adnan's colleagues, with his thick beard and completely
shaven head. He was wearing long trousers and was still trying
to fasten the waistband as he opened the door, yawning. Hisham

asked for Adnan and was shown into the sitting room. It was only a few moments before Adnan's thin, frightened face appeared at the door. Confused and agitated, and without returning his greeting, Adnan asked:

'Is everything all right? What's the matter, Hisham? I don't expect you to come visiting at this sort of time!'

'They're looking for us,' said Hisham, without preamble. 'It's our turn now ... Comrade!'

Adnan sat down without speaking. His hands trembled violently, and his face had turned a very noticeable yellow. Sweat covered his brow and his nostrils, although at that time in the morning the air was still cold.

'After all this time!' he said, his voice shaking. 'Who told you? It must be a lie ... Or else –'

Before he could finish, Hisham interrupted him:

'My father told me. He came to Riyadh last night, after our school principal told him they were looking for us in Dammam. It's quite definite, and I thought it my duty to tell you.' Adnan looked at him lifelessly.

'God bless you and reward you with good!' he muttered. 'God grant you a long life!' Every cell of his body was trembling and he was sweating profusely.

'What are you going to do?' asked Hisham. 'What have you decided?'

'I don't know,' replied Adnan, without giving it any thought. 'My father must know about this. He must have a solution.' Then he looked at Hisham and said, 'And you ... What have you decided?'

'My father is waiting at my uncle's house. We will go back to Dammam, and from there I will leave for Beirut. Why don't you come with me?'

'No, I can't. My father must know about it first. Please tell him when you reach Dammam.'

'Don't worry, we will.'

'God willing, you ought to say!'

'God willing!'

Hisham got up and walked over to the front door. Adnan followed him with dragging feet. Hisham looked at his childhood friend by the door, trying to put on a nonchalant smile.

'Don't worry,' he said. 'Everything will be all right. God willing!'

His optimism was disingenuous. Hisham's whole being was also gripped by fear, and he was not at all confident that everything would be all right. After taking a few paces, he went back as if he had forgotten something.

'Either way,' he said, 'it would be better for you not to go to college now, not until things calm down.' Adnan nodded in agreement.

'You're right,' he said. 'In any event, tell yourself that nothing will happen to us unless God has decreed it, and he is our Master and our best support.'

Hisham walked on. Before disappearing into one of the alleys, he gave a last glance behind him and saw Adnan still standing at the door. He waved and Adnan waved back, neither of them aware that this exchange would be their last.

43

When Hisham reached his uncle's house, Abu Hisham was the only person in the sitting room. He was sitting with a silver tray in front of him, containing a large pot of coffee and a plate of Sukkari dates. He could tell how many dates his father had got through from the pits scattered all over the tray. The coffee pot was almost empty.

There was nothing for them to talk about. Hisham picked at the dates, though he had no appetite, and poured himself a cup of coffee, which he drank without any real relish. He had to say something to break the silence:

'Sukkari, eh? Nice dates, aren't they father? Nothing so sweet except perhaps Barhi dates ... Sukkari and Barhi are the two best kinds!' There was more silence. He tried to think of something else for them to discuss. His father spared him the trouble by wrapping his headdress round his head and retreating into a corner of the sitting room, saying:

'I didn't sleep well last night. I'll snooze for a bit. We have a long journey in front of us.' It was only a few moments before the sound of his snoring filled the room.

It was still early, only a little after nine o'clock. There remained considerable time before they were to set out. Hisham had no wish to read or do anything else. He was extraordinarily tense and depressed. He thought of Suwayr and smiled … He had almost left without seeing her. He decided to meet her and try to explain why he was leaving, without of course telling her the whole truth. While his father slept, he slipped out of the sitting room and made for the front door. But before he could open it, he heard Moudhi behind him:

'Where are you going? Can't you bear to stay in this house?'

Startled by the unexpected interruption, he wheeled around, smiling, and said:

'Not at all … I just wanted to relax a little.'

Suddenly, doing something she had never done before, Moudhi grasped his hand and pulled him into the dining room. She sat him down in a corner, closed the door, then placed herself in front of him.

'Listen, Hisham,' she said firmly, without any formalities. 'You're my cousin. You know how much I have respected you ever since we were small.' She paused for a moment, then said, 'So I want to ask you a straightforward question, and I want an honest answer without any beating about the bush. You can be confident that what you say will go no further. What is this sudden journey? We're not in the holiday season, and your father wouldn't come to Riyadh for nothing. I have a feeling that there's something going on. Please, Hisham. Tell me the truth!'

She stared at him with eyes so wide they almost pierced her worn veil. He could hide nothing. He knew how intelligent Moudhi was, but he was afraid that she would find out about his relationship with Suwayr. Now that she had asked him directly, he hesitated to tell her the truth. It was not that he was afraid; he was fearful of hurting her. But Moudhi would not let go until she knew the truth, and if he didn't tell her, she'd have all sorts of ideas which might lead her to investigate his connection to Suwayr. Finally, Hisham decided to tell her everything. Her reaction was silence; just staring eyes and an open mouth. Then she screamed angrily:

'Oh, no! Oh, no! Oh, no!' as she beat her hand on her breast. Finally, she cried, weeping and weeping for a long time. Without realising he was doing it, Hisham took her hand and put it between his own, caressing it gently and tenderly, as he repeated:

'Don't worry … Nothing will happen to us if God has not decreed it.' He let her weep for as long as she needed, until finally her tears stopped. She pulled him to her breast, hugged him and started crying again, then got up, saying between her tears:

'All this was happening without my knowing … and I wouldn't have found out if I hadn't asked you. I believed that I was worth more to you than that!'

'You know how highly I regard you. God knows how dear you are to me. But … this is how it is,' said Hisham with great sincerity. Moudhi moved back to her place in front of him and sat down, squatting on her haunches. She moved her face so near to his that he could feel the warmth of her breath wafting onto his face.

'And what about Sarah?' she said, in a voice that was almost a hiss. 'Is she dear to you as well, or is she more than that?'

He leapt up as if bitten by a snake. His stomach churned so violently he thought it would rupture. His head boiled inside, but still he tried to control himself.

'Sarah? Who is Sarah?' he said, sounding like an idiot.

She looked at him with moist eyes, saying sarcastically:

'Oh! You mean, you don't know her? Sarah … our neighbour … Alyan's wife …'

'Ah … Alyan's wife. What about her?'

He was trying without success to control his body, every atom of which was in turmoil. His hands trembled as he hid them in his lap. Moudhi pushed her face still nearer until he could see through her veil the youthful freckles on her face.

'Don't play with me,' she said in a whisper. 'What is the relationship between you? She visits me all the time and speaks only of you ...'

God curse you, Suwayr, I visit you every day, why do you visit my uncle's house? The woman had gone mad, or else she had plans he didn't know.

'Believe me, Moudhi ... there's no relationship between us. You know me. I'm not that sort of person.'

'I believed that,' she hissed. 'Until I saw you slipping out of her house one afternoon!'

The bomb had exploded. He succumbed to a violent headache, as if he were in the middle of a whirlpool, or one of those violent winds in the deadly Nejdi desert during the burning days of summer. He saw, as in a vision, the glistening white statue of a Greek god explode into innumerable fine fragments. All his secrets were out. It seemed it was true that disasters never come singly. One last time, Hisham tried to defend himself.

'You must be confused,' he said. 'Couldn't the person you saw have been her husband or one of her relations?'

Then, realising the uselessness of this defence, and making as if he had suddenly remembered something, he immediately added:

'Howcome you say you saw me slipping out her house?'

Moudhi spoke calmly, though the sorrow and distress in her voice were plain:

'Of course there are always nasty surprises lurking beneath the surface. How cunning you are, Hisham! All this coming out about you! Anyone would think you were as meek as a lamb, but ... but you ... I don't want to say ... Women, politics and God knows what else ...'

She was lost for words and could not finish her sentence.

'I was in the upstairs room,' she went on, wiping away fresh tears, 'in your old room, looking around, when I found some leftovers on the window sill. I was about to clear them away when

I happened to glance into the street and saw you slipping out of there … I know perfectly well what you look like … if you'd been in a crowd of a hundred men, I would have known it was you!'

There was no way out this time. That cursed window. It was the window that had brought him to this crisis. He promised himself that from this day forth he would never open a window; then he looked at Moudhi with eyes that had lost their courage.

'I have made a mistake, Moudhi,' he said, 'and you're right to despise me and not to believe me in future. But believe me, my relationship with Suwayr is innocent, just a flirtation. It's not what you imagine.'

She frowned at him.

'You're still flirting with her,' she said. 'What sort of innocent relationship is that? Oh! I suppose I have to believe you, even though I don't!' There was silence for a few moments. Moudhi's eyes did not leave his face. Her gaze was too much for Hisham, and he shifted his eyes away. Then Moudhi said:

'What did you like about her?'

This unexpected turn in the conversation caught Hisham off-guard, but Moudhi didn't even give him the chance to be surprised:

'She's fat as a cow, and dark as a dry date … and I've always had doubts about her morals. I'm sure she led you on, and she's no doubt seduced others besides you. Believe me, Hisham, I know these sorts of women, who hunt out innocents like you … but you are inexperienced, you haven't tasted life yet!'

Hisham smiled to himself, thinking, 'If I'm innocent and inexperienced, what terrible things would I have done if I hadn't been so innocent?'

'Never mind Sarah and her games … what are you going to do?' asked Moudhi.

'About what?'

'About the trouble you are in … with the authorities.'

Moudhi's revelations about Suwayr meant Hisham had completely forgotten about his trouble with the authorities, but now he was instantly transported back into his whirl of terror. He sat up straight and clasped his hands around his knees.

'I will travel,' he said gloomily. 'I'll leave the country until things calm down.'

'Where will you go?'

'To Lebanon ... That's what I've agreed with my father ... No, that's what father wanted ... The important thing is ... that all this should end somehow.' He was talking to himself.

'Lebanon? You will leave one Sarah for a thousand others ...' Moudhi whispered, as if she, too, were talking to herself.

'What?'

'Nothing, nothing.' Moudhi stood up, wiped her eyes with the edge of her veil, and walked towards the door, saying:

'The important thing is for you to come back to us safely ... God preserve you.' She hurried out, but quickly returned again and stood beside the door.

'Hisham,' she said. 'If I showed you my face, would I have gone too far?'

'There is no "too far" between us, Moudhi. You will remain my beloved Moudhi whether you are veiled or whether you show your face.'

With a sudden movement, Moudhi tore off her veil to reveal her face, then went up to him and planted a quick kiss on his cheek. She looked at him with red, moist eyes, then stumbled from the room.

He stayed sitting in the dining room for a long time, daydreaming about nothing and everything, unable to move or think properly. He was only roused from his dreaming when Said informed him that there were two people at the door asking for him. Terror immediately overcame him and he began to tremble violently. Who could they be? The police? Suwayr and Alyan? Anything was possible when misfortunes all came at once. He got up, dragging his feet towards the door, almost fainting with each step.

At the door he found Muhaysin and Muhammad. He returned to his senses, feeling like a man recovered from a terrible sickness. Muhammad embraced him warmly.

'Don't worry. Everything will be all right. This is just a passing storm, God willing,' he said with emotion.

'God willing,' said Hisham, thinking: *So Muhaysin has told him everything.*

Muhaysin looked affectionately at Hisham:

'When I got up and couldn't find you, I was sure that you must be here. And I had to see you before you left. I didn't attend classes at college today. I went in to find Muhammad and told him everything. He insisted on coming here with me. I wanted to find Dais too but I knew that Dais wouldn't leave college no matter what the reason. There's no need to disturb him now – he'll find out everything soon enough.'

Hisham looked at his two friends with love and gratitude. It was good to know that he was not alone. Then he invited them into the sitting room and asked Said to make tea. Muhammad wanted to know every little detail, and Hisham did not disappoint him. He knew that he would be telling all sooner or later, so why should he not talk here, to his friends?

The three continued their whispered conversation until the sound of their voices woke Abu Hisham. Then the other occupants of the house began to arrive: Abd al-Rahman first, then Hisham's uncle, then the oldest son Muhammad. Hamad and Ahmad did not appear that day. Hisham's uncle insisted that Muhaysin and Muhammad stay to lunch, and it was not long before everyone gathered around the rice dish and plates of *jarish,* crushed wheat cooked with meat and vegetables, and *qursan,* made of fine bread with meat and vegetable stock poured over it.

During the meal, Hisham's uncle tried to find out the reason for this surprise visit and sudden departure, with questions that were frankly suspicious, but Abu Hisham maintained it was just some routine business that required Hisham's presence in Dammam. His uncle was grudgingly persuaded, knowing there was more to it but that he wasn't going to find out what it was. No doubt everything would become clear in due course. Abu Hisham didn't want to upset anyone unduly. He was optimistic that he could deal with the situation, and that all would be well in the end, and so didn't believe there was any need to worry the others with the facts. And indeed, if Hisham hadn't told Muhaysin and Moudhi, everything would have stayed a secret as his father wished.

The time came to leave. They said goodbye to everyone and Hisham took a seat beside his father in the green Peugeot. The car set off, and the boys chased it down the street amidst the cloud of dust it raised. As the car approached New Shumaisi Street, Hisham looked back and saw Muhaysin and Muhammad standing in the middle of the road, between his uncle's and Suwayr's houses. He felt sure Moudhi was looking from one of the windows, and that Suwayr would hear the noise of the car – but she wouldn't know it was carrying Hisham away, and that she would probably never see him again. He felt guilty at not being able to see her before he left. She would certainly ask Moudhi about him, but he couldn't predict how Moudhi would receive her – if she received her at all, now that she knew about their relationship. Suwayr would think he had abandoned and betrayed her, but now he could always say that he was thinking about her during his last moment in Riyadh.

At the junction, his father headed east and his friends and the house disappeared, leaving just their pale shadows in his mind … and one burning question: was the child in Suwayr's belly his, or Alyan's, or someone else's? At times he was certain it was his, at others sure that it wasn't. And now it looked as if he would never know. Or perhaps he would one day find out; for no one knows what the future holds …

44

When they reached Dammam, the night was almost a third gone. The city was dead; nothing moved except for a few police cars on routine street patrol. He had missed and yearned for this city so much! Last time he'd left, he had returned to missing it before a single week had gone by. But tonight it seemed lonely and repugnant, like a rotten corpse. Even the smell of the sea, even the smell of the vapour given off by the oil wells near Dhahran and Baqiq, now seemed putrid – more than they ever had in the past. On previous occasions, whenever they had returned from Riyadh and the blazing fires appeared along the route, he would breathe in the smell of the gas with pleasure and longing. Now though, it smelled far worse than it ever had before.

Camp Bedouin was the first quarter of Dammam. Soon they would reach Adama, where their house was. His father, however, did not turn left to Adama, but continued on the road towards the Workers' City quarter. Hisham was surprised at this and jokingly asked:

'Have you lost your way, father?'

'Our house will be under surveillance,' he replied, without turning towards Hisham. 'We'll go to Abdallah al-Zafarani's house. You'll stay with him for a bit, until your affairs are sorted out.' Fear overwhelmed Hisham again. It was true, then ... he really was being pursued. For a long time he'd willed everything to turn out to be a terrible nightmare from which he could one day wake, but now he was certain this was no dream.

Abu Hisham got out of the car and walked towards the decorated iron door. He banged on it so hard that Hisham could imagine the whole neighbourhood waking up and police cars surrounding them immediately. The silence was so intense he could clearly hear his own heartbeat and breathing as he crouched inside the car, staring wildly in every direction. The knocking continued. With each knock, Hisham's heart leapt out of his skin. Then he would start breathing again, looking in every direction, then staring at his father as if to beg him to stop knocking so that they could go back home to the security of his mother's warm embrace. At last the door opened and Abdallah's face peered out, looking furious. Who could this annoying fellow be, who went visiting people at such a late hour of the night? But his expression soon brightened when he saw Hisham's father before him. He greeted him with loud exclamations of joy, and invited him in.

Without saying a word, his father motioned to Hisham to get out of the car and they all went into the house. Abdallah closed the door, baffled by this nocturnal visit. They all sat down in the sitting room, saying nothing. Abdallah's tiny eyes, still full of sleep, betrayed intense curiosity as he scratched his bald pate through his ever-present skullcap. Hisham smiled when he glimpsed Abdallah's smooth scalp, with its dark skin; as a boy he had often asked to touch this scalp.

Finally, his father broke the silence.

'We have just arrived from Riyadh,' he said. 'Could you possibly help us with some cold water and coffee?' Abdallah's mouth fell wide open, and again he scratched his head.

'Riyadh!' he said. 'Everything's all right, I hope? What's going on? Tell me –' Abu Hisham interrupted.

'You'll find out everything later,' he said. 'The most important thing now is coffee!' Abdallah went off into the house, repeating:

'At once, at once!'

After a few moments, he came back, having changed his pyjama trousers for a white *tob*, and sat down opposite Hisham's father.

'Ha! ... what's going on?' he asked animatedly, sticking his neck in Abu Hisham's direction. 'Tell me your story ... I can't wait a moment longer!'

Abdallah al-Zafarani was one of four friends bound together by a close friendship. Abdallah, Abu Hisham, Hammud al-Shahham and Yahya al-Ali, Adnan's father, formed a close-knit foursome that was known as such to all the elite in Dammam. He was a very cultured man and loved books, although he could not himself read. He had a relaxed and happy face, with a natural smile. Easygoing and quick-witted, it was impossible not to like him from the first meeting, although his external appearance was not in the least handsome. He was short, with a hefty body and a large paunch, dark skin, thick lips and wavy hair. In the middle of his head shone an enormous bald scalp, and his nose was just two openings in the middle of his face. Hisham could only remember him ever talking about politics. He was famous among the Dammam elite for his political analyses – indeed, he had become something of a local authority. Many times Hisham had sat with his father, Hammud al-Shahham and Yahya al-Ali round the portable heater on a cold winter night, drinking hot milk and ginger and twiddling the knob on the radio in every direction to find news from one station or another; the dial would always settle eventually on 'Voice of the Arabs' or 'London Calling'. Then they would start their discussions and analyses, and Abdallah would soon take the lead. During the warm days of summer they would lie on the ground in the little garden, drinking tea and debating the weather itself. As for

Fridays, these were reserved entirely for the pro-Nasser journalist Haykal and his 'Frankly Speaking' column in *Al-Ahram*, which they listened to live on 'Voice of the Arabs', trying to read between the lines and decipher for themselves what the Great Leader was thinking. He remembered coming back from school one ordinary hot, humid Dammam day, and finding Abdallah parked in front of their house in his white Opel car. As soon as Abdallah saw him coming, he quickly got out of the car holding a carefully folded paper bag in his hand. Without a word, he led Hisham to a corner at the back of the house, then thrust the bag into his hand, glancing as he did so from right to left and saying hurriedly:

'Here's a present ... something that's just right for you, and no one else. I got it today, and I said to myself, "This is just right for Hisham, no one else, and it's come at the best possible time."' Then he thrust the bag towards Hisham, saying with a smile, 'You're going to like it,' and rushed back to his car.

Hisham had gone straight to his room, full of excitement, and opened the bag at once. There were two books – one of them al-Kawakibi's *The Nature of Tyranny*, and the other *The World is Not Rational*, by Abdallah al-Qusaymi. He was familiar with some of al-Kawakibi's ideas, but this was his first acquaintance with al-Qusaymi. He read *The World is Not Rational*, lost himself in al-Qusaymi's sceptical, playful, bohemian jaunts and found great pleasure, as well as confusion, in the exercise. *The Nature of Tyranny* he soon knew by heart. It was really an amazing gift, and whenever he saw Abdallah, the image of al-Kawakibi would come into his mind, with his turban, his beard, and his welcoming face ...

'Now, what's going on? I want the details,' said Abdallah, pouring the coffee that his wife had left in front of the sitting room door. Abu Hisham drank one cup of coffee immediately and poured another, from which he took a sip, then placed on the floor. Then he drank a glass of water. Abdallah's eyes never left Abu

Hisham's mouth the whole time. As for Hisham, squatting there like a forgotten quantity, drinking his tea, he might as well have been in his own private world.

After Abu Hisham had finished his third cup, he felt prepared. He looked at Abdallah, said, 'This is what's going on ...' then told him everything. He finished by saying, 'I've decided to send him to Beirut until things quiet down.' Taking another slow sip of coffee he added, 'But before that, he will stay in Dammam for a few days, so we can arrange things. My own house is no doubt under surveillance, so I thought that I could leave him here ... at your house, for a while. If you don't have any objection?'

Abdallah leapt up. 'Objection? Hisham is my son as much as yours! All this trouble,' he said, turning to Hisham and laughing. 'We were afraid for you, you were so introverted, such a loner! Hisham will be fine with me,' he added to Abu Hisham. 'You can go away feeling quite secure.'

'That's wonderful, Abu Salih. If I hadn't been completely confident, I wouldn't have entrusted you with him.' Abu Hisham made to stand up, then he and Hisham went to collect his things.

Hisham sat in the sitting room, waiting, while Abu Salih prepared a place for him to stay indefinitely in the interior of the house. Abu Salih soon reappeared and led him to his son Salih's room, saying:

'Umm Salih saw no need to make you up a special bed. You can use Salih's room. He is sleeping on the roof and no one is using this room. If you need anything, you only have to call Salih,' he said. 'Goodnight!' Abu Salih shut the door, leaving Hisham to the mercy of the dreadful damp filling every corner of the room.

Salih's was a small room, with a wide window overlooking a small garden like Hisham's family's own garden. In the middle of the room was a small carpet, and in one of the corners a small bed like his bed in Riyadh, but smaller than his bed in Dammam. In another corner was a study desk and chair, as well as a shelf containing novels and magazines. The heat and the humidity were intolerable, even though summer had officially not yet begun, for this was still the first half of June. But this was Dammam … it showed no mercy. Hisham was ravenous. He'd eaten nothing since the meal in Riyadh, which he'd hardly touched. Abu Salih hadn't offered him anything, and he was too embarrassed to ask at this late hour of the night – it was almost early morning. He took off his clothes and tried to sleep but the hunger, combined with the heat and humidity, prevented him. He tossed and turned on the bed, surrounded on every side by demons. Eventually he got up and browsed through the stories and magazines on the shelf. He picked a book called *Our Happy Golden Years* by Laura Ingalls Wilder, went back to bed and began to read. Soon he was in another world, escaped with Laura, Mary, Carrie and Almanzo to the plains of the American West.

45

In the morning a knock on the door woke him. He was drenched in sweat, and the humidity had made his body smell unbearable. He got up quickly, put on his *tob*, and opened the door. Umm Salih was holding a small tray, her veil over her face. She put the tray on the little desk. Hisham inquired about Salih and was told that he had gone to school early. He was forced to reflect that for most young people today was a normal school day and that the world did not stop for one person …

He took a quick shower in the bathroom next door, then gobbled down all his beans and bread. Then he drank his tea with something a little short of absolute pleasure, because he was so desperate for a cigarette. He wondered what Abu Salih had told his wife to explain Hisham's sudden arrival. No doubt he hadn't told her the truth. Her manner when she brought in his breakfast didn't suggest that she knew anything – unless she possessed a very cool head and was in complete control of her emotions; or perhaps she had no emotions at all; or she had concluded that the matter did not concern her in the least, as it was her husband's business. Umm

Salih was the epitome of the traditional Nejdi woman. Her world was restricted to pleasing her husband and master, and serving her children. This was why Hisham's mother hadn't grown close to her, as she had to Hammud al-Shahham's wife. His own mother's world and interests were much broader – without impinging on her husband's rights, of course. Hisham saddened when he thought of his mother. He missed her a lot. He wished she were beside him now, so that he could fall into her arms and give vent to his tears. Perhaps they would cry together – she always shared his suffering. Just having his mother beside him would make him feel secure, but where was she now? They were in the same city; he breathed the same air as she, they were scorched by the same heat and stinking with the same humidity, but she was further from him than she had ever been before. The image of Noura floated through his mind, but he banished it nervously, and soon the image of his mother returned to fill his whole mind.

He could do nothing but wait; a deadly boring waiting. He was extremely anxious about travelling to Beirut and terrified by the danger of arrest. At the same time, he was dying a slow death by boredom with every moment of waiting. He looked at the time and found that it was not yet ten. My God, how slowly time passed! He had showered, eaten breakfast and drunk his tea in less than half an hour. He got up and began to pace up and down the room, then stopped in front of the window and inspected the garden. It wasn't a garden in the proper sense of the word – just a patch of ground with some neglected couch grass scattered about. There was no one like his father for looking after a garden and bringing it to life. Hisham's mother was always saying, 'Abu Hisham, what wonderful hands you have … they are magic … you must have green fingers!' He smiled to remember that. His eyes travelled beyond the garden to the public road – or his ears, rather, for the wall around the house was too high for him to see over. Beyond the street stood the Middle School, where he and Adnan had spent three years.

What memories! His head spun with images; memories reeled in his mind like the films they used to watch at home on the projector they hired when they didn't want to go out to the cinema, when the film was of the exciting sort best watched at home. Events and faces crowded with amazing rapidity in his head; things he thought he had long forgotten still lurked there, just waiting for him to rediscover them in all their detail. Most striking of all was that for the first time Hisham understood how significant Adnan had always been. He was present in every event in his life he could remember. The pair of them had been like a single entity, and he had never realised this before.

Hisham smiled faintly to remember the day they had stolen something for the first and last time. It wasn't stealing in the true sense of the word, more a search for excitement. On their way home from school they passed a small shop owned by Hali. They used to stop by the shop and drink a bottle of cola or share a can of tomato juice or orange juice, which they would drink with a pastry. This particular day Hisham announced to his friend that they would eat and drink whatever they fancied without paying a single penny. He explained his plan. Adnan tried to dissuade but Hisham insisted, so Adnan had to accept. They stood in front of the counter. Hisham asked for two large cans of tomato juice, two cans of orange juice, two cheese-and-jam sandwiches and two pastries. It was a lot to order, and the shopkeeper doubted whether they could afford it, so he asked for the money in advance. Hisham replied brazenly:

'What's the world coming to? We're regular customers, we'll pay when we've finished, or else you can keep your stuff!' By this time they had already opened the cans of juice and eaten half the sandwiches, so the shopkeeper had no choice but to accept. Adnan looked at Hisham and whispered in a frightened voice:

'Hisham, the bill's two and a half *riyal*s, and I've only got four *piastres*, you've really got us in a fix!' Hisham laughed, his mouth full of bread and juice:

'Don't worry. I haven't even got a piastre, but don't worry ...'
They finished everything, then Hisham said to Adnan:

'You go now ... go on!' Adnan hesitated at first, but eventually did as he was told and left. The shopkeeper's eyes were glued to them, and as soon as Adnan left, he asked Hisham to pay. Hisham fumbled in his pockets as if he were fetching money, then suddenly took off at full pelt. This initially startled the shopkeeper, but his surprise didn't last long, and he abandoned the shop and gave chase. Hisham was very quick, but the shopkeeper almost caught him, and would have done had fate not intervened – at precisely the moment when the shopkeeper reached out to grab Hisham, his loincloth fell down, and he wasn't wearing anything underneath, so his private parts were completely exposed. The shopkeeper stopped to cover himself up, while Hisham disappeared into the distance, amazed at his escape. From that day on they took a different route to school, avoiding Hali's shop, but they remained terrified for several days. They were afraid that the man would complain to their school principal, and would look for them. Then the news would reach their families, which would be a real disaster. But 'God preserved' and nothing happened, though they never repeated the stunt.

Hisham left the window and paced around the room again, the memories still crowding his head. He would never forget the day when they'd almost lost the 'dearest thing they possessed'. This was a few days after the shop incident. They were coming back from school, talking and joking, as they walked along a side road from which several alleys branched off, trying to avoid the main road and Hali's shop. Three slightly older youths stepped out of one of the alleys. They stopped the two friends and searched their pockets, but found nothing. One of them, apparently their leader, blocked their path, took a cigarette from his pocket, lit it and inhaled deeply as he looked at the two of them. Finally he said:

'Since you haven't got any money on you, we shall have to –'
Hisham's heart began to beat faster, and every part of his body

started to tremble. Adnan's face turned pale and they looked at each other for help. This was his mother's worst fear – that which she had warned him about was going to happen. The leader stepped forward and the other two grabbed them and marched them to a pen in one of the narrow alleyways. Without thinking, Hisham started to shout and scream like someone struck by a fit of madness, and Adnan did the same thing. The youths tried to gag them, but Adnan bit the hand of his captor so hard that he let him go with a scream. Hisham hit the boy holding him with his school bag and he let go as well. They were both free and took to their heels, still screaming. The youths caught them up, but they had to stop and retreat when a man appeared from one of the adjoining alleyways. Fate had intervened to save them again. After this incident, they went back to walking along the main roads – let the shopkeeper see them, and be that as it may.

He looked at his watch again: eleven o'clock. It must be broken. Time stood still, and the heat was unbearable. How he missed his mother. He wanted to leave this 'safe house' and head off to Adama, come what may, but he didn't dare. He went to the bathroom and took another shower, then returned to the room, smiling thoughtfully. Perhaps this room was just a rehearsal for what was to come. His cravings for a cigarette had worsened and he considered going to the sitting room in the hope of finding some among Abu Salih's things, but rejected the idea. He looked around and found the book he had been reading last night thrown onto the bed. He picked it up but could find no enthusiasm for it it today, so he took *House of the Dead* out of his bag and escaped to Russia.

46

Life flowed through the house once more. Abu Salih came back from work and Salih returned from school. He was a boy of about Hisham's age, but he had failed twice in school. Abu Salih greeted him with a smile, then went to the bathroom to take a reviving cold shower and wash off the grime caused by the humidity. Salih sat with Hisham in his room, his eyes full of questions about Hisham's arrival, which he refrained from asking. They talked a lot about the adventures of Superman, the last 'Giant Beauty', the adventures of Sindbad and Tintin and Captain Haddock, then about Laura and her sisters and those vast plains of the American West, until Salih's father could be heard from the sitting room, calling them to lunch.

The three of them gathered around a large plate of white rice, with a whole chicken sitting on it, and three small plates of courgettes arranged around a bright red sauce. The air was beautifully refreshing since this was the only time of day when the one air-conditioning unit in the house was switched on. Hisham sat where Abu Salih indicated, at his side, while Salih sat opposite his father. They both waited for him to say grace before eating. But before Abu Salih began, he looked angrily at his son:

'Haven't I always told you to wash as soon as you come in from outside? Your smell would bring the birds down from the sky!' Salih was mortified. His brow glistened with sweat and he glanced at Hisham out of the corner of his eye.

Abu Salih began by dividing up the chicken. He threw one of the thighs to Hisham and quickly polished off the other one. Salih didn't eat much. It was clear he wanted to finish as quickly as possible, but couldn't leave the table before his father. He ate with his eyes downcast, occasionally glancing surreptitiously up at Hisham. When their eyes met, he looked away hastily. Hisham knew that Abu Salih had another son, several years younger than Salih. He asked about him, and Abu Salih replied sarcastically, crushing a bone with his teeth:

'Nasir? He's his mother's son. He only eats with her!' Forming a large ball of rice and sauce with his hand, he added, 'I've given up on that child. I've tried to teach him the ways of men, but it's useless!' He threw the ball of rice into his mouth, scattering grains of rice all over his lips. 'I've two sons. One is his mother's darling, and the other is a filthy brat!' Salih stopped eating, his gaze stuck fast to the floor. As soon as Abu Salih said 'Praise be to God', belching noisily and getting up, Salih jumped up and disappeared into the house.

Umm Salih had cleared the table when Hisham went back into the sitting room. Abu Salih sat there, his legs stretched out casually, smoking a cigarette and picking his teeth with a matchstick as he chewed the remains of his meal with a noise like the cooing of a turtle dove. Beside him was a large pot of tea. Abu Salih invited Hisham to sit beside him and poured him a glass of tea, which Hisham drank contentedly, feeling completely relaxed with his stomach full, the cool drafts of air from the air conditioning and the delicious smell of smoke lulling him to sleep. He was desperate for a cigarette but he couldn't smoke in front of Abu Salih. He breathed in the surrounding smoke with pleasure. Abu Salih stubbed out his cigarette and looked at Hisham:

'What have you been doing with yourself, my boy?' he asked. 'What have you been doing with your parents? The government never shows mercy in things like this, however straightforward they may appear.' He laughed. 'Anything except getting your father into trouble. Don't play around with him.' He poured himself another glass of tea, which he drank quickly, then turned to Hisham and said with some passion:

'You want the honest truth … congratulations! God be praised, you're a real man! I wish Salih could be a man,' he added, leaning back again. 'Even if he was put in jail.' Just then, Salih appeared at the door, his hair wet and dressed in a flowing white *tob*, from which the smell of lemon perfume wafted. His father looked at him and said sarcastically, 'Talk of the devil …' Salih's face betrayed failure and sorrow, but he said nothing and took a seat beside Hisham. He pulled the tea tray towards him.

When Abu Salih had finished the last drop from the teapot and smoked three more cigarettes, he pulled a cushion towards him and threw himself back on it with a loud sigh. It wasn't long before the sound of his snoring filled the entire house. Hisham smiled at the sight of his father's friend, then considered stealing a cigarette from his packet, but stopped himself, despite his desperate cravings. Instead he looked at Salih, and after some hesitation whispered:

'Salih … I need you to do something for me.'

'What is it?'

'I want you to buy me a packet of cigarettes … Is that OK?' Salih paused before answering.

'Anything you say, Hisham.' Hisham smiled happily, took a *riyal* from his pocket and handed it to Salih.

'A packet of Abu Bass,' he said in a whisper, glancing at the sleeping man. 'Quickly, for God's sake.'

Salih returned shortly with a packet of cigarettes and the box of matches that usually came with it. Hisham took them and went back to Salih's room, with Salih in tow. The air was extremely hot and humid, but still he locked the door shut and opened the window. Then he sat on the floor, while Salih sat on the bed. He lit the cigarette and inhaled deeply, the saliva flowing into his mouth. His head ached slightly as the image of Raqiyya appeared, shyly and hazily. Salih stared at him in amazement. This was the first time he had seen him smoking. Hisham ignored him. He was beginning to feel a little relaxed, despite the heat and humidity, and the fear and anxiety.

47

A week had gone by since he had been imprisoned in Salih's room. Hisham's father visited every day, but his mother hadn't yet appeared. He was fed up with his situation. It wasn't as if he could blame his incarceration on the authorities, yet still he had no freedom of movement and he had not travelled to Beirut. One afternoon, he stood in front of the window, watching the sun travel towards its inevitable destination, when he heard someone at the door of his room. Soon his mother's face appeared. He couldn't stop himself from throwing himself at her, shouting, 'Mother, mother!', as if he was a small child, not a hounded young man. He wanted nothing in the world more than to smell his mother's scent and feel her embrace. He kissed her brow repeatedly, and hugged her, while she in turn kissed him everywhere she could reach with her mouth. Their tears mingled as she savoured the smell of his neck. She was her usual brave self, and tried not to cry too much. Her mouth wore a calm smile, which didn't prevent Hisham from noticing the deathly pallor of her face, or her tired bloodshot eyes, their red veins more numerous than he had ever seen before. His mother's eyes were her most prominent feature – wide and clear, with very long eyelashes. He thought he could see wrinkles on her face for the first time, although his mother was no more than thirty-six years old.

The two of them sat on the bed, each examining the other closely. It was clear they were both trying to stop themselves crying, though the tears refused to emerge from their eyes, or find their way to the surface. A sad silence prevailed, only punctuated by their glances. Then Hisham spoke in a broken voice, full of sorrow and regret:

'I am sorry, mother. I have caused you and father pain that you do not deserve. I have not deserved your love and trust … I … I am a disobedient child.'

Then the tears choked him. His mother embraced him tenderly and stroked his hair with her hand, saying with affection:

'May God save you from any evil, my son … I never imagined that I would experience days like these … may God have mercy on his servants … A whole week you have been beside me, and I haven't seen you,' she went on, wiping away a tear that had fallen. 'When your father told me about it yesterday evening, I didn't believe it. I haven't been able to do anything, it's as if I've been paralysed. My instinct told me that something terrible had happened ever since your father travelled to Riyadh. I was praying to God for my feelings to be mistaken, but a mother's heart never lies, and a woman's instinct is never wrong …'

He felt the hurt from his aching wounds again, made fresh by his mother's words. Suwayr's tearstricken image entered into his mind. The image of Suwayr mingled with his mother's image, and he suddenly needed to vomit. He ran towards the bathroom and spewed up the contents of his stomach, then filled himself with water, washed his face and went back with a face resembling a freshly squeezed lemon. When he returned, his mother was drying her tears, the faintest of smiles on her mouth. Some trace of the sparkle of earlier days radiated from her eyes as she said, almost enthusiastically:

'Your father told me that he will be sending you to Beirut ... that is the best thing. You will study there and stay there until God grants relief ... But watch out for the women of Beirut,' she went on, smiling. 'There is no modesty there, and you are a handsome young man now. Take care! There is no God but Allah!'

His mother gave a short laugh as she said this, and he laughed with her, though images of Raqiyya, Suwayr and others floated through his mind. 'Better to have warned me about the women of Riyadh,' he said to himself. For a second he entertained the crazed notion of confessing to his mother what he had done in Riyadh and seeing her reaction, but it soon evaporated. He felt bad even thinking of it – he had caused his parents enough pain. His mother was still warning him about the temptresses of Beirut, when his father appeared.

'Hisham,' he said. 'I want to talk to you. Follow me to the sitting room.'

Hisham got up, followed by his mother, who embraced him again and kissed him on his neck. He could feel the warmth of her breath and tears. Then she went into the interior of the house, while he went into the sitting room.

His father and Abu Salih were sitting opposite each other, with a coffee pot between them. Their heads were close together and they spoke in whispers. He kissed his father's brow and sat down opposite him. His father looked at him sternly, though still affectionately.

'Today I've managed to get you a passport,' he said. 'It wouldn't have been so easy if I didn't have influential friends in the passport office.'

He sipped the last drop of coffee in his cup, then stretched out his hand with the cup to Abu Salih, shaking it and saying, 'They told me that your name was on the blacklist and that it was impossible to give you a passport. Then I had a brilliant idea ...'

He went on with all the enthusiasm of a man who has undertaken a successful adventure.

'I asked them to issue the passport with just your name and your father and grandfather's name, and without your family name. Hisham Ibrahim Muhammad. After some hesitation, they agreed. God bless them, they are exposing themselves to repercussions, and I'm extremely sorry for that, but what can one do? There's always something lurking behind to destroy one,' he said, looking at Abu Salih.

'Hisham is an excellent young man, but a bit of a hothead!' said Abu Salih.

'Oh, well! ... now the axe has come down on his head, and that's the end of it!' said Abu Hisham, sighing deeply.

Salih came in carrying a tea tray, which he put down in front of his father. Then he sat down, but Abu Salih rebuked him, ordering him out of the room. Salih left angrily, looking at Hisham.

'I've reserved a seat for you to Bahrain tomorrow afternoon,' said Abu Hisham. 'You will stay the night there, then leave for Beirut the following morning. Tomorrow morning I will try and send a telegram to Abu Muhammad in Beirut to meet you and help you sort out your arrangements.' He turned to Abu Salih. 'You know him, I think – a pharmaceutical salesman. He lived here some years ago, but it seems that he likes Lebanon. He married a Lebanese girl and lives there most of the time. He only comes at holiday times, despite the fact that his first wife and their children live in Riyadh ... he's besotted, that's for sure,' Abu Hisham laughed. Abu Salih laughed too.

'Yes, indeed ... could anyone see Lebanon, and the women of Lebanon, and not be enchanted? Or do you prefer the humidity of Sharqiyya and the drought of Nejd?'

The two continued to laugh, then Abu Salih said:

'God bless Abu Muhammad... Yes, indeed. I still remember well the flavour of evenings spent with him!' Abu Salih again laughed merrily, puffing smoke from his cigarette in every direction, while Hisham's father bit his lower lip and glanced at Abu Salih, unaware that Hisham saw this. Then silence fell, and everyone slowly drank their tea. Abu Hisham finished the last drop, then got up.

'God reward you, Abu Salih,' he said. 'Thank you! We have imposed on you more than we should have done.'

'Remember God, my friends! Hisham is my son and you are my brother. If we are not afraid now, when will we be afraid?' answered Abu Salih. Then he got up and walked off with Abu Hisham. Hisham followed them. His father shouted, 'Umm Hisham … we are going!' In a few moments, his mother appeared, still putting on her gown and veil.

'Okay, okay,' she said. 'I'm coming. Good evening to you, Abu Salih … we won't forget this favour!'

'Good evening, Umm Hisham. And God grant you happiness and joy. There are no favours in a family. I just hope that God will make it turn out for the best.' Then Umm Hisham embraced her son, giving him a final piece of advice about keeping away from women and anything that would displease God, and telling him to write as soon as he reached Beirut. Then the person he loved best in the world disappeared behind a door and Hisham went back to Salih's room, where he smoked cigarette after cigarette, his chest tighter than a tin of sardines.

48

The airport was quiet that afternoon, as it usually was, when their white Opel stopped in front of the terminal door. Hisham got out of the car. He wore black trousers and a white shirt, shiny black shoes and white socks, all brought to him by his father early that morning with his passport and tickets. Abu Hisham had given him the enormous sum of one thousand *riyal*s to draw on during his temporary residence in Lebanon. His mother had not come, forbidden by his father, who was frightened of attracting the attention of the people watching the house, who might suspect something if they saw both Hisham's parents leaving unusually early. She had reluctantly accepted, after instructing Abu Hisham to kiss her son on both eyes. It was easy for Abu Hisham to come – he left for work every morning – and it was easy for him to go wherever he wanted from there.

Abu Salih parked the car some ways away, then returned to Hisham, who had stayed by the door nervously looking in every direction. It was extremely humid. The humidity accumulated as moisture on his lenses and he was forced to take his glasses off to wipe them from time to time. Abu Salih marched past quickly, his eyes darting about in every direction, although his head stayed completely still. He picked up Hisham's black bag and hurried inside, taking a careful look round the whole hall, while Hisham walked behind him, hesitant and nervous, carrying a small school bag which held his passport and money. Despite Abu Salih's advice, he was unable to stop turning around nervously. The terminal was quiet and almost deserted. A few voices echoed around the enormous hall, and some workmen had found the air-conditioned hall a good place for a comfortable snooze. Abu Salih told Hisham to sit in a corner while he went to the airline counter with the passport and ticket in his hand.

Hisham took off his glasses and wiped them again. Once more memories flashed through his mind. He had often come as a spectator to the airport with his friends, or the many relatives and acquaintances who came to them from Riyadh and Qusaim as guests. It was the grandest airport in the country, with its original design and its door that revolved automatically as soon as you put your foot in front of it. This door, in fact, used to arouse the admiration and surprise of everyone, for it was the first time they had seen a door open by itself, so they would come and go through it repeatedly, laughing. On the terrace outside, they had a direct view of the planes leaving and arriving. They would cover their ears and laugh each time a plane took off or landed, then examine the new arrivals, searching out the women with rosy cheeks, crimson lips, and pure white complexions, coming from a beautiful world, some of which they could see on the television screen ...

Abu Salih returned smiling, carrying the passport and ticket with a boarding card. He sat down beside Hisham, saying in a whisper:

'Everything is OK ... Takeoff is in half an hour. Don't be agitated, just act calmly and normally. Come on ... have a safe journey, my son, and send us something in the post as soon as you arrive …' As he said that, he got up and laughed. Hisham wished desperately that his father and mother could be with him, but he also knew that it was in his interest for them not to be here. He was sure that they were, at that moment, sitting together in the TV room and that their hearts and thoughts were with him. He got up reluctantly, aware that he was embarking on an adventure whose outcome was unknowable. He kissed Abu Salih affectionately on the forehead, and they embraced. Then he made his way to the departure lounge, clutching the passport, ticket and boarding card in his fist. His heart beat faster and louder the closer he got to the small door behind which sat a passport official. When he reached it, he was shaking visibly, and his face and brow were completely drenched in sweat. The passport official sat at a small desk, with another stern-faced gentleman standing not far from him. He wore civilian clothes, which included a red headdress despite the incredible heat.

Hisham gave the officer his passport with an uncontrollably shaking hand. The officer noticed at once.

'I hope there's nothing wrong,' he said, leafing through the passport and looking at him.

'No, nothing … just the after-effects of flu,' he said in a dry voice, trying to smile. 'I hope you don't get the flu this summer!' The officer smiled.

'Don't come to any harm,' he said, and stamped the passport, which he handed back to Hisham. 'Have a safe journey,' he added mechanically, giving him a look that Hisham thought a little odd. The sound of the stamp on the passport triggered huge relief in Hisham, and he threw himself into the first seat he found, waiting to board the plane. He dried his face and wiped his glasses, perhaps for the thousandth time, then looked around. A small number of passengers had spaced themselves out in the seats scattered around the small hall, with several men in red headdresses standing in the corners or sitting between the passengers flicking through newspapers. After what seemed like an age, the plane's departure was announced. The passengers lined up in front of the departure gate. Hisham handed his boarding card to the airline official, who tore off the bottom piece and handed it back to him, then gave his passport to an officer standing beside him near the gate, who began to flick through it.

'Please wait a moment,' he said, and pointed to a seat just beside him. Then he handed the passport to one of the men in red headdresses standing behind him.

Hisham fell into the seat, hardly conscious of himself or of anything going on around him. He was seized by a violent headache, and was so afraid it was as if his fear had completely disappeared. His whole body had turned into a thumping heart. He tried to make himself believe this was just a routine operation that would soon be over and had no connection with his fears, but he knew the game was up when, as soon as he sat down, two men with red headdresses took up positions on either side of him while a third sat down on a seat opposite. The other passengers glanced pitifully at him, impatient to embark. He thought of trying to run for it. But how? And where to? It was all over, he just had to surrender. Was there anything else he could do?

After the last of the few passengers had left, the gate was closed. The roar of the plane outside deafened Hisham, and pained the inside of his chest. The hall was now empty, except for a few officers and men in red headdresses. As soon as the gate closed, one of the men sitting beside him shook Hisham.

'Come on,' he said sharply. Another grabbed his arm while two more stood behind him, then they all moved out of the small departure lounge. They led him to a secluded room near the automatic door to departures, and Hisham noticed Abu Salih sitting where they had said goodbye. He was smoking voraciously, as was clear from the quantity of smoke pouring from his mouth. Abu Salih noticed Hisham too. He threw the cigarette to the floor, jumped up, eyes starting from his head, and stood rooted to the spot until Hisham had disappeared inside the room. Hisham longed to run towards him for help, but asking for help or running away was useless with these people, and in any case Abu Salih could not help him. In fact, he might harm him if he did anything that revealed their relationship.

They led him into a small room containing a small desk, behind which sat a smart gentleman in an impeccable white uniform. A smell of strong perfume wafted from him. Beside the desk were two large sofas, and between them a shining glass table. On one of the sofas sat another man, looking just like the man at the desk. The two were smoking and laughing when Hisham entered. The man at the desk looked at him in an offhand way, then went on laughing and smoking, blowing the smoke in Hisham's direction. They sat him on the empty sofa and the two men who had brought him in sat either side of him, while a third sat on an armchair opposite. The fourth stayed standing by the door. Hisham smiled sardonically to himself despite his terror. Was it so dangerous? The man behind the desk dialled a number on the telephone and spoke rapidly to someone, with a few cryptic words, looking around at the people present as he did so. Then he replaced the receiver.

'They're coming,' he said, and went back to talking to his colleague about the weather and the dreadful humidity. Hisham felt as if he was taking part in some horror movie. All his emotions had become mixed up, as though he inhabited a region outside time and space, a region with no dimensions. He took out a packet of cigarettes, lit one and drew heavily on it, before the man behind the desk sharply rebuked him.

'Where do you think you are?' he asked, glaring at him. 'At home? In a café? Smoking is forbidden.' Hisham stubbed out the cigarette with trembling hands. His heart was racing. The man behind the desk immediately took a packet of Kents from in front of him, lit a cigarette, and blew the smoke in Hisham's direction, smiling happily.

After about half an hour, the door of the room opened, and two men appeared, both wearing red headdresses. They greeted the man behind the desk and handed him a piece of paper, which he signed and returned to them. Then he gestured to Hisham, telling him to get up. They grabbed him by the wrists and hustled him outside to a grey Land Rover waiting immediately outside the door. Beside the driver sat another man. They pushed Hisham into the back seat and got in beside him, then the Land Rover sped off. No one said a word. Before they left the terminal building, Hisham looked back and thought he saw Abu Salih stamping out a cigarette just by the door.

49

The sun had turned red and was on the point of setting when the Land Rover left the airport. It took the road towards Khubar, which they reached after less than a quarter of an hour. The car raced along al-Baladiyya Street, then headed straight for the shore, where it pulled up finally at a four-storey building surrounded by soldiers. The roof was a forest of aerials.

Hisham walked with his companions along a narrow corridor inside the building. He caught a strong smell of the sea. At the end of the corridor they came to a metal desk, behind which sat a well-built officer wearing three stripes and holding an enormous ledger. The two men saluted the officer and handed him a piece of paper, together with Hisham's papers.

'We caught him trying to escape,' said one. The officer took the passport and flicked through it.

'Hisham Ibrahim Muhammad,' he said, as if talking to himself. Then he looked at the two men who had brought Hisham and said, 'Okay, your job is done, you can go.' He gave them back their now-signed piece of paper, and they saluted him again and left.

'Corporal Musad!' shouted the officer. He opened the ledger in front of him, scribbled something in it, then closed it and threw Hisham's papers in one of his drawers, while another soldier, wearing two stripes, arrived, stamped his feet on the ground and saluted. The officer behind the desk studied the corporal.

'Take the prisoner to the third floor,' he said. The corporal stamped his foot on the floor once more, then dragged Hisham hard by the wrist.

'Move it, prisoner!' he said. The word 'prisoner' grated on Hisham's ears. He was used to hearing it and reading it, but he never imagined it would ever be applied to him. Although he knew that not every prisoner is guilty, using the term made him feel that he was, and this caused him considerable distress. He had become guilty.

Hisham and Corporal Musad made their way along a corridor that branched off from the first corridor, until they reached a crumbling staircase. On the third floor, Corporal Musad put him into a room with a wide door entirely made of bars. A young soldier stood beside it. Once the door was closed, the corporal said to him, 'If you need anything, just call the guard.' Then he left, giving him a look that seemed to Hisham sad. If he had been in a different situation, the corporal and the soldier on guard duty would perhaps have made him laugh. They were feebly built – short and extremely thin – and wore baggy military uniforms that gave them the air of smugglers.

The room was very large and painted white – or what had once been white. Humidity had leached away the colour, leaving great chunks of the wall just bare cement. One tiny barred window looked out over the sea, and there were three straw beds. The floor was bare but for a scattering of broken tiles. Cockroaches poked their heads out of the cracks. It was clear that the whole building had been designed as residential flats, but was now converted into a prison. Hisham stepped towards the window. He gazed out at the still waters of the Gulf, watching the last remains of the reddish twilight struggle against the darkness. He was no longer quite as terrified as he had been, though he was certainly still apprehensive – his greatest fears had now been realised.

Nausea overcame him, and with it a biting cold that numbed his spirit and his body. He closed his eyes and tried deeply inhaling the humid atmosphere of the sea, but the air of the Gulf does not invigorate … it just made him more nauseous, and now he wanted to vomit. There was no toilet or basin in the room and he could not bring himself to ask. He thrust his face against the bars on the window, giving his stomach and his soul the freedom to vomit, but he could only bring up a little yellow, bitter-tasting liquid, despite the fact that he retched so hard he almost heaved his stomach from his belly. He put his finger into his throat, but nothing came out. He carried on trying until his stomach almost came up in his hand. It was then he remembered that he hadn't eaten anything since morning. He hadn't had any appetite, and he had no desire for food now, although he felt as if the walls of his stomach had met and threatened to consume each other.

Hisham left the window and crossed the room to call the guard. He asked for the bathroom. The guard opened the door, led him to the bathroom, then stood at the door, waiting. A foul stench filled the air; a stench of rotting fish, humidity and excrement. Hisham stopped his nose and breathed through his mouth, putting his head under the tap and letting the water run for a long time. Then he filled his stomach with water and went back. The nausea had eased a little, so he lit a cigarette, which he inhaled deeply. He felt a slight headache, which soon cleared. He looked at his watch. It was almost eight o'clock in the evening. He smiled … About this time, Noura would bring them their milk, and at about this time he would sit with his parents in front of the television drinking tea. His throat hurt, so he stamped the cigarette out on the floor, lay down on one of the beds and read the faint graffiti on the walls: *Isam ... 10/3/1970 ... Say, nothing will befall us unless it be the will of God ... Our steps are preordained, and if steps are fated for a man, he must walk them ... A man's heartbeat tells him that life is but minutes and seconds ... If a people wants life one day, fate must respond ... Alas, the darkness of prison has set in ... Every night has its dawn ... Stand firm by your view in life and struggle. Life is faith and struggle ...* He looked around at the walls until he dozed off for a bit, but he soon woke again, aching all over, with a pain in his stomach. Sweat ran from every pore in his skin, his body shook violently and he was as cold as ice despite a temperature of almost forty degrees. He got up and went over to the window again. Darkness covered everything, except for a few lights glistening in the distance. Perhaps they were the lights of Bahrain! He sighed deeply, feeling nothing but sorrow and regret. He could hear the voices of children playing on the beach below him, and a child nearby singing in a gentle voice: *O dove that sings so sweetly, what's wrong with you that you cry for my eye ... my family blames me and does not know that the fire is burning the foot that steps on it.* He wanted to vomit again, but nothing came up except water and yellow fluid. He went back to bed, still shaking, and tried to sleep, but his eyes burned him like pieces of hot charcoal while the cold was almost killing him. He got up and called the guard, who came grumbling.

'Yes ... What is it this time?' he asked. Hisham explained that he was bitterly cold and asked for a glass of water, two aspirin and a blanket. The guard laughed.

'What is this?!' he asked sarcastically. 'You think you're in your mother's arms?' Hisham felt bitterly insulted, but he implored the guard. The guard snorted.

'All you bring us is your heartache,' he said. Then he looked at the floor and shouted:

'Private Mahbub!'

'What is it, Private Ali?' came a voice.

'A glass of water, some aspirin and a blanket for his mother's darling here ...' Hisham swallowed the insult despite himself. He went back to bed and dozed a little more, until he heard the voice of the guard:

'Hey, prisoner! ... Hey, rubbish!' Hisham opened his eyes, dragged himself over to the door and took the water and aspirin, while the guard chucked the blanket on the floor. He swallowed the aspirin, drank the water and picked up the blanket, suddenly feeling as if he wanted to break down and weep, but he pulled himself together and went back to bed. The blanket was old and tattered, and stank of stale urine, but he wrapped himself in it anyway and after a few minutes got used to the smell. He felt a little warmer, and closed his eyes. But he soon started up again when the guard rapped on the iron bars of the door and shouted:

'Supper ... supper, prisoner!'

'I don't want it ... I don't want it,' he replied shakily, hardly conscious of his surroundings. He covered his head with the blanket and dozed off again, to sink into a fitful sleep of phantoms and hallucinations.

50

He was drenched in sweat when he woke the following day to the sound of the *muezzin* calling the dawn prayers. His own smell had mingled with that of the blanket; together they smelled like an abandoned toilet. He got out of bed, feeling extremely weak, with a needle-like pain in his bones and joints. He must really have caught flu, as he had told the officer at the airport. His shirt was a soaking wet rag and his underwear smelled foul, as if it had been steeped in a barrel of excrement. He took a long time adjusting to his surroundings, then got up and moved wearily over to the door. There was a new guard there, older than the previous one, but with the same loose clothes. He was fighting off sleep. Hisham asked permission to go to the bathroom, promising himself a cold shower, but once there he could see no shower. He took a bowl from beside the lavatory and filled it with water which he poured over his body, until he felt a little better. Then he dried his body with his vest and went back to his room.

The nightmares returned. He read the walls again, and leaned against the window to gaze over the waters of the Gulf, listening with pleasure to the sound of car horns coming from the distance. He went on switching from the grafitti on the walls to the window over the sea, until he heard the guard's voice calling him for breakfast.

Breakfast came in a grease-lined paper bag, the contents of which Hisham spread out onto the blanket on the ground ... a loaf of bread, a plastic bag containing some warm beans, a boiled egg and some pickles. He asked the guard for a plate and a glass of tea. The guard grunted, called another soldier, then brought a plastic plate and a glass of lukewarm tea, which he gave to Hisham.

'God strengthen the government,' he said, looking Hisham straight in the eye. 'Amen,' replied Hisham casually, then went back to his breakfast. He didn't feel hungry but he knew he had to eat – he'd eaten nothing since yesterday. He forced down the boiled egg and some of the beans, then lit a cigarette, which he smoked with the glass of tea. His nausea had completely disappeared, but he remained gripped by an anxiety he could not overcome. He finished the tea and asked for another glass, but the guard refused in a harsh voice.

'It's forbidden, prisoner,' he said. 'Do you think you're at home? God bless the government that feeds you!' Hisham went back to his bed, but soon felt the familiar nausea return. He got up, lit another cigarette and moved back to the window, looking at the horizon and puffing his smoke into the distance, envying it as it blew away into the sky. Everything was perfectly still, both time and space – the very waters of the Gulf seemed to have died ... everything had conspired to assassinate time.

51

The sun blazed in the middle of the sky. The heat was unbearable, the humidity dreadful, and the stench intolerable. In the distance, a *muezzin* called the faithful to prayer in a fine and captivating voice. Other *muezzins* followed, all mingling with each other until the city seethed with so many voices calling the faithful to prayer, the sound became a scream. In the middle of all this he heard a voice nearby singing in a sad, soft tone. It was the same voice he had heard yesterday. Could he be imagining it? Was the voice coming from within or from outside? Hisham couldn't tell, but it hardly bothered him. The important thing was to listen and enjoy its melancholy, penetrating melody.

He took to pacing about the room for a time, then lying down on the bed, then getting up and standing at the window, smoking joylessly and enviously watching the smoke evaporate into the air. His joints ached and his bones felt as if they had been crushed. His nausea came and went. He was smoking the last cigarette in his packet when he was startled to hear the voice of the guard call out his full name – Hisham Ibrahim Muhammad al-Abir. He went over to the door, where the guard asked him:

'Are you Hisham Ibrahim Muhammad al-Abir?' Hisham's sarcasm got the better of him.

'What's wrong with your eyes? ... Unless there are other people here I can't see – or perhaps a *djinn*?!' The guard glared at him angrily.

'Are you taunting me, prisoner?' he scolded. 'Are you making fun of the government, prisoner? Come on, the sergeant wants you.' He opened the door and dragged Hisham out by the wrist. Hisham's heart stopped beating completely; then it pounded violently – then it stopped again. He was hardly conscious of his surroundings. The dreadful hour had arrived. He forgot his bones and joints, aware of nothing but these dreadful contractions tearing him apart from within.

The guard led him into a neighbouring building very like the first, but cleaner. They stood in front of an enormous officer wearing four stripes, who reminded him of Sergeant Atiyya in Ismail Yasin's films* – he was the spitting image. The guard went out – once Sergeant Atiyya had given him permission – leaving Hisham standing there while the officer perused some papers in front of him, sipping milky tea and smoking without uttering a word. He didn't know how long he stayed standing there – in those moments of eternity, time ceased to exist. Meanwhile, the officer drank his tea and smoked.

Then, lighting another cigarette, he looked up at Hisham and asked:

'Are you Hisham al-Abir?' The urge to be sarcastic surged in him again, but his fear stopped him from saying anything.

'Yes,' he said. 'Yes, may your life be long!' Sergeant Atiyya's

---

*   Ismail Yasin was an Egyptian comic actor who starred in a series of films playing on his own persona, beginning with *Ismail Yasin in the Army* (1955).

features relaxed at Hisham's use of this phrase, which is usually only said to important people or to the very old. He puffed vigorously at his cigarette.

'It seems you're a good lad,' he said at length. 'What's brought you here?' Hisham was confused and hesitated.

'God must know,' he stammered. 'Because I don't.' The officer laughed, displaying his brown, gap-filled teeth.

'You mean,' he said. 'they're doing you an injustice?' He picked up his cap from the desk and got up. 'Either way. The cane always reveals everything. It will loosen your tongue!'

Sergeant Atiyya led him down a long corridor with several rooms on either side. It ended in what appeared to be the largest of these, with a bigger door than the rest. The sergeant knocked, then entered, pushing Hisham in front of him, and stamping his foot quietly on the floor. It was an extremely spacious room, painted a fresh-smelling white gloss. A large red Isfahani carpet with blue and yellow decorations covered most of the floor. The middle of the room was taken up by an enormous desk, obviously made of expensive wood, behind which sat a trim gentleman dressed entirely in white civilian clothes. Hisham caught a powerful smell of perfume that reminded him of the perfume of the man behind the desk in the airport … yesterday … God! Yesterday seemed a long way off, almost centuries ago. Flanking this desk were two huge shiny black leather sofas arranged around a large glass table. It held a giant crystal ashtray. Beside the desk was the largest radio Hisham had ever seen in his life – completely covered in knobs and dials. The table was covered with carefully arranged papers and files and displayed a small black plaque, on which was engraved in golden letters: 'Colonel Masrour al-Sayyaf.'

The colonel was reading a file when they entered. He carried on for some time, before raising his head.

'The prisoner who was summoned, sir!' said the sergeant. The colonel nodded, and Sergeant Attiya stamped his foot on the ground again and went out. Smiling broadly the colonel looked at Hisham, inviting him to sit down on the sofa to his right. He studied him for some time before saying:

'Brother Hisham al-Abir, isn't it?'

'Yes, sir, yes,' said Hisham, using the same form of address that Sergeant Atiyya had used. Everyone was checking his identity here; it was as if he was no longer himself. He'd even started checking himself that he was who he said he was. The man's smile grew wider still, and he relaxed on his leather revolving chair, took a cigarette from the packet of Kents thrown on the desk, and offered the packet to Hisham.

'Cigarette?' he asked, 'Or don't you smoke?'

Hisham took a cigarette and the man lit them both with a stylish gold lighter, then leaned back in his comfortable chair.

'Aren't you too young to be smoking, brother Hisham?' he asked. 'How old are you?'

'About nineteen, sir.' The man made gestured with his hand in the air, and twisted his mouth a little, saying:

'My word ... you *are* very young. Even though your thick moustache would suggest the opposite.' He laughed, while Hisham secretly cursed moustaches and those who grew them. Then the man said in an apologetic tone:

'I've forgotten the duty of hospitality ... Would you like to drink coffee, tea, a cold drink, or something else?' *Arak* immediately suggested itself to Hisham, but he replied:

'Tea, please.'

'With milk, or black?'

'Black, please.'

'With sugar, or not?'

'With sugar, please.'

'A lot, or just a little?'

'Just a little, please.'

Finally the hot tea came. He sipped it pleasurably and smoked another of the colonel's cigarettes. He was utterly bewildered. Was this the investigation that had terrified him for so long? Tea, cigarettes, and a kindly face ... Where was the torture they talked about, where was the cane that Sergeant Atiyya threatened him with? How people exaggerate! He finished the tea and the cigarette. His spirits revived, and he was feeling quite relaxed when the colonel suddenly asked him, still smiling:

'Why were you trying to escape, brother Hisham?'

Instantly his nerve failed him again, and he lost all trace of calm, stammering:

'No, no ... I wasn't trying to escape, sir, I was travelling to Bahrain. Then again, why should I escape? Escape from what?' The colonel laughed.

'Then to Beirut, wasn't it?' he said. 'Be truthful with us,' he added, wagging his finger in the air. 'The truth is always the best solution.' Hisham started to shake.

'Yes, yes,' he said. 'I was travelling to Beirut. I want to study there.'

'That's understandable,' said his white-suited interrogator, 'But why didn't you travel before now? You passed your school-leaving exams almost a year ago, and your university reports show you are doing well, so why travel now?'

'I've always wanted to study abroad, but my mother wouldn't agree. Now she's agreed, after we insisted. That's all there is to it, sir.'

'Really? A fine thing. And which university will you be studying in? The American University, the Arab University, the Lebanese University, the Jesuit University, or somewhere else?'

'I don't know. Whichever one will accept me.'

'Strange! Are you going to enrol in a university without having got an acceptance, and without any papers or documents?'

Hisham started to tremble again. He hadn't taken his file to the airport. They'd all been so agitated that they'd forgotten all about it and the things needed for registering at a university in Beirut.

'Actually …' he tried in desperation. 'Actually, I sent the documents by post some time ago, because things had to be done in a hurry, as you know, sir …' The colonel laughed again.

'Sent the documents to whom? Didn't you say that you didn't know which university you were going to enrol at? So who did you send the documents to?'

By now Hisham was drenched in sweat and shaking uncontrollably. The tips of his fingers were cold.

'I didn't send them to a university, I sent them to a friend of my father's in Lebanon so that he could look for a suitable university.'

'What's his name?'

'Who?'

'Your father's friend.'

'I don't know.'

'You sent something to somebody and you don't know his name?'

'Actually, it was my father who sent the documents.'

'You mean, your father knows …'

'Knows what?'

'Knows that you are trying to flee.' Hisham got up.

'No, no. Father doesn't know. I mean, Father has agreed that I should travel,' he continued, sitting down again, 'because I insisted, and because I want to study abroad.'

'And does your father know about you joining secret organisations?'

'No. I mean, I haven't joined any secret organisations for him to know about or not know about.'

'Then why did he have a passport issued for you with an incomplete name?'

'It's me that had the passport issued.' The colonel laughed again.

'How did you get it issued when you were in Riyadh, or

supposed to be in Riyadh, when it was issued by the passport office in Dammam?'

The colonel leaned forward and rested his elbows on the desk.

'Didn't I tell you that the truth is the best policy? You don't need to lie. The passport has "Granted at the request of his father" written on it.' Now Hisham was seized with fear for his father. But the colonel showed no mercy. 'And since your father had the passport issued with an incomplete name, he must know something that he wants to hide. Isn't that so? You're an intelligent university student. You must understand logic!'

Hisham was no longer bothered about himself, he just wanted to get his father out of the mess he had landed him in. His brain began to work furiously.

'Logically, you are right, sir,' he said, trying to smile. 'But you know the chaotic state of the passport office. Sometimes they write your family name, sometimes the name of your tribe or sub-tribe, and sometimes none of those things. You can get two passports issued with two different names. There's nothing for my father to hide ...'

The colonel grinned and settled back in his seat.

'An intelligent young man,' he said, pointing at Hisham. 'An intelligent young man, but very devious.' Then there was a knock on the door and a soldier came in, carrying a tray with two cups of coffee and two glasses of water. He put one of them in front of the colonel and the other in front of Hisham, then left after stamping his foot again. The colonel offered Hisham a cigarette.

'Does your father know that you smoke, Hisham?' he asked, lighting it.

'I believe so, sir. You can't hide a smoker's smell from anyone. But I don't smoke in front of him. Anyway, I've only smoked for a short time, about three months.'

'Do you drink, Hisham?' Hisham hesitated before replying.

'Sometimes, sir ... On special occasions.' The colonel shook his head and slurped his cup of coffee noisily, then blew smoke at the ceiling. Only the noise of the air-conditioning disturbed the silence. Then suddenly the colonel spoke again:

'Hisham. Who brought you to the airport? Don't say your father. He wasn't with you.' Drops of coffee spilled onto his shirt. He put the cup down on the table with an unsteady hand.

'No one,' he managed to say. 'Believe me, sir, no one did. I came by taxi.'

'OK, where were you last week? You weren't at home and you weren't in college. Where were you?' Hisham sank into his seat. He could think of nothing to say. Sweat poured from him as he gazed dumbly at his questioner. The colonel put an end to his dilemma.

'Listen, my lad,' he said. 'We know who brought you to the airport, and how. A white Opel ... I think that's enough to let you know that we know.' He paused briefly and clasped his hands together, resting his elbows on the desk. A fresh anxiety now gripped Hisham. He feared for Abu Salih. Still leaning on the desk, the colonel went on:

'We know that your father was trying to get you out of the country, and I know what is going on in your mind. Don't be afraid for your father or Abdallah al-Zafarani. Nothing will happen to them. What they did is perfectly natural. We wouldn't expect a father to hand over his son under any circumstances, or a friend not to offer a friend a bolthole. That's how people always behave, we understand that perfectly well. We're from this country as well. Or did you think otherwise?' He lit another cigarette.

'We're not trying to put people in prison for no reason, my lad,' he went on. 'We're not putting people in prison for the sake of it. We want to get inside the secret organisations, that's all ... we want information and certain people.' Hisham's fears subsided a little.

'But sir,' he said, 'I don't have any connection with any secret organisation.' The colonel laughed.

'Really! And what about those books on Marxism and nationalism and Baathism that we found in your house this morning?' *They had searched the house. God help you, Umm Hisham!*

'I like to read everything,' said Hisham. 'Reading everything doesn't mean believing in it …'

'That's true,' said the colonel, offering Hisham another cigarette. 'But finding leaflets means a lot.'

'What?'

Hisham was caught off-guard by the officer's words. He hadn't expected there to be any leaflets in the house – he had gradually been getting rid of them. The colonel laughed again, and shook his head.

'Yes, leaflets,' he said. 'We found one in one of the books in your library.'

Adnan was right when he accused me of being careless in those days, Hisham said to himself, struggling to find a way out of this latest corner. 'A leaflet doesn't mean someone belongs to a secret organisation,' he said aloud. The colonel looked at Hisham for a long time, then said quietly:

'You're an intelligent young man, but unfortunately you are barking up the wrong tree … Anyway,' he continued, trying to find some dregs of coffee in his cup. 'We're just chatting here. The investigation will be in Jeddah. Everything will become clear there. By the way, your father is here. He came with us this morning.' The colonel pressed a button beside him on the desk and Sergeant Atiyya appeared again. He asked him to bring in Abu Hisham.

Hisham's father came in hesitantly, but with his usual dignity. Hisham kissed him on the brow, feeling that he wanted to burst into tears and run away. He felt his throat choking him, and his stomach contract. His father sat on the sofa opposite Hisham and handed him a small leather bag.

'These are some clothes that your mother put out for you,' he said. Hisham took them and placed them beside him. The image of his mother filled his mind. He could almost smell her in front of him.

'Don't worry, Sayyid Ibrahim,' the officer said. 'Hisham will be perfectly okay. All his needs will be supplied. We want some information. It won't take long, and then Hisham will be back at home again.' His father smiled as he thanked the colonel, praised the government, and prayed for a long life for the ruler. Then he looked at Hisham.

'Your mother sends her greetings,' he said, 'and says to you, be honest, as you always have been. An honest man has nothing to fear.' Then he looked at the colonel, who was smiling, his fingers pressed against each other, relaxed on his chair. Abu Hisham looked back at his son. 'Don't worry, and don't be afraid, son. Everything will be all right, God willing!'

He knew that his father did not mean what he said, for he was several times more anxious and afraid than Hisham was, but he was trying to encourage him, even now that the game was up. Then his father put his hand in his pocket and took out a bundle of ten-*riyal* notes, which he pushed towards Hisham.

'They gave me your hand baggage today … I know that the government never fails in its duty … take this, in case you need it!'

'Sayyid Abu Hisham,' interrupted the colonel. 'There is no need for that. He will be looked after and provided for. Don't worry!'

'You are right, colonel. God strengthen the state! But a little extra never does any harm!' Abu Hisham tried to smile. The colonel shook his head.

'All right, all right,' he said. 'Though he doesn't need money, believe me, Sayyid Ibrahim!' Then he pressed the button beside him on the desk again and Sergeant Atiyya returned, as usual stamping the ground with his foot. 'Take Sayyid Ibrahim outside,' ordered the colonel. Abu Hisham got up, embraced Hisham and they kissed. Then he disappeared behind the door, Hisham feeling that his heart had been torn from his body. It was the first time in his life he had seen tears in his father's eyes.

He remained standing, looking at the door for he didn't know how long, barely conscious of anything around him. His parents occupied all his thoughts. Then the sound of the sergeant's footsteps brought him back to reality and to the colonel, who was ordering him back to his room.

'Don't make yourself anxious, Hisham,' he said. 'As I told you, telling the truth is the safest course of action. One way or another you'll own up to everything ... so don't worry, my lad.' Then he returned to the file he had been reading before Hisham's arrival.

52

Two skullcaps, plastic sandals, underwear, a bar of soap, toothpaste and a toothbrush. When Hisham got back to his room, he went straight to the bathroom, washed and put on clean clothes. He felt a little calmer afterwards. Then he gave the guard five *riyal*s and asked him to buy two packets of cigarettes and a glass of hot tea, and to keep the change. This time, the guard did not hesitate. He called one of the soldiers downstairs, and it was only a few minutes before he was enjoying a glass of warm tea and a cigarette, while the sun was once again sinking into the waters of the Gulf.

It was nearly eleven o'clock at night when he heard a noise at the door of the room. Then it opened. He had been standing at the window, gazing at the distant lights of Bahrain, all sorts of thoughts and ideas clashing in his head as he strained his ears in the hope of hearing that sad voice singing again. But every voice had disappeared, and there was only a total silence, as calm settled over the surface of the Gulf.

Two men in civilian clothes entered. One of them held a piece of paper in his hand.

'Hisham Ibrahim Muhammad al-Abir, isn't it?' he asked, looking at the paper. Hisham answered with a nod. The man told him to get ready to leave.

'Where to?' asked Hisham.

'To where we're going,' the man replied offhandedly. 'Come on, we don't have much time.' Hisham put on a skullcap and headdress, stuffed his feet into his sandals and picked up his bag. They all hurried out to a waiting Jeep.

Before the Jeep moved off, one of the guards put his hand into the boot and took out some steel handcuffs, which he handed to the other guard in the back seat, who quickly snapped them onto Hisham's wrists. Hisham felt utterly powerless, as if a snake had bitten him and the poison was even now oozing into his veins. All he could do was wait for a death as inevitable as it would be slow. A strange coldness held him in its grip, making his limbs shiver violently, despite the heat and the suffocating humidity. The whole way to the airport, images chased one another across his mind with amazing speed. It was as if the monotonous sound of the Jeep's engine spurred them on in their frenzy. The whole of his life – his friends and acquaintances in Dammam and Riyadh – became a series of rapid images that his mind consumed in a mad rush. Amongst them he glimpsed Suwayr, her belly swollen, and he felt himself contract with nausea and pain.

The smart airport terminal appeared on the horizon. He had been told they would be travelling to Jeddah, that most beautiful of cities, a sort of bride among cities. He still remembered how beautiful Jeddah was, and how rude the people there were, from the time he had gone on the pilgrimage with his parents more than two years ago. When they got to Mecca, everything on the *Hajj* itself had been fine: the running, walking around the Kaaba, standing on Mina and sacrificing the sheep on the morning of Eid. Even more enjoyable than all that, however, had been Jeddah itself and its beauty – for it had many beautiful qualities you find nowhere else.

The only place to come close to the beauty of Jeddah was Khubar, even though there was a big difference. He'd found there were two sides to Khubar. The Khubar that he knew, where he had spent his childhood and those happy days with his friends, concealed another frightening Khubar, with no beauty and no spirit at all. Could there be another Jeddah just as ugly, or even uglier? It seemed that God and the Devil were not just sharing the universe, but every human soul, and every city and place. Beauty implied ugliness, and good implied evil. How different would that beautiful Jeddah appear? How would the bride look when her wedding dress was taken off? He was afraid even to imagine it ...

For the whole two hours of the flight, he smoked without break. He gazed into the darkness beyond the window, as if he was looking inside himself. There was no one in the first-class cabin except himself and the guard, while from tourist class came the happy noise of laughter. He had so much wanted to travel in first class, but he had not known that his wish would come true in this way. Today he wished he was in tourist class, with the passengers laughing without a care in the world. In fact, he wished he could be packed up with the luggage, or hanging on to the airplane's wing. He hated all first classes ...

Jeddah appeared beneath them. How beautiful she was! A shining jewel, lights diffused on the clear surface of the water surrounding it, a sight as bright and beautiful as you could find. He had travelled to Beirut, Damascus and Amman; but there was no city to rival Jeddah in its beauty and warmth, and the fragrance of its nights and its days.

But the Jeddah that he knew was not the Jeddah he was arriving at today. This was another Jeddah, a Jeddah that not everyone saw. He had been destined to see it, and he wished that he had not. He was as afraid of Jeddah now as he had been delighted with it the first time he visited it. How could the same place inspire such fear and such happiness? The plane began its descent towards the airport. Hisham's heart pounded as they approached the runway. The mysterious heart of Jeddah awaited him, and he knew nothing of its nature.